ghost towns

also by

betsy thornton

HIGH LONESOME ROAD

THE COWBOY RIDES AWAY

ghost towns

BETSY THORNTON

THOMAS DUNNE BOOKS
ST. MARTIN'S MINOTAUR
≈ NEW YORK

THOMAS DUNNE BOOKS.
An imprint of St. Martin's Press.

www.minotaurbooks.com

Library of Congress Cataloging-in-Publication Data

Thornton, Betsy.
        Ghost towns / Betsy Thornton.—1st ed.
            p.   cm.
        ISBN 0-312-28041-6
        1. Newcomb, Chloe (Fictitious character)—Fiction.   2. Victims of crimes—Services for—Fiction.   3. Murder victims' families— Fiction.   4. Arizona—Fiction.   I. Title.

    PS3570.H6645 G49   2002
    813'.54—dc21

                                                                2001051270

First Edition: February 2002

10   9   8   7   6   5   4   3   2   1

TO BOB

acknowledgments

Thanks to John McKinnon of the Cochise County Attorney's office for his help with land development issues.

This is a work of fiction, not a guidebook to Cochise County. I have added or distorted places and buildings at will.

ghost towns

IT WAS A SUNDAY, LATE SPRING IN DUDLEY, *Arizona, and the purple irises were blooming. California poppies, pink and blue larkspur covered the hillsides. Craig and I had dinner reservations at a new upscale restaurant on Main Street. He came over early and planted a bunch of sunflowers next to my driveway. They didn't look like much, little brown sticks.*

"Mexican sunflowers. They're the best." Craig tamped down the dirt carefully around the last sunflower and stood back. "You'll get a fantastic display in the fall."

"I thought you just threw down a bunch of seeds for sunflowers."

"These are perennials. Forever." He smiled.

I loved Craig's smile—wide and open and warm, it creased long lines down his cheeks. He was tall to the point of gangly, but well muscled from working in gardens. His brown hair was streaked with sun, his French-blue, knit shirt set off his tan. Forever was fine with me, at the moment. I'd known him for six weeks.

Before he took up landscaping he'd taught high school English, years ago in another life when he'd had a wife. He still wrote poetry. Just the other day I'd gotten a postcard in the mail with a line from one of his poems. The tin roof of her house flames in the sun!

I wanted to be careful, not to collapse into myself, but when I looked at him, chemicals from various parts of my body travelled up to my brain, canceling out my intelligence; brand-new chemicals no one had known the names of a few years ago— dopamine, norepinephrine, endorphins, enkephalins, serotonin.

"So what are you *grinning about?" he said.*

"*Who, me?"*

"*Smug, like a Cheshire cat."*

It was Sunday Jazz Night at the Ole! Cafe. Craig and I sat at a little candlelit table eating pesto crustini and warm seafood cocktails with lime juice and cilantro. The shrimp had a perfect rubbery bounce and I could die for cilantro.

"*I hope my cat doesn't dig up the sunflowers," I said.*

"*Worry," said Craig. "Worry, worry, worry. Just don't." He smiled. "When you learn not to worry that's when you become fully alive 'cause you're not all tied up in the future."*

"*Right," I said. "One day at a time. That twelve-step stuff."*

Craig *cocked his head. "What's wrong with that? You don't like twelve-step stuff?"*

"*I'm just bored with it, it's over used."*

"*You say that 'cause you've never needed it."*

"*Come on," I said. "It is over used."*

"*Never mind," said Craig. "All I'm saying is, have fun, enjoy yourself. Like right now. Stop. Listen."*

I *was having fun, but I sat still, heard over the murmur of diners, the lead singer of the jazz band, a woman, singing softly "Where or When."*

"*Rodgers and Hart," said Craig. "You know who did a rendition of that?"*

"*Dion and the Belmonts."*

"*Very good!*" said Craig. "*And what's the best doo-wop song of all time?*"

"*I give up.*"

"*The Flamingos. 'I Only Have Eyes for You.' That's why I never worry.*" Craig's eyes were bright in the candlelight, his smile was dazzling. I smiled back, dizzy with love, or maybe an excess of endorphins. "*When you worry,*" he said, "*you don't have time for the things that really matter, like remembering the way the Flamingos sang 'I Only Have Eyes for You.'*"

"*The sunflowers,*" I said, in spite of myself. "*I forgot to ask about watering.*"

"*Some deep watering now, while they're getting established. There's people that think after that you don't have to water at all anymore.*"

"*But not you,*" I said.

"*Everything does better if you pay attention to it.*"

HE LIVED IN SIERRA VISTA, ON THE OUTSKIRTS, in the Foothills, with a wife, a small son, and a mother-in-law who hated him. But this October night he was twenty-five miles away in Tombstone, parked in his red Toyota under a streetlight next to the old black Packard that was always there, at the Boot Hill Trading Post. The only thing you could trade with at the Boot Hill Trading Post nowadays was money, in exchange for Indian blankets, cowboy mugs, stuffed iguanas, scorpion paperweights and bolos, wild west T-shirts, spears, tomahawks, and arrowheads (one free with any purchase). But the place was closed now of course, just a night-light burning.

A sheriff deputy's car drove by slowly, too dark to see who was at the wheel, if it was one of the ones he knew. The Trading Post being in the city of Tombstone, it wouldn't be the sheriff's jurisdiction but if he were doing his job properly, the deputy would still check out a car parked there with a man sitting in it. He watched as the white car, with its blue and gold Cochise County emblem, made a U-turn and came back past.

And went on by.

He exhaled, realizing he'd been holding his breath, then reached in the upper pocket of his jacket and pulled out the note. The light was dim and he'd misplaced his reading glasses, but he knew what it said by heart anyway. Computer printed, not handwritten, anyone could have done it. So what he was doing was not just foolish, it was possibly—He stopped the thought, fumbled in the glove compartment and pulled out a plastic bottle of Tums Ultra, took four. The minty antacid soothed his burning chest almost at once, but he knew it was only a mask, the pain was still there underneath.

Yes, he thought, I am a fool. He brushed his hair self-consciously back from his forehead. An old fool, and people are beginning to realize it. Now he felt sad and fell into a kind of dream, back to the days when no one had thought him a fool, back when he'd been a hotshot, a go-better, a prince, if you will—prince of the realm of Cochise County. Dances at the country club and too much liquor, plenty of friends and a beautiful wife.

He looked at his watch, a Rolex, her gift twenty-some years ago on their fifth anniversary. But Lee, she was something else he didn't want to think about and he stopped those thoughts too. For weeks now, he'd felt such an overwhelming sadness in his bones.

He looked at his watch again, the time hadn't registered. 11:45. Windy City was twelve miles away. Why Windy City, for God's sake?

It's not from her.

He felt exhausted, more exhausted than he'd ever felt before in his whole life, as if the note not being from her made everything final. And then he had a sense that what he was doing was extraordinary and had to do with his exhaustion. Then it seemed to him that exhaustion had been stalking him for years and had only now finally caught up with him.

He folded the note, put it back in his pocket. Gripping the steering wheel, he stared out at the old black Packard. A hearse. He'd passed it a thousand times, driving through Tombstone on his way to somewhere else and never registered till now that it was a hearse. Words written all over it in white paint.

When You Are Shot and Before You Are Stiff, We'll Be There in Just a Jiff. Why Go Around Half Dead When We Can Bury You?

Jesus Christ. He began to laugh, banging his hands on the steering wheel. He laughed and laughed. Then abruptly he stopped. The laughing had cleared his head and a line from a commercial came to his mind. *Just do it.*

He backed out and continued north past the OK Corral, the Best Western, and the big RV park for the tourists, into the dark of the desert until he reached the sign pointing to Windy City. Half shrouded by clouds, the moon three quarters full, the desert was silvery gray. Through the open window he smelled a hint of rain, autumn rain. And no other cars, no headlights coming at him before or behind. He turned onto the narrow blacktop road.

Five miles down and five to go, he pulled over to the shoulder, opened the glove compartment and took out the forty-five. He put the gun on the seat beside him, then slowly drove the last five miles. Bunnies and jackrabbits darted out and froze in his headlights but he managed to miss them all.

He passed the sign announcing Windy City, the hotel ahead on his right. Not really a hotel anymore, just the ruins of it, a few adobe walls, just as Windy City wasn't a city anymore or anything much at all, a ghost town.

And not a single car was parked at the side of the road, waiting for him, at Windy City.

He looked at his watch. A couple of minutes after midnight, should he wait? How long? Five minutes? Ten? Cautiously he slowed almost to a stop and peered over the low adobe walls that had once been the hotel.

And he saw someone sitting on the rubble. A slim figure in the moonlight, wearing something long, dark; head bowed, hands covering the face. *Her* face. Yes. Hers, because he saw the hair cascading down her shoulders, her beautiful rich hair, what was the word? Pearlescent. Pearlescent in the moonlight. She's all I want, he thought, it's so simple.

The note had been from her, after all; a test. He'd taken a chance, and he'd been rewarded. Suddenly the tightness in his chest was gone entirely, muscles that must have been tense for years, relaxed. He felt twenty, thirty years younger. A whole new life ahead of him. And I'll do it right, he thought, this time.

A smile twitched at his lips; she was so foolish, so melodramatic. He would be stern with her at first. What if I hadn't come, he'd say, and you all alone in a ghost town in the middle of the night.

He pulled over to the side and stopped in the dirt near the ghost hotel in the ghost town of Windy City. He unlocked his door and got out, leaving the forty-five behind him on the seat.

chapter one

IT WAS FRIDAY, A CRISP FALL DAY IN THE
high Arizona desert when Nate Pendergast called me at the County
Attorney's office where I work as a victim advocate, helping victims
of violent crimes through the criminal justice system in any way I
can.

"Chloe. I really need to talk to you." His voice was full of its usual
urgency. "Can you meet me at the Tombstome Cafe? Right away?"

I smiled. Nate always made me smile. A reporter for the *Sierra
Vista Dispatch*, he was twenty-three years old, full of fire, always
with something urgent cooking.

"This isn't a good time," I said. "Melvin's here and he's in a bad
mood." Melvin Huber was the county attorney.

"Come on," said Nate. "Half the time, you're not in your office."

"Hush."

"It's *important*."

Outside, the wind was torturing the Arizona cypress by the big pink
art deco courthouse, whipping at the short short skirt of a lone secretary as she teetered up the wide steps on stiletto heels.

Down the hill and across the street from the courthouse, the
Tombstone Cafe had started life as a wooden miner's shack but was
now a coffee shop. Nate was standing in front, shoulders hunched

against the wind: teddy-bear face, nerd glasses, dark brown hair in a buzz cut.

It wasn't cold but the wind scurried yellow leaves across the asphalt and blew my hair over my eyes. "Let's go inside," I said.

"Just a gentle breeze," said Nate, his thrift store madras jacket from the fifties flapping wildly. On the lapel was a ribbon boutonniere he claimed had belonged to his great-great-grandfather when he was in the French Foreign Legion. "Outside's more private. Come on, it's more sheltered over here."

Nate's khaki pants were ordinary enough but God knows where he'd got the high-top canvas shoes. They were white gone gray with rubber caps on the toes, manufactured in some distant era before Adidas and Nike.

I brushed the leaves off the bench to a slatted wooden table and sat down. Nate didn't sit, he was too revved up.

"Okay," I said, "what's this all about?"

"Judge Thomas."

I raised my eyebrows. "Oh?"

Cal Thomas, a judge of the Superior Court of Cochise County, had been missing since late Tuesday. Steady, reliable, popular around the courthouse, adored by his mostly female staff, he'd always reminded me of Gary Cooper; courtly, patrician, with sweet, old-fashioned manners and not so sweet old-fashioned views on women. What I thought of as a Republican in human form.

"He was last seen at the Copper Queen Hotel Tuesday night," Nate said. "He had dinner there with this old friend of his, Jack Townsend."

For a judge to simply vanish was absurd, unheard of. "So?" I said. "The unfounded rumors are flying."

"This isn't a rumor. I know the waitress who served them. Patti. This Townsend guy, he's from Phoenix. He was a little smashed but the judge was completely sober. She overheard them talking."

I looked at my watch. "Why don't I run in and get us some coffee?"

"I'll do it. Just a sec. *Listen.* Patti heard the judge say to this Townsend guy, 'Have you ever wondered what it would be like to start over again, have *a whole new life?*' "

"*Really.* What was so wrong with his old life?" A disgruntled attorney had said to me once, "Judges are the closest thing we have to royalty in Cochise County."

"Don't you keep up with the gossip? A whole lot's wrong with the life of Judge Calvin Thomas."

I raised my eyebrows.

Nate looked smug. "Tell you in a minute. Just coffee?"

I nodded and tried not to look curious.

Nate disappeared into the cafe and I opened my purse, took out the postcard I'd gotten this morning from my younger brother Danny and read it over.

Hi, Chloe!!!! Left Vermont two weeks ago and been on the road since. Just want you to know I'll be OK when I get everything worked out. Love, Danny.

Okay when he got everything worked out? He wasn't okay now?

"What's that?" Nate brushed aside leaves and plunked down two cups of coffee on the table.

"Postcard from my brother," I said.

"Hey, wow, *Danny.* The Buddhist. How's he doing?" Nate grabbed the postcard and looked at the picture. "Who is this guy? Or is it a guy?"

"A Buddha," I said.

"Nine Sarasvati," he read. "The Buddha of intellectual and artistic achievement: consort of Maniushri. *Cool.*" He flipped it over. "Ogden, Utah? I thought he was in a Buddhist colony in Vermont."

"So did I. I thought he'd finally settled down." I shivered and looked away. Across the street, beyond the courthouse, old shabby frame houses mingled with the newly renovated. On the hills, the mesquite trees were feathery fronds turning gold, heavy with pale tan pods. Overhead, a gust of wind twinkled the cottonwood leaves.

My mind drifted, remembering years ago, when I was sixteen and had just gotten my driver's license and Danny and I had gone for a joy ride out in the country around the little college town where we lived.

It was summer, the corn was ripening in those midwestern fields, tall and green. The roads there were two-lane blacktops, a series of hills, and I'd taken those high roller-coaster bumps at eighty miles an hour, the car flying up, leaving the ground for one brief heart-stopping second, then coming down, Danny and I whooping like banshees with the sheer thrill of it.

We were still whooping when the car left the road, plowed in slow motion through row after row after row of green corn before it came to rest. That day had turned me into a cautious driver, but Danny, Danny was still flying.

I shivered again. "It's going to *snow* in Utah pretty soon."

Nate pushed his nerd glasses farther up on his nose and said kindly, "He'll be okay. I mean it snows in Vermont too."

"He's always had this way," I said, "of screwing up. Damn. But, anyway, you've got me now, *so tell me*—what was so wrong with the judge's old life?"

Nate's round brown eyes gleamed. "His wife Lee, for one. From some rich old-money family back east, New York. That's right—you used to live in New York. Long Island, the North Shore."

I nodded.

"I hear she's a knockout—or was. When she first came here she blew everybody away but she hasn't been any support to him for years. Like it's beneath her or something—his whole staff hates her. They call her 'La-di-dah Lee.' Imagine coming home every night to someone like that. He couldn't take it anymore! He's made a run for freedom!"

I perked up. "Amazing." The thought that a judge of twenty years, dignified, powerful, *conservative,* could leave everything behind and blossom into an entirely new life was exhilarating. I looked at Nate suspiciously. "How do you know all this?"

He smirked. "Etta told me."

"God," I said. "His court reporter? Not very professional."

"In confidence, she trusts me. I let her feed me lemon bars. Seriously," he added, "a real reporter never rests. I make it a point to be on good terms with the courthouse staff."

I bit my lip so I wouldn't smile. Nate had been around just a few months and his ambition was exceeded only by the lack of high profile cases he was assigned to cover.

He looked wise, like he knew all the secrets. "There've been plenty of signs, haven't you noticed? Sometimes you had to wait almost an hour before he showed up in court. And he dyed his hair last month, you must have noticed that."

"God, it looked awful," I said. "Like some dead *thing* perched on the top of his skull."

Nate twisted the small gold hoop in his right ear lobe. "So he wakes up one morning, looks in the mirror and sees this *old* guy. Suddenly realizes his whole life has passed him by. Midlife crisis. Male menopause."

I looked at my watch and stood up. "Is that it? That's what was so important? I absolutely have to get back."

"Wait!" said Nate urgently. "*No.* That's *not* all. I was building up to it. I've been working on this story . . ." he paused. "Well, it has to do with Judge Thomas, pretty sensitive stuff. *Dynamite* stuff actually. I wanted your opinion. It's kind of involved."

"I don't have time for involved." I hesitated. "Listen, why don't you come to dinner tonight? You can tell me then if you come early. Craig's coming at seven."

"How's Craig?"

"Fine. Actually he hurt his back a few weeks ago. Poor thing. He's been a little irritable."

"Oh?"

"It's nothing. Anyway it's time you met."

"I don't like meeting my friends' significant others," said Nate. "You'll spend all your time worrying if you're leaving him out. Besides, what if we hate each other?"

An image floated in front of me: Craig's polite, withheld expression when I babbled on about Nate. Could he be jealous? What an idiot.

A large tour bus rumbled noisily into one of the parking spaces in front of the cafe, filling the air with the stink of its exhaust.

"Chloe?" Nate yelled over the noise. He looked worried. "I'm really in a quandary about this. I—Oh, shit," he said, as the door of the bus opened and a slew of elderly tourists in bright running suits emerged and hobbled past us. "Never mind."

"Call me," I said.

Gigi, the county attorney receptionist, fortyish with green eyes, Cleopatra-mascaraed under rigid blond bangs, looked up hopefully as I came in. "Guess what," she said in a hushed voice.

"What?"

"Someone saw the judge in Show Low. With a good-looking brunette, *half* his age." She looked worried.

"Gigi always gets thing wrong," said Marilu, one of the legal secretaries, who was washing dishes in the break room, under the sign YOUR MOTHER DOES NOT WORK HERE—PLEASE CLEAN UP AFTER YOURSELF. "Not Show Low, *Vegas.* The Mirage."

"Vegas," I said. "Wow." I'd always wanted to go to Las Vegas. *"Casino, Leaving Las Vegas, Bugsy."*

Marilu looked at me over what she called her power glasses, which were tinted pink. *"What* are you talking about?"

"Movies. *Honeymoon in Las Vegas, This is Elvis!"*

She looked at me sternly. "You need to live more in the real world, Chloe." Her hair was piled on her head in a whirl of frosting. "They're saying he must have had some kind of amnesia."

"Really." The coffeepot had been turned off so I carried my cup to the microwave to heat it up. They served incredible gourmet food in Vegas now, I'd read somewhere. I opened the little glass door and inhaled the banal stink of hundreds of microwave meals.

"Amnesia," Marilu repeated scornfully. *"Sure.* So he heads to

Vegas? With a gorgeous showgirl type, to help him forget. Anyway they're sending someone there to—"

She stopped as Melvin appeared at the door. He was tall anyway, over six feet but the fancy cowboy boots added another two inches. A man dedicated to being large, a kind of perpetual rage made his handsome perfect features stony, except around campaign time.

"Clare!" he boomed in his big lawyer voice.

"Chloe," I said.

"Did I see you talking to the press over at the Tombstone Cafe?"

My toes clenched up involuntarily like they used to do years ago in the principal's office, but I said gamely, "It wasn't work related. Nate's a friend of mine. Anyway it's important to have good relations with the media."

"Forget about that media stuff." He raised his voice another decibel. "This is the time for *a low profile*. I don't want *one damn soul* connected to this office talking to anyone about anything that's goes on here concerning Judge Thomas. That includes friends. That includes relatives—husbands, wives, kids. Is that clear?"

"Yes, sir," said Marilu.

Melvin retreated.

"What were you saying?" I asked her. "They're sending someone to Las Vegas to get Judge Thomas? Who? The police?"

"We better not." She glanced at the vacant doorway. "Not when Melvin's on the rag."

At five o'clock, I got into my old Dodge Omni and headed for home. I live here in Dudley though most people that work at the courthouse drive the twenty some miles from Sierra Vista, which is the largest and fastest growing town in Cochise County. Dudley is the county seat left over from the days when the copper mines were going and it was the biggest town (according to the tourist office brochures) between New Orleans and San Francisco.

Once, glamorous imported opera singers sang on Opera Drive, but the theater is a meditation center now and Dudley, shrunken and struggling to survive off the tourist industry, is a much mixed place of old timers from the mining days, painters and potters, retirees, drunks, wandering kids, and refugees from the big city like me.

I passed the nineteenth-century storefronts on Main Street, boarded over for years after the mines closed down but now filled with antique and collectible stores, galleries, restaurants; turned and started up the hill to my house, passing tourists with plenty of money relaxing over drinks on the terrace of the old and elaborate Copper Queen Hotel. Last sighting of Judge Calvin Thomas in Cochise County before he headed for the bright neon lights and the luscious show-girls?

It was exciting, as juicy as gossip can get, but there was a poignancy, a sadness to it, as well. How long could he keep it up, literally as well as figuratively? Pretty humiliating for his wife, too, no matter how la-di-dah.

At the top of the hill I made the sharp left turn and pulled into my driveway. The sunflowers Craig had planted last spring were now a magnificent mass of blazing orange flowers. Maybe things weren't quite as perfect now but I'd run the dating gamut in Dudley, from auto mechanics to lawyers and suddenly here I was in the safe harbor, the freedom, of coupledom.

Not like some. Across the street, a couple in their forties had moved into the once shabby adobe and transformed it into a cutesy Santa Fe cottage in terra-cotta with turquoise trim. But Sarah had moved out three weeks ago, gone back to California. Roy Orbison's rich and plaintive voice drifted out of the open windows, singing "Only the Lonely."

As I got out, Bill appeared suddenly from behind one of the to-mato plants that filled the tiny yard, wearing a grass-stained T-shirt, frayed L. L. Bean shorts, holding a clump of weeds.

"Come *on,* Sarah," I remembered hearing him yelling, in military tones, a couple of months ago, "It's still *light.* If we finish up the last coat today we can start on the trim first thing tomorrow."

Now beige stubble softened the clean-cut face and his blond hair, once neatly trimmed, was beginning to curl around his ears. He raised an arm, let it fall. "Hi, Chloe."

"Hi," I said back. "How you doing?"

"I'm fine. Great." As if to prove it, he smiled a wide grin that seemed to crack his face in half as he leaned down and pulled at more weeds. "Besides"—his eyes glittered—"I still got *tomatoes!*"

And I still had Craig.

Inside in the kitchen, Big Foot, my enormous mottled tomcat, crouched on the floor guarding a lizard, eyes baleful as if I might snatch it away and eat it myself. I'd moved here from New York City when I inherited this house from Hal, who had been the partner of my older brother James. James was already dead from AIDS when Hal died, and Hal hadn't seen any of his own family in twenty years. I was the closest thing to family he had.

James was brilliant, handsome, perfect, which hadn't left much for my little brother Danny to do but be the kind of kid who stands on the tops of buildings and threatens to jump. Danny had been suspended twice in high school, spent time in prison for drugs in the state of Michigan, almost died once when he was pushed from a car.

I carried the phone into the living room. For a long time this room, its French doors, elegant white couch, bright chintz cushions, had still seemed to belong to Hal, but gradually the couch had yellowed, the cushions faded, the French doors warped and become hard to close. Plus I'd bought an old brown velvet recliner at a yard sale and it sat amidst all that shabby good taste, like a rusted-out old pickup in an English cottage garden.

I sat on the recliner and dialed the number for Karme Choling, the Buddhist colony in Vermont and asked for Michelle, Danny's wife.

"She's on retreat now," a young woman told me.

I left a message. On retreat? Trying to deal emotionally with Danny? Then I heard Craig's truck coming up my hill. Early.

His tires crunched on the gravel in the carport as I opened the kitchen door. John Prine was blasting out "Bad Boy," stopping in mid-sentence as Craig turned off the ignition. He jumped out. His eyes were hidden by sunglasses and he carried a white paper package.

"Aren't you early?" I said.

He held the package aloft. "Brought the steaks for tonight. I picked them up on my way into town. I've got to finish up a job and I didn't want them warming in the truck."

He walked past me into the kitchen. Big Foot was sitting on the counter, but when he saw Craig, he jumped down, scuttled away. "He hates me, that cat," said Craig, putting the steaks into the fridge.

"Listen, I got this postcard from Danny. He's in Ogden, Utah. I'm really worried he . . ." I stopped.

Craig was by the sink, an amber pill bottle in his hand, filling a glass with water.

"What are you doing?" I asked.

"Taking a couple of Percodans."

"Your back again?" I didn't want to seem unsympathetic but I must admit I was weary of his back. He'd hurt it hauling rocks for a wall and when it bothered him he got snappish.

He nodded, taking off the sunglasses. The lines around his mouth, his eyes, seemed deeper, as if he hadn't slept the night before. I'd never seen him look so tired.

"Are you okay?" Anxiety pricked at my heart like some wormy little virus. I tried to keep it out of my voice. Craig hated anxiety as much as he hated worry.

"Fine." He swallowed the pills.

"Aren't they bad for you, all those pills?"

"Better than the pain."

"Danny's in Ogden, Utah," I said. "He didn't explain why."

"Chloe. Sweetheart," Craig said patiently. "I think you worry about him too much. He's all grown-up. I'll be back seven, seven-thirty. Got to run."

"Wait." Things seemed too unsatisfactory. I walked over to him and put my arms around him, my arms under his arms, and massaged the muscles of his poor hurt back. It felt good to hold him. I flicked my tongue at a spot on his neck. He tasted salty, as if he'd spent the day digging a bunch of fence-post holes.

"You know what Nate told me this morning?" I said but as soon as I said it, I felt him tense up the way he always did when I mentioned Nate.

"What?" he said flatly.

"Nothing," I said.

I showered, put on black sweats and a black T-shirt and was just applying blusher when my phone rang.

"Chloe?" said an unfamiliar man's voice. "This is Hector Estrada."

"Hector," I said. "Hey there." Hector was a detective with the sheriff's department. Need a good reason for an illegal stop and search? Hector would kick out that taillight if he needed to. But when he made detective, he'd risen to the occasion. He was very very good, everyone said so.

"We need Victim Witness for a call out in Sierra Vista and I don't want to use volunteers, so don't bring a partner. Can you meet me at the Mesquite Tree out on Highway Ninety-two at six-thirty?"

"What's up?"

"We found the judge."

"You did?" I sat down abruptly on the brown recliner. "In Vegas?"

"Vegas? Hell, no. It was that ghost town east of Tombstone— Windy City."

"*What?*" I said. "Windy City? What's he doing there?"

"Chloe. He's dead. Shot twice in the back of the head."

"Yikes!" I said. "My God, who?"

"No one's been charged. We got to tell the family before it gets out. Are you in?"

"Of course."

So Cal Thomas wasn't in Las Vegas after all; no brunette show-girls, no neon lights. A judge, who Nate had been pursuing a story about, a sensitive story, *dynamite,* murdered. Wow. I wanted to call Nate, but there wasn't time.

chapter two

IT WAS REALLY SOMETHING, THE JUDGE
murdered and me going to deliver a death notification to his snooty
wife. Well, I thought, as I drove into Sierra Vista, maybe she wouldn't
want some ordinary stranger there and order me imperiously out the
door. Banners flapped gaily from car lots, traffic honked and growled.
Seemingly reborn every fifteen minutes, Sierra Vista had every big-
box store known to man, Sears, JC Penney, Kmart, Wal-Mart, a brand
new Club Tar-jay. I turned left onto 92 at the light by the Desert
Market, drove four miles south to the Mesquite Tree and pulled into
the parking lot.

The restaurant was old weathered wood, built low to the ground.
A slew of battered pickups and newish cars were parked in front, a
deputy's white car near the entrance. I parked by a stand of pink
salt cedar and got out, looked at my watch: just a hair before six-
thirty.

The air smelled of creosote. Cars whizzed by. My ears were ringing. I gulped involuntarily, swallowing air. Where was Hector?

Then the door of the restaurant opened and he came out, a uni-
formed deputy behind him. Hector had salt-and-pepper hair and
matching mustache, a little swagger to his walk. He wore dark blue
pants, a pink shirt with a blue and pink tie, his suit jacket slung over
one arm. Hector was always immaculate, but as he came near I saw
rings of sweat under the arms of the pink shirt.

He smiled. He was a notorious flirt but this evening his smile didn't reach his eyes, as if he were operating on automatic pilot. He fumbled in his shirt pocket, pulled out a pack of cigarettes, aimed the pack at the deputy.

"This is Deputy Ken Bradshow. Ken, this is Chloe Newcombe, from Victim Witness."

Ken ducked his head, jaw muscles working, his young pink skin so clean shaven it looked plastic. In fact, he looked exactly like a Ken doll.

"He and Justin, they're pretty good friends," Hector said.

"Justin?"

"The judge's nine-year-old."

I winced. Thrilling to the juiciness of the judge leaving his cold cruel wife and living it up in Vegas, I hadn't thought about children.

"He should be home, along with Mrs. Thomas and her elderly mother. There's a daughter too, Cornelia, but she's away at college."

A daughter too. Shit. "I'll do the actual notification," I said with more confidence than I felt. "Just give me the details."

"Hector!" someone called. "You about done?"

I turned, stared. Two men had come out of the restaurant. Mutt and Jeff. The shorter was Freddy Archer, the county sheriff, looking up at the world even with his boots on and his tall cowboy hat. His skin was pockmarked, features bold, craggy, as if an inept sculptor had set out to chisel the face of a handsome man and not quite succeeded. The other was Melvin Huber.

"Five minutes!" Hector called.

"What are they doing here?" I asked.

"They want to pay their respects."

"Great," I said flatly. "Actually, I'd prefer to do this without the county attorney and the sheriff looking on. And the family will probably feel the same way."

"They'll come in later, when everyone's, uh . . . calmed down," said Hector.

At the back of my mind, a twitter of voices from the astral plane sang *dum dum dum dum de doo wah, yeah, yeah, yeah, yeah* and *doowah*, the chorus from "Only the Lonely." I struggled for focus, wondering if the judge had been lucky, had died instantly, hadn't lain there in the dark for hours, bleeding to death, maybe looking up at the sky as the stars went out one by one. I bit my lip. The salt cedar was such an unbelievable pink.

"Tell me everything you can," I said to Hector.

"He was found this morning, at the old Windy City hotel, it's just ruins now. Couple of hours later we located his car a mile away, in a wash. Body's at the medical examiner's. That's about all I can tell you. This is a homicide investigation, we want to keep it clean." Hector shifted, looking down. His elegant black shoes were covered with dust.

"Hector!" Melvin bellowed out. "Get going. You got forty-five minutes from the time you leave. We ain't got all night." The "ain't" was for the voters; Melvin was perfectly capable of speaking grammatically.

"Yes, sir!" Hector tossed his cigarette. "Anyway," he said hurriedly, "the plan is, you follow me and Deputy Bradshow to the house and we go in with you while you do the notification, get people calmed down before the sheriff and Melvin show up." He pulled out a handkerchief and moistened it with his tongue.

"You said no one's been charged. But do you have a suspect?" I asked.

Hector looked up from where he was polishing his shoes, getting them spick-and-span for the judge's wife. For La-di-dah Lee Thomas. "Not at this time," he said.

The sun was low on the horizon, tinting the sky shades of peach and mauve and apricot, the Huachuca mountains over to my left a deep shade of indigo, as I followed Hector down Highway 92 a few miles to the Foothills where the people with money lived, including Lee Thomas. According to Nate, the judge's staff hated her.

Did what Nate hadn't had time to tell me concern Lee too? Again according to him, there were big problems. I shivered. Just how big? If Nate knew anything important, *relevant,* he needed to talk to Hector right away. I'd call him as soon as I got back home.

Hector turned right, then right again onto a narrow dirt road, winding around clumps of manzanita, ending in a circular driveway. By now it was dark, the house, built of stone was only a meandering shape. Inside lights were burning. Inside was a *family* about to be irretrievably shattered.

Hector parked and I pulled in behind him. Knees shaky, nervous, wondering about Lee, I got out. Death is death, I told myself, it doesn't change anything if it's a judge. Standing on the gravel, I had the feeling I wasn't here at all, but at a distance watching a woman get out of a car. Get everyone inside, I rehearsed, people screamed sometime, fell to the ground, you had to get them sitting. Give a quick summary, try to keep it to a sentence, then say the words.

"He's dead."

I reached into the back seat and pulled out my victim advocate hideous pink plastic tote bag. In the time it took me to do that a light came on over the door and it opened. The collective feet of the three of us crunched on gravel, shockingly loud, as we walked toward a silhouette standing in the light.

Someone tall, very slender. At first I thought it must be a boy, a teenager, but then I saw it was a woman in jeans and a white T-shirt. Her hair was held back with a headband and in the yellow light her face, void of makeup, was classic as a cameo, the high cheekbones finely wrought.

"Lee Thomas?" I asked.

"Yes," she said. "Who are you?"

"My name's Chloe Newcombe, I'm with Victim Witness. Could we—"

"Victim Witness," she broke in. "Oh no." She looked past me.

"Hector, Ken. You found Cal, didn't you? And you brought *her* with you. That means—"

"Lee, where's Justin?" Ken asked.

"Out." Her voice rose. "Aren't you going to *tell* me?"

"Please," I said. "We need to go inside."

chapter three

WE ENTERED A LIVING ROOM. THERE WAS
another woman there, who Lee introduced as her mother, Mrs. Gladys
Alexander. Still nervous, I barely registered her presence.

"Mrs. Thomas—" I began.

"Please," she said, as if to forestall what she knew was coming.
"Call me Lee."

"Lee. Your husband was found this morning by the hotel in Windy
City. He was shot twice in the back of his head. He's dead."

A large vase of dried grasses in the stone fireplace filled the big
room with a musty smell. It was so quiet, you could hear the tiny
grass seeds dropping. Lee's face had turned white.

"You said 'Windy City'?" she asked finally, turning toward me on
the big couch, slipcovered in a faded chintz. Her gray eyes stared at
mine, but she wasn't seeing me.

"Yes." I tried not to stare back. Obviously we'd caught her in an
off moment; her pale hair was lank, her white T-shirt dotted with tiny
holes, her fuchsia ballet flats badly scuffed. Instead of the la-di-dah
lady I'd expected, I felt as though I were looking at a snapshot
dimmed with the smudges of a hundred fingerprints.

"Ma'am," said Hector, "does that mean something to you? Windy
City?"

"It's the name. Windy City. It sounds so cold and *lonely*." She
shivered and took a deep breath. "Who—?"

"No one's been charged," Hector said.

"Lee!" Gladys Alexander waved a cigarette so imperiously, it could have been a scepter. A white-haired, hawk-faced woman in a cream silk blouse and red silk pants that were too big, her feet dangled from her chair, not quite reaching the floor. "Who *are* these people?" Her voice was surprisingly deep; husky, like an old time movie star's.

"Mummy, please," said Lee. "You were introduced."

Mrs. Alexander flicked the cigarette at nothing, scattering ash down the front of her cream silk blouse. "Tell them to go away, I'm far too old to sit around and make bird noises at people I don't know."

"Then you can hush." Lee's voice was unnaturally patient. In her gray eyes I seemed to see the knowledge of her husband's death still dawning.

"Calvin Thomas," Mrs. Alexander barked out. "Judge of the *Superior* Court." Her blue eyes were bright and cold. "The superior court of nowhere!"

I wanted to get up then and there, go over and bop that snobby hideous old woman on the head. Instead I looked away, and with a shock encountered Cal Thomas himself. Alive and well, in a red down vest and cowboy hat, smiling from a silver, framed photograph on an end table.

"Cal's dead," Lee said gamely. "You heard them, Mummy . . . Someone shot him. They don't know who."

"Well," Mrs. Alexander said, "why are you just sitting here? You'll have to tell Cornelia."

Lee jumped up, face pale, forehead moist. "Excuse me," she said and left the room.

"Chloe," said Hector. "Mrs. Thomas didn't look too good."

I got up and went after her.

Smaller halls led off from the sautillo-tiled main hall with front door at one end, kitchen at the other. I stopped in frustration. Where had she gone? Then I heard the faint chimes of a touch-tone phone from the hall on my right and followed it down almost to the end. Through a half-open door I saw white carpeting, Lee on the phone, her back to me, sitting on the end of a bed covered with a pale blue satin comforter.

"Willy, if you're there, pick up the phone. If not then call me when you get in, whatever the time." Her voice was tense, desperate. "*Please.* You're the only one I can trust."

I backtracked to the main hall, turned the corner, counted slowly to ten. "Lee?" I called.

"Yes?"

I clomped as loudly as I could in my tan rubber-soled Aerosoles back down the smaller hall, knocked on the half-open door. "It's Chloe."

"Come in."

I pushed the door open the rest of the way. King-size bed, pale blue-and-white striped armchair, cherry wood dresser and chest of drawers. The room was large but it felt claustrophobic. Lee turned toward me, looking small on the big bed, holding the phone like it was a defensive weapon.

"I didn't mean to disturb you," I said, "but are you all right?"

"Yes." She glanced down as if surprised to see the phone, then set it down on the bed. "I . . . I just called Cornelia. My daughter." Her hands were trembling. "But she . . . she wasn't there." She put her renegade hands together, fingers interlocking.

But she'd left a message for *Willy.* Okay, it was none of my business. There was a silence. I waited it out in case she wanted to say more. At each side of the huge bed was a cherry wood nightstand. One held a reading lamp with a blue-and-white striped silk shade, stacks of magazines, a book, a half empty glass of water. The other, nothing.

Uh-oh. Who was Willy? A lover?

"*Cal,*" said Lee. "I keep thinking. When I met him, he was so straightforward, so honest. I thought he was the first real person I'd ever known. Except for Daddy. Mummy dragged me out to the Grand Canyon, the summer after Daddy died. I was sixteen."

"Oh," I said. "Oh dear."

"That's where Cal and I went too, on our honeymoon. The Grand Canyon. It doesn't seem . . ." Her face crumpled. She covered it with her hands.

Then I had an image, lover or no, how she would be adrift tonight, haunted with memories and rudderless in her wide king-size bed.

"I can't . . ." she fumbled.

Somewhere a car door slammed. "Oh. That's *Justin.*" She jumped up and went past me. I hurried after her out to the main hall.

"Detective Estrada!" A skinny kid in jeans and running shoes, dirty sweatshirt, stood at the living room door. "You need a search warrant or something?" He brightened. "Ken!"

"Justin," said Lee quietly.

He turned, peeling sunburned nose, his mother's hair and eyes and the excitement drained from his face. "Mom?"

Lee walked toward him. knelt. "Sweetheart," she said. "I have terrible news, the worst . . ."

"Then don't tell me, Mom!" said Justin. "Okay?"

"I have to. Somebody killed your daddy. He's dead. That's why all these people are here."

Justin stared at her. "You're a liar," he shouted, backing away. "Mom, you're a liar! Ken! She is, isn't she?"

Ken put his hand on Justin's shoulder, man to man. "Let's take a walk," he said. "Okay?" he asked Lee.

She faltered, touched her son's cheek. "Just bring him back soon."

The silence in the living room thickened, became so heavy it felt as though some giant beast were sucking in all the air.

Lee exhaled. "I keep thinking how Daddy—"

"Stop that," Mrs. Alexander cut in. "Where's Cornelia?"

Lee sighed. "Mummy, I don't *know.* I called her but no one was there."

"Well, we need her here. It's time she came home."

Gladys Alexander's bossy tones grated on me, but I tried to look neutral.

"Corney's not a ditherer, she'll take charge," Mrs. Alexander went on.

"Oh, what difference does it make." Lee closed her eyes. "Just let me sit here."

"Where did Justin go?" Mrs. Alexander complained. "He never talks to me."

Hector combed his mustache with his fingernails, antsy, dying to ask a few questions. He gave me a significant look. "Chloe, why don't you go check on Ken and Justin."

I went back to hall again, one way led to the door outside but they'd gone the other way. Lee hadn't called her daughter, she hadn't had time. Or maybe Willy lived with Cornelia? *The only one she could trust?* At the far end of the hall was the kitchen. The room was darkish but a small light shone down on a young woman standing in front of the sink. She turned when I came in.

She was maybe early twenties, dark, with blunt features: black hair pulled back in a thick braid and bangs cut straight across her forehead. Hispanic, maybe a little Indian.

"I'm Sylvia Montano," she whispered. "I work here."

"And I'm Chloe Newcombe—"

"Victim Witness." She picked up a cloth and began polishing the clean counter. "I heard everything," she said, still whispering. "Shot dead, just like he was an ordinary person . . . Well," she put down the cloth, "maybe he was."

It seemed an odd thing to say.

"How about you?" I caught myself whispering too, as if this conversation were not quite legitimate. I changed to a normal tone of voice. "Are you okay? Have you worked here long?"

She nodded. "About a year. I go to Cochise College. It's a good deal here, I get room and board, so I can save a lot."

She seemed so calm, so self-assured.

As if she knew what I was thinking, she said, "I don't see him much." She made a face. "Didn't. Or her either. She walks all the time, or thinks. I'd be lonely except for Mrs. Alexander."

"Oh?" I said in a neutral voice. It seemed to me being around Gladys Alexander would be the loneliest thing of all.

"She's old," Sylvia's voice was defensive. "She lives in another time like my *nana*. She taught me this game, backgammon, we play for pinto beans." She paused. "I owe her three hundred and twenty-one."

I decided I'd had enough of this. "Do you know where Ken and Justin went?"

"They're in his bedroom."

"Where?"

"I'll show you." She led me out of the kitchen back to the hall. There she paused. "Look," she said whispering again. "That's Mrs. Thomas. When she was twenty years old."

She pointed to a photograph, a cameo face above an evening gown, one strand of pearls. A studio portrait, Bachrach maybe—like those pictures of debutantes I used to skip over back when I lived in New York City and read the *New York Times*—relegated to a wall near the kitchen.

I stared at it. Despite the standardized formality of the setting, intensity burned in Lee Thomas's twenty-year-old face—only the actual features resembled the diffused woman in the living room.

"She left *everything* behind to marry the judge," Sylvia said. "She left her whole life. I don't understand why a person would do that."

Ken and Justin sat side by side on straight-backed chairs, in front of a computer. A tangle of clothes on the floor, closet door standing open. On the wall a poster of some black athlete, NIKE emblazoned across a corner.

"I've been in this tower dungeon for two weeks," Justin was saying. "I can't figure out how to get out."

When he saw me, Ken stood up. "Hold on," he said to Justin. We went out to the hall. Ken's pink skin had paled. Under some kind of aftershave, I could smell the perspiration.

"He's kind of blanked things out," said Ken. "He wanted to turn on the computer."

"So we'll see," I said. "I'll sit with him for a while."

We went back into the room.

"I got to go, Justin," Ken said. "This is Chloe. You can show her. Okay?"

"Sure," said Justin tonelessly.

I sat where Ken had been. "Show me what?" On the computer screen was a vividly colored sixteenth-century room, backed by eerie sounding music.

"Myst," said Justin. He clicked the mouse, exiting, exiting, exiting. "I hate it. It's stupid. I got it for my dad actually. For Christmas." He picked at a bit of skin, peeling off his nose, and added mournfully, "It's too hard for me, but somebody has to use it."

"Your dad." I waited, hoping he would say more. "Did he like it?" I asked finally.

Justin made a face. "He said he did, but he probably thought it was stupid. Ken says they don't know who did it yet. When they find out, I'm going to kill him." His voice was still toneless, without affect, as if he were reading from a script that held no interest for him. He clamped his mouth shut, muscles showed along his jawline. "Bam." He pointed his finger at me. "Bam, bam. Just do it."

"I was wondering about your sister, Justin—Cornelia? Does she live with someone called Willy?"

"Willy's my mom's friend, stupid." Jason wrinkled his nose and looked at me confidingly. "Corney hates this family. You know what else?"

"What?"

"Gramma hates Dad. And he hates her." He blinked.

"Oh," I said.

"Gramma wants me to go to some stupid school back east when I'm thirteen. St. Mark's. Dad said I don't have to. He promised. I want to go to Buena with my friends. Buena's stupid too but it's better than stupid stupid St. Mark's. They make you wear a stupid tie so you look like a dork." He pushed his chair back from the desk and stood up. "It's all just stupid."

I stood up too. Justin closed his eyes so tight they vanished into his skull. His mouth trembled. *"Stupid,"* he said.

On instinct I leaned over and hugged him. He hugged back hard, almost knocking the breath out of me.

"My mom," he said pleadingly. "Can I go see my mom now?"

I stood at the door of the living room, Justin behind me. Melvin and the sheriff had arrived. Hector Estrada and Ken had been relegated to chairs near the door. Melvin sat where I had been and was patting Lee's hand.

"This is not a crime that's going to go unpunished in Cochise County," he said awkwardly. "I can promise you that."

Lee removed her hand. "Thank you, Mel," she said politely. Exhaustion fairly shimmered off her. Couldn't he see that?

Cowboy hat placed brim up on the floor beside him, Sheriff Archer sat on a footstool by Gladys Alexander. "I'll pay all the overtime it takes!" he boomed.

Mrs. Alexander said, "We had ourselves a time. The Plaza! Danced all night. Nothing like it, the Plaza, back then." She paused. "I could use a good stiff drink." She tugged flirtatiously at the sheriff's sleeve. "Would you mind fixing it for me?"

"Justin would like to see his mother," I said loudly.

Lee patted the place beside her. "Come here, sweetheart."

"Our victim advocate lady has to go now but isn't she wonderful?" said Melvin as Justin, keeping his distance, walked a careful half circle round him and sat down. "Our victim advocate lady. Clare!"

"Chloe," I said. "I was wondering—maybe Lee has people she needs to call, and there's—"

The phone rang. I jumped. Willy, returning Lee's call? Communication between Victim Witness and victims was confidential, but I'd overheard this. Shit, was it something I should tell Hector later?

"Phone's ringing," Melvin said.

No one moved.

"You go home," Melvin said to me, "get a good night's sleep, we'll look after Mrs. Thomas."

I left, closing the door behind me on the sound of the phone, still ringing.

chapter four

I SAT IN MY CAR FOR A MINUTE, TRYING TO rejoin the normal world; staring at the house, thinking about my job as a victim advocate. An image came of an old-fashioned undertaker, someone out of Dickens maybe, rubbing his hands together and smiling unctuously. The thought was so unpleasant I hurriedly started the car and spun the tires on the gravel a little as I drove back down the dirt road. I needed to get my life back. Craig was waiting at my house. Oh no.

Or was he? I forgot to leave him a note. My last thoughts before I left were of Nate, what he'd been going to tell me about the judge. Did Nate know abut Willy? I decided I didn't have to tell anyone about Lee's desperate phone call. If he was a lover, people would already know. Someone would tell Hector.

How could I have forgotten to leave Craig a note?

I drove out to the highway, feeling a little anxious. Something Craig had said earlier when he was taking the Percodan swam up in my mind, *"better than the pain."* At Highway 80 I turned right, drove out into the cool air of the desert, into the dark.

It was just past nine when I got back to Dudley. Water from the monsoons still ran in the drainage ditches choked with the fennel Italian miners had brought in many years ago, making the air smell of licorice. I drove fast up the hill to my house. Craig's truck wasn't there. I bit my lip.

I pulled into the empty carport and when I got out my knees almost buckled under me. I was exhausted and I hadn't even noticed.

A man in a baseball cap, a dark blue windbreaker, and jeans came up from the dark and stood under the streetlight.

"Mark," I said in surprise.

How odd. Mark Flannery was a detective with the county sheriff's office, a blunt-featured strawberry blond. I knew him fairly well. Under the lights he looked just like a big old golden retriever.

He hesitated. "I wondered if I could have a word with you."

Craig? I thought. Had something happened to him? My God, was this another death notification, my turn this time, and they'd sent Mark to do it? Adrenaline kicked in and suddenly I wasn't tired anymore.

"Come in," I said. I saw the yellow paper, torn from a legal pad, lying on my counter as soon as I walked in the door.

"Not in the habit of locking up, I see," said Mark from behind me, always the cop.

"Only when I'm inside." I picked up the piece of paper, scanned it. *Hi! I waited a long time but it's nine and I'm half asleep so I'm going home. What's up?* I glanced at my watch, nine-fifteen now, so he must have just left. It would be too soon for someone to be showing up with bad news.

I smiled at Mark so radiantly, he stepped back a pace. What was he doing here anyway?

"Hector called you out on the death notification for the judge, I heard," said Mark. "Lee Thomas. She okay?"

"How could she be?" I said. "Do you know her?"

"Everyone in Cochise County, practically, knew her at one time," said Mark. "Then, all of a sudden no one saw her anymore."

I looked at him, curious. "Why is that?"

He sat down heavily on one of the stools at the counter. "No one knows."

I gave up. Besides I wanted to call Craig right way. Then Nate. *Why* was Mark here?

"Things are jumping." He rubbed the back of his neck. "It's double overtime for the weekend. Judy and me went to see *The Thin Red Line* last night. Didn't make a bit of sense. I liked *G. I. Jane* better. You like that Demi Moore?"

"She's okay." He came to chat about *movies*?

"I kind of like Thursday nights, you know? To do things. Not so crowded. Bet you and Craig wait for the weekend."

"You know about Craig?" I said in disgust. "Honestly, this county, you can't have a private life."

"You guys really serious, get together every night?"

I sighed. "Not every night."

"You see him say, Tuesday night?"

"No. I had—" Suddenly I felt as if a door had opened somewhere and a cold wind was blowing in. "Wait a minute. Did I see him *Tuesday*? How did Craig get into this?"

Mark looked apologetic. "He ever talk to you about the lawsuit in front of Judge Thomas?"

For a second I was stunned speechless. "What lawsuit?" I said finally.

"Well, he lost. The judge directed the verdict, made the damages higher than the jury recommended, and I understand your boy wasn't too happy about it."

I could feel my face getting red. "Oh," I said scathingly. "Oh, *really*. What are you saying, that Craig's a suspect?" I was so mad, it scared me. I dug my nails into my palms to keep the tremor out of my voice. "Because of losing some lawsuit? It wasn't exactly preying on his mind or he would have talked about it, don't you think?"

"Hey." Mark put up his hands as if to ward off blows. "Blame Hector. He sent me. It's just routine bullshit. I was in the neighborhood. I figured he'd be here and I could mark him off my list."

* * *

Didn't Mark have anything better to do than pursue some lame lead about an old lawsuit? I watched through my front window until he disappeared down the hill; he must have left his car parked in the lot below, in case anyone recognized it. Polite, so people wouldn't see a cop's car in front of my house. I went quick into the living room and called Craig. He answered on the first ring as if he'd been sitting by the phone.

"I'm sorry," I said. "I had a call-out and in the excitement I forgot to leave a note. This judge has been missing, and it turned out he'd been murdered."

"No kidding! What judge?"

"Judge Thomas."

"Jesus Christ. I know him."

"You do?" I said, in relief. Why? Had I thought Craig was going to deny knowing him? "How?"

"Well . . ." He hesitated. "He was the judge . . ." He sighed. "Actually he was the judge in this lawsuit. I was sued. A guy had me build him a rock garden, I did a great job and the asshole never paid me."

"So *he* took *you* to court?"

"Well—not exactly. I knew he'd be out of town, and I dismantled the rock garden and took all the plants home. So he sued me."

"What a jerk," I said.

"The jury thought so too. They had to find in his favor but they made the damages minimal. But Judge Thomas directed the verdict, and upped the damages a lot." He paused. "And now he's dead. Jesus, who did it?"

"I don't think I can talk about it. No one's been charged. I had to tell his family."

"That must have been tough," he said. "I'm sorry I left. I got pissed, I didn't know where you were."

"It's okay," I said. "I'm exhausted anyway."

"Come over tomorrow. I called a guy I did some work for who still owes me. He promised to drop off a check before noon so I'm rich. We can go to Tucson. Come early so you can go with me to see Roy and Flame. I have to pick up an apple tree."

There was a pause.

Then Craig went on, "Listen, Chloe, I know I've been a jerk lately."

"Um."

"Things are going to be a lot better for us soon. I promise."

We hung up. Things were going to be better for Craig and me soon. Well, good. I called Nate.

"I wanted you to know," I said. "Judge Thomas was murdered. They just found his body today."

"No shit! Wow!"

"Look," I said. "What you said to me, at the cafe?"

"Where?"

"At the cafe. The story you were working on."

"Hold on, I'm still taking this in. *Where* was he murdered, Chloe? *How? Who?*"

"They don't seem to have a suspect but you can find out all the details officially. You're the press, I might say something I'm not supposed to. I just wanted you to know because I'm concerned about what you said to me at the cafe, the story you were doing about him?"

"Jesus Christ, Chloe," Nate said worriedly. "Did you mention that to anyone?"

"Mention what? You didn't tell me anything."

"I told you I was working on a story. Listen, don't say anything about it, okay?"

"Why not?"

"Murdered. Wow."

"*Nate.* Why aren't I supposed to mention it? There's going to be a homicide investigation." I couldn't seem to get my tone of voice right, it felt as though I were talking down a long tube. "If you know something that might be relevant the very best thing you can do is tell the police right away."

"I don't think so."

"What do you mean you don't think so?" I squawked. "Is it possibly relevant?"

"Actually, yes. Possibly."

"Well, you *will* talk to the police, okay?"

"I can't promise. Look, I can't talk now. Nola's here."

Nola was his girlfriend. We'd never met.

"Why can't you promise?" I persisted, unheard like the tongueless nightingale. "There's a murderer on the loose. For God's sake, Danny, why are you being so difficult?"

"Danny?"

"Nate. God."

"Nola! Cut it out! Gotta go! Bye!"

Danny. He *was* just like Danny. Danny who hadn't listened to me years ago in Michigan, when I'd told him never, ever to drive with marijuana in his car. Danny ... My head ached. I went out and sat on my porch in the dark.

There I seemed to see my little brother bent double in a raging blizzard, all alone on some dark deserted street in Ogden, Utah. The image merged into Justin, eyes closed, *stupid, stupid, stupid.* Why had Lee lied to me about calling her daughter? *Who was Willy?* Let it go, I thought, you did all you could. But I couldn't.

What could Nate know anyway? He was pretty new to Cochise County, it could just be gossip that everyone already knew, except me. I tried to relax, let my mind blank out. A full insect orchestra was playing in my yard, cicadas backed by crickets. The day had been windy but warm, the night was clear; a beautiful fall night, with just the hint of a chill.

chapter five

ROY HARVEY HOBBLED ROUND THE CORNER
of Flame's studio in an ancient plaid flannel shirt and baggy jeans,
half carrying, half dragging a young apple tree, with its roots wrapped
in plastic. His fine white hair stood on end like a halo, his dopey,
happy smile seeming to precede him, float toward us, all big horse
teeth.

"Here it is, all bundled up and ready for you!" he shouted.

"You okay with that, Roy?" said Craig. "Here, let me take it."

No, no, I thought, like some anxious mother, your back.

"No problem!" shouted Roy, Adam's apple bobbing vigorously. He
hoisted the tree over the tail gate and into the pickup. "Hi there,"
he said to me. "How're you doing . . ." Doubt clouded his faded blue
eyes.

"Chloe," I said.

Roy banged the side of his head. " 'Course. What's the matter
with me?"

We stood together, smiling at each other in the dirt driveway. In
the empty blue sky the sun felt bright and warm, almost too warm
already. Old friends of Craig's, Roy and Flame Harvey had met in San
Francisco where he'd been a dentist and Flame a potter. Forty-seven
years old to Flame's thirty-seven, he'd given up everything—job, wife,
nearly grown kids—to wander the country with Flame.

Thirty years later they lived in the desert, ten miles from Craig, in a house that was half wood, half adobe. Red marigolds grew in rampant disarray by the wooden porch, and wind chimes made of glass, brass bells, and old silverware hung from the front beam.

"Don't you two leave now, before you say hi to Flame." Roy took a step, stopped. He scratched his head, looking abashed.

"Let's try the house," said Craig.

We went across the yard, up the wooden porch steps and into an enormous kitchen. The floor was brick, the stuccoed walls covered with odds and ends stuck up with whatever would hold them: old postcards, snapshots, bright pages ripped from magazines, God's eyes made from colored yarn, strings of beads, tiny plastic skeletons from the Day of the Dead.

In the center of the kitchen was a round table covered with an oilcloth, cream-colored dotted with red cherries, full of little crackles like an antique painting. There was a big old-fashioned range and a wooden counter stacked with bright bowls. On top of a child's school desk in the corner, like a spaceship landed among the early pilgrims, was a Macintosh computer.

"Flame!" Roy called.

Craig went over to the counter, leaned against it. He'd kept on his black sunglasses, but behind them, I had the impression his eyes were closed.

Flame came in from the hall. "Hi there, you two." Her cheeks were wrinkled, but her hair, though faded to dull brown, was thick and her movements quick. She had on a blue denim apron over a Mexican peasant blouse, the embroidered flowers faded and frayed. "Roy gets so agitated. He thinks I'll run off and leave him."

Roy looked worried. "You did, Flame, remember? Back in nineteen seventy-two you run off with that cartoonist fellow. And in 'seventy-eight in Palo Alto there was that big handsome sculptor! Brent, was his name."

Flame looked at us. Her eyes were odd, one brown and one blue. Fascinators, Craig called them, because you couldn't stop looking at them.

"Hands like big old hams!" said Roy. "Size twelve shoe. At least."

"Did you get your tree?" said Flame.

"Yes," said Craig. "Thank you. We just wanted to say hi, we have to go."

"Now hold on," Roy said. "You got to sit down, have some tea with us." He looked at me. "Melissa wants some tea, don't you, Melissa?"

"Chloe," I said. "It's Chloe."

"He's having a senior moment," said Flame.

Roy went on, oblivious. "You used to bring us all kinds of tea. Chamomile and raspberry leaves and peppermint."

"Roy, sweetheart, why don't you go into the living room," said Flame. "Find that book I was looking for, with the flower pictures. Go on, now."

She walked over to Craig, put her hand on his arm and said inexplicably, "I'm sorry."

"Forget it." Craig stood up and winced. "Chloe and I are going to Tucson, we're behind schedule already." He took my hand. "Come on, Chloe."

Outside the three of us stood next to Craig's black truck. The fruit trees behind the house were golden, the blond landscape fringed with deep lavender mountains.

"You've kept those sunglasses on the whole time." Flame waved her hand in front of Craig's eyes. "I'd like to see you for just a second without them."

He backed away. "Thanks again for the tree," he said as if he hadn't heard her, and got in the truck. I went round to the passenger side and got in too.

Beyond Craig, Flame stood in the driveway. Her arms were thin, but ropy, strong from throwing pots; her strange eyes hidden as she squinted against the sun.

"Sweetest apples in the world," Craig said out the window. "And they're almost extinct."

"Next time you come," she said, "you might bring those strawberry plants."

"Shit. I'm sorry. I forgot."

"And Craig?" Flame said.

"What?"

"I've known you for fifteen years. You might fool everyone else, but you don't fool me, even with sunglasses. I want you to take care of yourself, you hear me?"

The two-lane blacktop curved through the desert, as we headed back to Craig's. Mesquite, smoky buckwheat flowers, sunflowers lined the road.

"What was Flame talking about, you couldn't fool her?"

Craig accelerated, as we hit a straight. "Sometimes only Flame knows what she's talking about and right now she's in massive denial. This senior moment stuff. Roy's worse every time I go over."

"You think it's Alzheimer's?" I said.

"I don't know. And Flame refuses to take him to a doctor."

It was too sad. I wanted to change the subject. "Who's Melissa?" I asked. "Roy called me Melissa."

There was a pause. We hit a curve and the truck moved into the other lane. The mesquite, the sunflowers were so high they blocked the view of another car coming but Craig didn't slow down. "Someone we all knew," he said shortly.

"She liked tea, I guess," I said lightly.

Biting off the words one by one so they came out of his mouth like little explosions, Craig said, "Who—the—fuck—cares. Let's—not—talk—about—Melissa? Okay?"

"What's wrong with you?"

"Nothing." He floored the accelerator. "We're running late."

Here we were side by side, but he might as well have been in Afghanistan. Maybe we were late but I wished he wouldn't drive so fast. If there was a slow-moving tractor round a curve he wouldn't have time to slow down. I held the door handle on my side tightly, scrunched up my toes in my black Aerosoles. We would smash into the tractor, the front end of the pickup would crumple, engine parts ramming into the front seat crushing our rib cages, blood trickling from our mouths.

"I see you," Craig said. "Hanging on to the door handle. Relax, I'm only going sixty-five."

"I'm fine," I said.

"No, you're not." He braked. "Here, now I'm going *forty*-five." He turned his head and smiled, but I couldn't see his eyes behind the sunglasses. "Better?"

"Great."

Now we seemed to inch along. I could pick out details of the tiny yellow flowers of the snakeweed, identify the mangled remains of roadkill on the blacktop's gravel border—javelina.

Suddenly Craig whooshed out a breath. "Sorry again," he said. "I'm being a shit." He accelerated a little. "Don't hate me."

I relaxed. "I don't hate you in any way, shape, or form."

We pulled into Craig's driveway, lined with the same brilliant Mexican sunflowers he'd planted by my carport. The white cinder block house was bordered with lavender, allysum, and bright pink cosmos and had a desert willow in the front yard. Adobe bricks formed a patio on the side.

My car was parked next to the little office by the nursery. We got out and Craig reached for the apple tree.

"No, let me," I said.

"It's okay," he said, a little snappish. "Stop mothering me."

He lifted the tree out and carried it over to the office, then took out his keys, unlocked the door, and opened it wide. "Goddamnit!" he said.

"What?"

He walked inside and stomped all around the cement floor.

"*What?*" I said again.

"Goddamnit to hell! There's *no* check. I told Carson to drop it in the slot in the door."

"Oh."

"The asshole said he'd drop it off by ten. I said noon at the latest and he said no problem." He looked at his watch. "It's almost one."

It was unseasonably hot, maybe ninety-five degrees. Suddenly I realized how tired I was. Wired from doing the death notification, I'd hardly slept. "Call him," I said. "Maybe he forgot."

"The hell he did. I told him it was important and I spent my last dime on supplies. You know I don't spend money until I know I have it."

Sweat beaded on my forehead, drying almost instantly. I wanted to be on our way to Tucson in my newly air-conditioned car.

"Call him," I said patiently.

Craig vanished into the office. I sat in the truck until I got sick of sitting, then I went into the office. He was just hanging up the phone.

"I talked to a damn house-sitter," he said. "He went to goddamn Santa Fe." His voice rose. "For a *month.*"

The heat made what I usually saw as Craig's vibrant energy, seem like a kind of violence. "Well, forget it then," I said, finally letting my irritation take over. "We can use my credit card."

"You know I don't believe in credit cards."

"You don't have to believe in them, it's *my* card. Come on. We can still have fun. You don't have to let some jerk wreck everything."

"Well he did. He fucking did." Craig pushed at a rack of seeds, set it whirling. Little colored pictures of California poppies, black-seeded Simpsons flashed past. "I told you I don't spend money until I have it. I don't want you to have to pay for everything."

"You can pay me back. I don't care."

"Well I do." He walked over and aimed his black sunglasses at my eyes.

My stomach tensed. He didn't seem like Craig anymore. My impatience vanished, replaced with a deep willed calm.

"Do you understand?" he said menacingly.

I backed off a couple of feet. "Understand what?"

"That I care, goddamnit," he shouted.

"Craig . . ."

"Goddamnit, I *care,*" he shouted. "I don't want to owe anybody a goddamn thing because I'm in debt right now a thousand dollars. I never go into debt! That goddamn judge! I don't give a fuck that he's dead!"

He kicked a big galvanized metal watering can, sent it clattering across the floor. He kicked at a bag of manure. Kicked it again. Picked it up, threw it across the room. It hit the cinder block wall and split open. I inched toward the door as he picked up another bag, threw that. It hit the table with the coffeepot and the pot fell, shattering on the floor.

Adrenalin filled me with a strange excitement, scarier even than what Craig was doing. He was starting on the third bag of manure when I slipped out the door, got in my car, and drove off. It was fifteen miles back to Dudley. My foot trembled on the accelerator all the way.

Bill was outside in front of his Santa Fe house fiddling with his damn tomatoes when, stone-faced, I pulled into the carport.

"Hi, Chloe!" he called.

I waved and escaped inside. A cup sat on the counter, where I'd had coffee before I left early to drive to Craig's. A dead fly drifted in the remaining murky liquid. My stomach turned.

Big Foot meowed at me, a starving bottomless pit and he had a full bowl of cat food, not to mention the numerous grasshopper and lizard parts that littered the floor.

"You're glad," I hissed. "You always hated him."

Nate, I thought. There was an upside to everything. Now at least I could call Nate, talk without interruption. I could get him to tell me just what the story he'd been working on about the judge was all about. Nate was always fun. I dialed his number but I only got the machine, some punk rock band shouting "kill the poor" over and over. "Nate," I said, "It's Chloe. If you're there, pick up."

But he wasn't, or didn't.

I yanked out the plug in the answering machine and turned the phone ringer off, in case Craig tried to call. *"That goddamn judge! I don't give a fuck that he's dead!"* My hands were cold and tension knotted and grew in the muscles above my shoulder blades. I walked through rooms, picking things up and setting them down. My house seemed strange to me, shabby and diminished, as though I'd returned here after a long journey from a better world.

chapter six

I OVERSLEPT THE NEXT DAY, WOKE UP NUMB
and battered inside. I showered groggily, made coffee, walked out to
get the paper lying in my driveway. A few thin clouds streaked the
blue sky. Thoughts of Craig kept rising in my mind, exploding like
little bubbles on the surface.

I opened the paper.

Cochise County Rocked by
Murder of Long Time Superior
Court Judge Calvin Thomas.
New Life Only a Mirage.

Judge Calvin Thomas talked about
"starting a new life" over dinner with an old
friend, Jack Townsend, the night he myste-
riously disappeared. Fueled by this comment
and an alleged sighting at the famed Mirage
hotel, authorities believed the judge to be
in Las Vegas until Friday morning when his
bullet-riddled body was discovered in Windy
City, a ghost town a few miles out of Tombstone.

I stopped reading. "New life only a mirage." "Bullet-riddled." Nice
touches. I hoped Lee Thomas wasn't reading the paper. Speaking of
which, I should do a follow-up, refer her to counselors. Sometimes

people stay away from homicide survivors, murder is embarrassing. What was her number? A judge's would be unlisted, but somewhere I had an internal directory for county employees with home phone numbers. I found it between two out-of-date phone books, looked up the judge and dialed the number.

She answered after two rings. "Thank you so much for calling, Chloe," she said. "Actually there is . . . something I'd like to talk to you about."

"Whatever I can do."

"I thought . . . well . . . it's so personal. If you were in the neighborhood . . . later today, maybe after three . . ."

"No problem," I said.

I looked at my watch. I had hours before I had to show up. Plenty of time to call Nate again. Obstreperous Nate. But no one answered, just the machine again.

Anything seemed better than staying home, worrying about Nate, wondering if Craig was trying to call me, wondering if he would show up and what I would do if he did. I changed clothes, turned on my ringer, plugged in the answering machine, and took off for Windy City.

Though Dudley has its share of tourists, Tombstone is the real tourist town of Cochise County. The town too tough to die was now living off its past: Wyatt Earp, Doc Holliday, the gunfight at OK Corral. They reenacted the whole thing a couple of times a year but you could see the OK Corral any day, stop in at the Cowboy Museum, the Boot Hill Trading Post.

I drove past the John Wyatt Cooper High School, past the sign to Allen Street where the tourists would be walking along the boardwalk and paying three dollars to peer in at the largest rose bush in the world, or so it said on the plaque outside. At the Circle K I gassed up, went inside, and bought a peach iced tea Snapple.

The store was empty except for the clerk, youngish, permed hair a storm of gold and silver—your basic cowboy sweetheart type. She looked bored.

"Slow day," I said, as I paid.

She brightened. "Sure wasn't couple of days ago, the cops were everywhere. That judge that got murdered in Windy City?" She lowered her voice. "He was parked at the Trading Post, just down the road, *Tuesday night.* Around eleven-thirty. One of the deputies saw him."

"Alone?" I said.

"Come again?"

"Was he was parked alone at the Trading Post?"

Her eyes widened. "Brad didn't mention there was anyone with him." She patted the mass of hair. "Brad Holloway. He came in here right after. Wondered what a judge was doing sitting there in his car that time of night. The Windy City turnoff's just up the road about a quarter mile."

"Interesting," I said. "I wonder why he was going to Windy City."

"On his way to meet his maker." Her voice was hushed, reverent.

I drove away, past the Boot Hill Trading Post. Cal Thomas had been parked there late at night? Was someone with him, crouched down, a gun to his head? At the Windy City sign I turned and headed east.

The blacktop cut through the uninhabited desert, past the stands of mesquite and desert willow, sand verbena, brilliant purple, down and then up, up and then down through the washes. Craig had a big patch of sand verbena behind his house. He'd gathered the seeds from the wild flowers one fall, planted them.

I shut off the air-conditioning, rolled down the window. The hot air shimmered, noisy with cicadas. But it was fall, the heat would be gone soon enough. Why had Craig wrecked things? It was so stupid. Thinking, I passed the sign marking Windy City before it registered, braked, backed up, and pulled over. I got out and stood on the dusty roadside.

The cicadas climaxed, started again.

I guess I'd expected the whole nine yards: tattered curtains drifting from the broken windows of wooden buildings along the street, the hotel big in the middle, maybe the saloon beside it with the ghost of Miss Kitty just coming through the swinging doors and the whiff of hard liquor drifting out behind her.

What I saw were the minor ruins of a few small adobe buildings, low to the ground, well on the way to vanishing into the red desert dirt from which they'd come. Any one of them could have been the hotel. And I could smell nothing human: only desert dust, the dry prickle of weeds.

I had on black shorts, a black T-shirt, Aerosoles. The shorts were longish—I would be paying a visit to the judge's wife after this—but my calves were bare, so I walked gingerly around the tumbleweed, prickly pear, and devil's claw with its barbed seed pods, and kept my eye out for rattlesnakes.

At the highest wall, I stopped. It was just knee high and I peered inside at more tumbleweed, prickly poppies, and crumbled adobe bricks. Mexican generals, giant grasshoppers marked with red and green, jumped around where two walls met. Someone had spray-painted one of them in big white letters, FUCK YOU TOO, WYATT EARP.

Craig would get a kick out of that, the dumb shit. Craig would . . .

But I was distracted by a battered pickup rattling noisily down the road toward me. I watched as it slowed, pulled over, and parked. On the side was painted *B. W.'s Collectibles, Tombstone, AZ.* A little old man in a straw cowboy hat jumped out.

"Hey there!" he shouted over at me. "You look like you could use a cold drink!"

"What?"

He strode to the back of his pickup, bowlegged in high-heeled tan cowboy boots, and the big white top of a cooler came up. "Pepsi, Diet Pepsi, Mountain Dew, and some Fanta Orange! I'd have beer too, only the boys from Liquor Control would be all over me!"

Actually I was pretty thirsty in spite of the Circle K Snapple which was long gone. "Sure." I walked to my car and got my purse. "Maybe a Mountain Dew. How much?"

"Three bucks!"

Jesus Christ. For a mere soda. The Snapple had been eighty-nine cents at the Circle K but I counted out three singles and handed them over.

"I'm B.W. Watkins," he said now that he had the three bucks. He handed me a Mountain Dew.

"Chloe," I said.

He didn't ask what my last name was, maybe he'd met too many people in his life already to care.

"Thought there'd be more folks here," he said. "There sure was this morning. 'Course it's pretty damn hot now."

His wizened old face was tanned to leather and covered with sweat. Sweat stained his faded denim shirt. His jeans were too big, cinched in tight at the waist with a stamped leather belt fastened by an engraved silver and turquoise belt buckle.

"Way back in the fifties," he said, "I had a refreshment stand here, made some decent money, but the buildings were a lot bigger then. People stopped coming but now they're back, least for a little bit. 'Cause of the judge." He looked proud. "I'm the one that found him."

"Really?" I said, suitably wide-eyed.

"Couldn't see him from the road but I wondered why the damn buzzards was collecting. Didn't recognize him but damned if I didn't come to find out, thirty years back he was my ex-wife's lawyer. Thomas and Townsend." He spit in the dirt. "Took everything I had. Which was just a damned trailer."

He lowered his voice. "Had a little rain before they found him, washed away the car tracks. I helped 'em find his car. Figured one place it might be, wash near here. And there 'twas, gun on the front seat, big old forty-five."

"Really?" I said.

He took off his cowboy hat revealing a bald head, put it back on again. "They took away the crime scene tape, I can show you exactly where I found him. Come on. You bought your drink, you get the tour."

I followed him to the far wall with the FUCK YOU TOO, WYATT EARP. He went behind the wall and pointed down toward the dirt at a large dark stain.

"Lying on his back. Dropped right down when he took the bullets. I might of heard the shots, I live just a couple miles away but there's so many of them military retired from Fort Huachuca round here that I'd of thought it must of been one of them."

"Military?"

"Sure, militia types." He winked at me. "Bunch of 'em dresses up in camouflage clothes and plays games."

The dark stain was for real, though. I looked down at it but my eyes skittered away, up to the mountains in the distance. The thin clouds this morning had thickened over the peaks. Maybe it would rain. They were predicting a rainy fall, because of El Niño.

The air was very still, oppressive. Its weight seemed to preclude all thought, much less action. But at night the heat would vanish rapidly, nothing here to hold it in. At night it would be cool in Windy City.

I looked around me. "Not much of a town," I said.

"That's 'cause over the years damn people carried away everything for souvenirs. First the fixtures, then the wood. Used the wood to build other stuff, burned a lot of it." He looked disgusted. "And what's left they got to put that graffiti on it. No respect for history."

A grasshopper whirred, hit my leg, jumped back out onto the low wall. The grasshoppers were everywhere, perhaps they were the greatly diminished souls of the former inhabitants.

"Why did everyone move away?" I asked.

"Same reason they called it Windy City," he said. "You can't tell it on a day like this, but that's what it was here, situated all wrong, so what was a breeze anywhere else was a damn hurricane when it got here. Windows rattlin' loose all day long, all night long too, dust'd blow in your eyes the minute you stepped outside. You can only take so much aggravation then I guess you got to move."

He chuckled. "Tell you one thing, nothing good goes on out here, not at night anyway. It ain't the first time something bad has happened."

"Oh?" I said. "Like what?"

He shook his head. "Nothing on earth can hush up a rumor, you ever notice that? Teenagers like to come out here, think it's fun to come to a ghost town with a six-pack and a sweetie." He smirked. "Maybe the judge had a date."

"Maybe," I said. "Any reason you'd think that?"

"Just seventy-eight years of studying human nature, that's all. Some little sweetie, finds out he don't love her no more after she come all the way to see him on her bicycle."

"Her *bicycle*?"

"Yep. Skinny little track, right by the side of the road, bushes kept the rain away. Couldn't be nothin' but. Sheriff's deputies liked that, oh boy, I found 'em a clue. Thought they might give me a medal." He paused looking at me with his watery eyes. Then he spat at the ground. "You ask me it's the same damn thing over and over. *Sershay la fame.*"

"And fortune too," I said brightly.

I looked at my watch. Close to three. "Have to go," I said to B.W. "Thanks for the tour."

I got in my car. If I kept on this road, it would take me straight to Sierra Vista. As I drove off, in my rearview mirror I saw a car approaching. Turquoise and cream, a '56 Chevy. Nate's car. I grinned. Nate, "a real reporter never rests," going to check out the crime scene. For a moment I kept going, then thought, no, he couldn't escape me now. Not Chloe, the nag, the surrogate big sister. I braked and turned around.

But B.W. beat me to him. Nate, in a beat-up tan cowboy hat that looked bizarre with the madras jacket, was shaking his hand. Nate had on big silver-tone metal clip-on sunglasses over his nerd frames. He looked so normal, for Nate, I wondered why I'd spent so much time worrying.

"Hey!" I shouted out my window.

"Not now." He motioned me to back off. "I'll call you, I promise, okay?"

chapter seven

IN DAYLIGHT THE NARROW ROAD TO THE
Thomas house wound through clumps of manzanita, mesquite, and
live oak, turned sharply and then stopped at a gravel drive. Even now
that I could see it clearly, the gray and beige stone house merged
with the landscape and was defined mostly by its red tile roof. The
drive circled a stand of woody-stemmed red roses and weeds pushed
up through the gravel, clumps of wild grasses choked the roses.

Craig would have gone at those roses, hacked off the woody
branches, cleared away the weeds, given them new life. Damn Craig.

Overhead the clouds were building up but they parted suddenly
and sun winked off the many windows of the Thomas house, like eyes
looking out at me. I parked near the front door but didn't get out
right away. Thinking of Craig, I saw that there was no excuse for the
way he'd acted. No excuse. For a moment I felt even worse than I
had yesterday.

Get a grip, I told myself, you're going to see the widow of a man
who's been murdered. Self-consciously I brushed at the dust on my
black shorts, ran my fingers through my hair.

Then I got out and walked up two low steps to the front door,
which was painted a muted shade of terra-cotta. I pushed a white
doorbell button ringed with tarnished brass, listening hard for a
chime inside, footsteps. I heard nothing so I waited a minute and

then knocked. There was no knocker, the wood was dense and my knuckles hardly made an impact.

I looked at my watch; nearly three-thirty. Lee had said any time after three. Wouldn't she be listening for my car? I walked back down the steps and onto the gravel, crunching as loudly as I could, looking around for a car parked somewhere, anything to indicate someone was here.

There was a garage at the far end, but the door was closed and there was no window. Ill at ease, I stood very still, listening intently over the hum of the cicadas. Nothing. Suddenly I was spooked— visions of bloody bodies inside, a silent killer waiting for me. I got back in my car and drove fast down the driveway, hairs prickling on the back of my neck.

I wasn't really watching the road, but even if I had been, it appeared out of nowhere. A small red car rounding the curve, going way too fast. An idiot! Coming right at me! I swerved off the road, stalled and came to rest against a large mesquite.

For a moment I watched the mesquite shedding its tiny yellow leaves all over my windshield, thinking, Craig should hear about this, now I have a really good reason to call him. Then I heard a noise, turned my head and saw a large white-haired man with an extremely handsome mustache tapping at the side window. I rolled it down.

"Are you okay?" His eyes were a brilliant astonishing blue, his skin so deeply pink I wondered about heart attack. New jeans, immaculate white shirt, antique bolo tie. In one hand, a fawn colored cowboy hat.

"Fine," I said. "I guess."

"Jesus Christ, I'm so sorry. Damn little rental cars, so light it seems like they jump out of your hands." He stepped back, walked around my car, inspecting it.

A big man, formidable, even. His cowboy boots were ostrich skin, surely custom made. Watching him, I thought suddenly of a poem by e. e. cummings. *Buffalo Bill's defunct who used to ride a water-smooth silver stallion and shoot onetwothreefourfive pigeons, just like that.*

Jesus, he was a handsome man.

"Don't see any damage," said Buffalo Bill. "Why don't you get out, let me make sure it starts."

He looked like a person of substance but I was a grown woman, perfectly capable of turning the key in the ignition. Still, I got out of the car. He jumped in and turned the key. The car started at once, of course. He backed my car out to the center of the road, jumped out. His hand came out at me like it was on a spring. I took it.

His grip was firm, warm, reassuring. *You're safe with me.* "Jack Townsend," he said.

"Oh, I know who you are then," I said. "You used to be the judge's partner. You had dinner . . ." I stopped, embarrassed.

He released my hand. My fingers tingled. "And who might you be?" he said.

"Chloe Newcombe, I'm the victim advocate with the County Attorney's office."

"Ah," he said. "How's old Melvin doing?"

"Just fine."

"Hah." He grinned conspiratorially. "Coming from Lee's?"

I nodded. "I was supposed to see her this afternoon, but no one's home."

"You mean I came all this way and she's not . . . Son of a bitch." His skin turned even pinker and he seemed to deflate, right there in front of me. "Excuse me." He sat down on a big rock.

He smoothed his mustache, then took a white silk handkerchief out of his breast pocket and wiped his forehead. "I should of called ahead. When I heard the news I jumped the first plane out of Phoenix. Well, I guess I'll sit here on this rock till Lee comes by. You know her very well?"

"I met her for the first time Friday night. I did the . . . um . . . death notification." I felt my face flush, the words sounded so bureaucratic.

Jack Townsend's blue eyes caught mine, seemed to understand my embarrassment, my reason for it. Not only that, they seemed to understand other things as well, deeper, possibly not even known to myself. "That's one hell of job you have there," he said.

I bent and pulled a sticker off my shoe, to get away from all that understanding. "Um."

"How'd she take it?"

I straightened. "Shocked, of course."

"Damned if I don't have butterflies, thinking of seeing her." He ran his fingers through his hair. "I been through two marriages and my third's pretty much down the tubes. They were married twenty-five, twenty-six years."

"Long time," I said.

"That's right and the damn newspaper got hold of that quote about a new life and won't give it a rest. Closest he's come in years to confiding in me, and damned if I knew what he meant by it. Did Lee say anything?"

"I'm sorry, I can't talk about what Lee says to me."

"Sure. Of course." He paused. "Damn. There's the kids too. I hardly know the boy, but that Corney. She's something. An artist."

"Really?"

"I stopped in and saw some of her work in Tucson once. Didn't understand it." He shrugged. "I first met Lee right after they got married, when Cal first brought her to Sierra Vista. Which is now just like Phoenix except smaller but back then you knew everyone, where they were from and where they were likely to end up. Back when Cal and I had our law firm. We were all best friends."

I nodded.

"Lee was a real lady, I don't mean all prissy priss, I mean she had guts, not afraid to try anything. Kind of person lights up the room. Men falling all over themselves just to get a look from her. Me too, I guess, but I'll tell you one thing, she was crazy about Cal."

The wind gusted up a bit, clouds overhead met and parted. I thought of the empty nightstand by the bed. I said, "How long has it been since you've seen her?"

Jack didn't answer for a moment. My words seemed to drift in the air.

"Quite a while," he said finally. He picked up a rock, threw it into a scrub oak bush. "All the way here," he went on, "things kept coming back. How we used to go to the country club, dance, flirt, sometimes we'd get ourselves a six-pack and ride around this big old empty county, see the sun rise. Lee and Cal, me and my first wife Mary. All so young and we didn't even know it." He looked stricken. "How am I going to face her?"

"All so young and we didn't even know it." All the way home I wondered about Lee. What had happened to her? Everything changes, nothing stays the same. One day you lit up a room, the next you could barely get off the couch.

But she'd had the energy to call someone right away, after I'd told her her husband had been murdered. Someone named Willy. Who was he?

I dashed to the answering machine as soon as I got home, one hang-up but no message. Still, yesterday Craig could have called me all afternoon and into the night and I'd never have known it. He might have given up. Poor Craig—lost his lawsuit, back pain, stiffed by a client, who wouldn't blow up the way he had? I was ready to assume full responsibility.

I picked up the phone.

If you call him now, my mind whispered, in the confident liberated voice of a stranger, a bossy know-it-all acquaintance, *he'll think he can throw a tantrum in front of you anytime he likes.* Tantrum? It was no tantrum, it was a violence, pure and simple. I hung up the phone, picked it up again and called Nate. Got the machine.

"It's Chloe. Pick *up,*" I said, futilely. Still talking to B. W. probably, spending a fortune on marked up sodas.

Thinking of Nate made me think of Danny. Danny's postcard had been from Ogden, Utah. I took down my atlas and turned to the map of the U.S. There was Utah, wedged between Colorado and Nevada,

Ogden in the upper corner. It was a lot closer to Arizona than Vermont, anyway. I closed it, went out and sat on the porch. The ash tree in my garden was shedding. A breeze had sprung up and the tree's remaining leaves flickered in a peculiarly annoying way. My head felt unpleasantly light, giddy from conflicting emotions, as if I'd jumped on a roller coaster and couldn't get off.

chapter eight

"GOOD MORNING," SAID GIGI, THE COUNTY
attorney receptionist, not as brightly as usual. She twisted an earring.
"It's so terrible about the judge. Who's going to take over, anyway?"

I grabbed my messages and, distracted, said shortly, "They'll have
a procedure, I'm sure."

Her lower lip trembled. Poor Gigi. No one ever told her anything.

"Are you okay?" I asked.

She bit her lip and nodded.

I scanned the messages quickly, one from a victim who couldn't
make it to the arraignment today in Division Three, asking would I
call her when it was over, one from Yolanda Sanchez, Judge Thomas's
clerk.

Hurriedly I pushed open the door to the inner offices. No reso-
nant lawyer voices came from the break room, no clerks and secretaries laughing at their jokes. It felt as though the whole office were
holding its breath. The door to the law library where conferences
were held, usually open, was closed.

I walked as softly as I could in my inch-high black heels. Monday
was law-and-motion day, a busy day. Marilu was sitting at her desk,
drinking coffee and shuffling paper around. She looked up at me over
her pink-tinted power glasses. "Unbelievable, isn't it?"

"So how are they handling everything?"

"All of Division Two's even numbered cases are being handled by

Division One, the odds by Division Three." She pushed her glasses up on her nose. "Soon they'll bump up the juvenile judge and then eventually they'll appoint a judge pro tem."

"What's wrong with Gigi?"

"Melvin yelled at her." Marilu sneezed. "Excuse me. I think I'm getting a cold." She sneezed again. "I was fine when I woke up this morning."

"Where is everybody?"

"Melvin stormed in at eight o'clock and called a meeting of all the lawyers." She lowered her voice. "You know most of them never get here right at eight. So that really pissed him off. That's when he yelled at Gigi." She sniffed. "Everyone's walking on tippy-toe."

"Lots of pressure on him," I said.

"You're not kidding." She lowered her voice again. "He's been wanting to run for judge for years, and now there's a opening so he must be salivating. But if don't they catch who did it, it'll reflect on him as much as the sheriff. Voters don't think. Then there's the prosecution, if he blows that, come the next election we could all have a new boss." She rested her chin in her hand for a moment, contemplatively.

We grinned at each other.

"I didn't say a word." She looked at me with interest. "I heard you went on the call-out to tell his family."

I nodded. "Melvin showed up too."

She looked disgusted. "That dog! Politicking before the corpse is cold. Lee Thomas still has some power in this county." She paused. "She even started up a rape crisis center. People remember."

"What rape crisis center?"

"Before your time. It closed down when she went off the board. It's a shame—the judge didn't really understand women's stuff. I mean I liked him, he was always a perfect gentleman, but . . ."

"A chauvinist."

"Yeah. They're still using that word?"

"I wonder why she dropped out of everything."

Marilu shrugged. "Maybe she just got bored."

* * *

I sat at my desk with the messages. Work, wonderful work, so sooth-
ing. Craig wouldn't call me here, so I could rest. Nate hadn't called
me last night, but he was always in court on law-and-motion day. I
wasn't handling the Nate thing right, too pushy. *Losing the grip,*
that's what I was doing, the good things in my life slipping out of my
hands.

I looked over the messages—didn't need to call the victim until
after the arraignment. But Yolanda—how were they doing over there?
Not just Yolanda, but his bailiff, his secretary, Etta his court reporter.

A judge's staff, they were family too, a second family of equal
and sometimes greater value; they propped him up when he needed
it the most, knew where he was, well, usually, where he had been
and where he was supposed to be; they were the equivalent of lighting technicians, sound men, prompters, makeup people, all so the
show could go on.

I found the phone buried under a clutter of brochures—"Death
of a Loved One," "Domestic Violence," "Testifying in Court," "When
Your Child Has Been Molested." I dialed the number for Judge
Thomas's court, but no one answered, even the message machine was
turned off. It was five to nine. I grabbed the calendar for Division
Three and took off for the courthouse.

I slipped into Division Three, Judge Coleman's court. The judge was
plump cheeked and roly-poly, not nearly as inspiring as Cal Thomas
had been.

"Counselor," he was saying to one of the lawyers, "this is your
client's second escape."

The wood and wrought-iron seats attached to the floor of the
courtroom were filled with a motley collection of defendants and relatives, in clothing that ranged from torn jeans to cocktail party dresses.
The jury box was full of defendants in orange and red jumpsuits.

I looked for Nate, but he wasn't there. He was always there, law-and-motion day. In the far corner Ollie Menton, the official courtroom reporter for the *Sierra Vista Dispatch*, overweight, in red beard and wire rims, was in the act of yawning hugely. Nate hated Ollie, he got all the good stories. I walked back and sat in the chair in front of him.

"My client's changed, your honor," the lawyer was saying, preppy in a blue-and-white striped seersucker jacket, one fatherly arm around the shoulder of his scruffy client. "This has been a wake-up call for him. His mother's very sick. If you could reduce his bond to fifty thousand dollars his mother will put up her house . . ."

Ollie snickered.

I turned. "Where's Nate?" I asked.

"Beats me." Ollie fingered his upper lip fondly. "Could it be he's actually somewhere doing his job instead of hanging around trying to do mine?"

"I guess," I said noncommittally.

Once I got the trial date for the victim who couldn't be there, I left the courtroom. The big hall was empty, light gleaming on the marble floors and off the art deco brass. Across from me, the door to Division Two was closed on the empty darkened courtroom. I wondered if the judge's staff, his second family, were back in his chambers. Or had they all stayed home to mourn? But I knew Yolanda was there because she'd left that number on the message slip.

I started down the narrow hall to his chambers just as the door opened and Yolanda herself came out, young, pretty. But the hall was dark, her face shadowed. She had on a white blouse buttoned to the neck, a short black skirt. Her high heels clicked on the marble floor as she came toward me. A couple of feet away, she stopped abruptly.

"Oh!" Gold bracelets jangled as she put her hand on her heart; a *semanario* of gold bracelets, one for each day of the week. "You startled me." Her hair was pulled straight back, gold earrings shone at her ears, and now I could see her eyes, red and swollen, her eyebrows two wings against her white face.

"I'm sorry," I said. "I got your message so I was coming to see you."

She glanced over at the security guard way down the hall by the door, lounging back in his seat reading a paperback. "Right now, I can't think very well." She touched an earring, her hand trembling. Her voice was breathless, hyperventilated. "And just to go over to your office, everyone around . . ."

"We can talk somewhere else, if you like," I said.

"I live in Naco," she said tentatively. "I work out between five and six-fifteen, over at Googie's Gym, so could we possibly meet after that, say seven this evening at my house? Wait, not tonight. Tonight there's someone I have to . . . Tomorrow?"

Naco was a tiny town on the border, five miles from Dudley. "Tell me the address," I said. "I'll be there."

"Chloe! Wait!"

I turned. Cars were pulling out all around me. It was five o'clock and I was headed for my own car in the County Attorney parking lot.

Nate was just getting out of his turquoise and white '56 Chevy, in the back window was a FOR SALE sign that had been there for as long as I'd known him.

"Where were you this morning?" I asked as he approached.

"Running around." He was wearing a pink and green southwestern aloha-type shirt printed with sombreros and postcards of Mexico, and khakis aged to a sublime limpness. "Did you have a good weekend with *Craig*?"

"Don't ask."

"Why not?" Nate looked concerned. "Are you guys fighting? Didn't you say he'd been touchy lately?"

I felt weary. "Never mind. How was Windy City? Did B. W. sell you a three-dollar soft drink?"

Nate smirked. "He gave me one. He said he knew life was hard for young people." He paused. "And you're mad at me, I can tell. Because I never called you back."

Cars were pulling out around us. I hoped Melvin had left earlier and wouldn't see me talking to the press. "Sort of," I said.

"I couldn't," Nate said. "I knew you'd just ask me about that story I'm working on. Then you'd bug me about talking to the cops and telling them everything."

I leaned against the cement wall by my car. Yellow leaves littered the windshield. Arizona didn't have much in the way of red leaves. The lot was empty now, except for a couple of county cars. "Does that mean you're not going to?" I tried to make my voice neutral.

"Not yet."

"God. Nate." I paused. "I don't even know what we're talking about. Maybe it doesn't have any relevance whatsoever. Maybe it's common knowledge, you know? Part of the rumor mill and you haven't lived here long enough to realize that."

"It's more than that. Believe me." Little fires burned in Nate's big brown eyes behind his nerd glasses. "I want in on this. And Ollie's covering the actual crime. Does he seem to you like a man who'll go out of his way? He doesn't have a clue about being an investigative reporter. All he'll do is call up Hector Estrada and write up whatever Hector tells him to. He's old and tired, you know?"

"Nate, I don't think he's even forty."

"Spiritually. I meant spiritually." He put his hands in the pockets of his baggy pants and looked down, kicking at leaves on the asphalt. Below the short sleeve of his southwestern aloha shirt, I could see the peace sign that I kidded him about, tattooed on his forearm, as if he didn't know which decade he longed for.

"The judge died a rich man," he said, looking up. "Land deals, a lot of them, *quasi legal,* if you know what I mean."

"Kind of." But I felt relieved. "A lot of people would know that." I stared at one of the sombreros printed on his shirt. Once probably red and green it was now only pink and sage but it hadn't lost its jaunty tilt.

"People got screwed in those deals. Under all that high-class charm Judge Thomas was a jerk," he said. "Take a look at his family. Talk about dysfunctional. There's a daughter, Cornelia, who hasn't been home—"

I put my hands over my ears. "Nate, hush. That's their business. You know I can't discuss the judge's family with you. It would be a violation of confidentiality."

"Look, I'm telling you this stuff because I want someone I trust to know about it, in case—Right now it's somewhat unconnected, but if I keep going I think I can pull it all together."

"Nate," I said, "how about this: you go talk to Hector Estrada, tell him everything you know and let him do the investigating. If you play it right probably he'll give you some kind of exclusive. You know how he likes to wheel and deal."

"Hector Estrada." Nate sighed. "I can't believe you're talking about Hector Estrada."

"Why not?"

"You think you can trust him? Everyone knows Hector makes his own rules. He lied to me about one thing I know of for sure, so who knows what else?"

"What did he lie to you about?"

Nate shook his head. "Look, I'm on my way to talk to someone. If they tell me what I think they're going to then maybe I'll think about what you're saying." He lowered his voice, though by now the parking lot was empty. "I already talked to them once. I think they're ready for the whole shebang."

That's the dumbest thing I ever heard, was right there on the tip of my tongue. *This isn't a game, it's a homicide.* "Nate, *listen* to me," I said in frustration.

"No, you have to listen to *me,*" said Nate. "I have to do this stuff. I have to take some risks. That reporter, Don Bowles, you ever heard of him?"

"Don Bowles?" I stared at him. "Nate. Don Bowles was blown up with a car bomb. You really are an *idiot.*"

"Don't worry, I'm not going to get blown up. This is how I keep my integrity. You think I want to get cheesy? And you know what else, Chloe? You have to let your brother do what he has to do too."

"My brother's nuts," I said.

"So? That's who he is then. Chloe, you're my best friend in Cochise County, but—I don't care if it's not politically correct—you're still not a guy, so you can't understand." He looked at his watch. "Gotta go."

I stood there speechless for a moment.

He walked away over to his car, postcards, sombreros receding. "Say hi to Craig," he said over his shoulder.

"Anyway, at least be careful," I called, as he got in.

I stood in the empty parking lot and watched him drive off. Under all that ambition, Nate was just a kid. The FOR SALE sign in the back window of his car was crooked. He needed air in his back left tire and one of his brake lights was out. The other one blinked at me as he stopped at the parking lot exit. Then he turned and was out of sight.

chapter nine

IT WAS ALMOST SEVEN THE NEXT EVENING
as I drove to the roundabout that separated Old Dudley from New
Dudley. Halfway around I made a right onto Highway 92, then a left
just after Lily's Cafe, heading for Naco to see Yolanda. I still had heard
nothing from Craig. I didn't know if I even wanted to. A waning moon
hung low in the sky, the mountains outlined in the light of the setting
sun like cardboard cutouts in cheap movie scenery. Ahead of me,
Naco was a bowl of lights—a tiny town that straddled the border,
half in Mexico, half in the U.S.

Yolanda's house was a white frame, very small, on a road a few
blocks before the street that led to the border crossing. I parked
under an Arizona cypress and got out to the scent of pine. I'd brought
my victim advocate tote bag, full of brochures, resource book, flashlight, rubber gloves, Kleenex. The pink plastic donated tote bag.
Maybe that's why Gladys Alexander found me so unacceptable. Jeez,
I thought, you let Lee's snob mother get to you.

A light was on over Yolanda's door, shining on a bed of orange
and scarlet marigolds bordered with tough spiky grass. Yolanda
opened the door before I had a chance to knock.

I looked at her with semishock—I was used to her prim courtroom clothes, but now she wore a short-sleeved white turtleneck,
white pants, her hair drawn back loosely; dark, thick, charged with
electricity. She looked like a movie star.

"I was watching." She shivered though it wasn't cold. "I get so *nervous* when a car pulls up."

"Hypervigilance," I said. "You've had a big shock."

"No, it's that reporter. He came over on Saturday, he didn't call before or anything. I keep thinking he's coming back to ask me more questions."

"What reporter?"

"The young guy with the funny glasses? Oh." She put her hand to her mouth. "I'm sorry. You guys are friends, aren't you? I've seen you together at the cafe."

"Nate?" Nate had had the nerve to come and talk to the judge's clerk? "You don't have to talk to reporters," I said. "Whether they're my friends or not."

"He was polite," she said, "kind of sweet, but then he asked me . . ." She stared past me at the Arizona cypress, as if Nate stood there listening, notebook in hand, light gleaming off his funny glasses.

"Asked you what?"

"Nothing." She smiled apologetically. "I didn't mean to keep you standing outside. Come in."

The door led directly into the living room. Long, deep red curtains, floor to ceiling, were drawn closed at the windows, deep red wall-to-wall carpeting on the floor. A red and cream flowered couch, two cream armchairs, small red cushion on each one, a television in a corner. On the end tables were little doilies perfectly centered. There was a smell of burning wax.

In the middle of the room, Yolanda paused. "Sylvia Montano's mother told me you were the one who told Judge Thomas's family."

"Sylvia?" I said in surprise. "Who works for the Thomases? You know her?"

She nodded. "We both grew up in Naco. Her *nana* raised her. She was born into an old family, they lost everything long ago in the Revolution, except for a way of thinking. She's a hard worker, so I mentioned her to Cal." Her voice was edgy. "Please, sit down. Would you like coffee?"

"That would be nice."

I sat on the flowered couch while she went into the kitchen. A long line of framed photographs, family pictures, stood on a shelf against the far wall. In the middle under a small statue of the Virgin Mary, a votive candle burned. I wondered how long Yolanda had lived here; except for the icon and the photographs, the room was somehow empty. It seemed to convey expectations gravely diminished.

On the coffee table was a stack of magazines, very neat, corners squared, and a book on the top, upside down. I turned it over and read the title on its glossy cover: *Getting Mr. Right: What You Need to Know to Keep Your Man.* A woman, perfect blond hair, perfect teeth, perfect red-framed glasses, smiled at me promisingly. I opened it up.

Nora was a bright, attractive woman in her early thirties, with a good job as a sales manager for a computer firm, but when she showed up at my office one winter day, she was at the end of her rope. "Susan," she said, "I just don't know what to do about Tom—

Oh, please. I flipped pages, paused at,

Twelve Danger Signals to Look for in Your Relationship
1. You're always the one to make up after a fight.

Hurriedly I closed the book as Yolanda came back into the room. She set a brass tray down on the coffee table and the dark liquid in the cups sloshed over the rims and beaded on the tray.

"Sylvia's *nana* is dead now," she said. "Sylvia worshiped her, she almost went crazy when she died. Sylvia's not very stable in some ways. Her *nana* was beautiful, so white skinned, poor Sylvia got all the dark Indian blood from her father. One quarter *mestizo*. We Mexicans can be terrible snobs." She sat down, giving me a quick sidelong glance. "Just like I think Cal's wife must be."

I dabbed at the spilled coffee on the tray with a napkin, keeping my face noncommittal.

"You were there," she persisted. "How did she take it?"

"Yolanda, I can't talk about that," I said. "It's confidential, the same as it would be if someone asked me about you."

The *semanario* of gold bracelets slid down her arm as she reached out and picked up her coffee cup, took a sip. Her hands were slender, beautiful, except for the nails, bitten down to the quick.

"I saw her once when I was in Sierra Vista," she said. "At Fry's." Drops fell from the bottom of the cup onto her immaculate white turtleneck, leaving small brown spots. She didn't seem to notice.

"I was with a friend and they whispered, look, there's the judge's wife." Yolanda set the cup down and put her hand over her heart. "I couldn't believe it. I thought she was supposed to be so glamorous. She was wearing a dress like an old sack and her hair needed washing. I was so embarrassed for her, I looked away."

Too much. Had she gotten me out here just to gossip about Lee Thomas? So she could report back to his staff who hated her? "You're the one I'm concerned about," I said to her. "He was your boss. This must be a terrible shock."

"My boss." Yolanda stared at me. She picked up the cup again but she didn't take a sip. "Yes," she said. "It was. Not just for me but for all of us that worked for him. Everyone stayed home today except for me. No one knows if they'll even have a job when we get a new judge."

She set down her cup, missed the tray. The cup teetered on the edge of the coffee table. I caught it just in time. "I just want to know," she said. "Did she even *cry*?"

"Look . . ." I began, then stopped in frustration.

"Please." Her voice shook. "Hector came and talked to me. I never said a word about her, never brought up anything. But, Chloe, things were terribly wrong in that marriage. We all knew." Her mouth quivered. "Some nights he couldn't even bear to go home." She put her face in her hands and began to cry.

I reached into the tote bag, pulled out a couple of Kleenex. Then I let her cry, sipped my coffee; it was strong, bitter. After a while her sobs died down. I handed her the Kleenex and she blew her nose.

"It goes around and around in my mind," she said, thickly. "What if he didn't die right away, lying there all alone in the dark? Why did he go to Windy City? I asked Hector, *why*? Then he told me something I wasn't supposed to know. No one's supposed to know." She paused then added nervously. "But this is confidential, everything I say to you, right?"

"Yes," I said.

She lowered her voice. "They found a *note* in Cal's pocket."

"A note?"

"Yes. It said"—she closed her eyes—" 'Sweetheart, meet me at Windy City midnight, tonight. We'll start again. I love you.' "

"Sweetheart? I love you? Start again?" I said, sucked in, in spite of myself. "A girlfriend? My God, so that's what he meant by 'a new life.' "

"It fooled poor Cal." Her voice trembled. "But Hector's not fooled. The note was done on a computer. It could have been from anybody." She blinked rapidly, eyelashes heavy with tears. "Someone who knew him well. Someone who *hated* him." She paused significantly. "We all wondered," she went on, "why live that way, why not get a divorce? Cal wasn't even Catholic and neither is she."

"What? You think his wife wrote it? And what? Got him there and shot him? Or hired a hit man or something? Yolanda, you don't know . . ."

She shrugged and sighed. "Let's just drop it, okay. I mean, that's Hector's job." She ran her fingers through her hair. "Poor Cal, I feel so guilty, Chloe. Like it's all my fault."

"Why on earth would it be your fault?"

"He'd never have gone to Windy City if he was himself. He'd have known. Anyone could see he wasn't himself lately. His hair, when he dyed it. It looked so awful." She winced. "I tried to say it nicely—I thought he'd understand, he was always so fatherly, so mature, but no, he got angry, like a teenager."

"Wait, you lost me back there," I said.

"Isn't it obvious?" Yolanda looked at me, pityingly. "He had this power, all this power but he couldn't get to my heart anymore."

"Your heart?" I said faintly.

"But I had to do it. I knew he was never going to leave her, not ever. So I finally broke it off with him, a few weeks ago."

I stared at her.

She looked a little taken aback. "You didn't know?"

I shook my head.

"I thought everyone knew. Cal and I were lovers since I was twenty-five. Almost three years. But it was over . . . really over."

Whoever Nate had been going to talk to he'd said he already talked to them once. He'd talked to Yolanda on Saturday. Was that who Nate had been going to see last night? Yolanda? To do a story about their affair? Would Nate be that tacky? Had he miscalculated, actually shown up? Was that why she'd been so hypervigilant?

"Yolanda," I said, "did you tell the reporter about this?"

She looked at me in horror. "Do you think I'm crazy?"

"Did he ask you?"

"Not exactly. Oh, Chloe." She wrung her hands. "I keep thinking—about Cal lying out there in the desert, *dying*. It gets so cold at night and Chloe, he didn't have any religion at all." A tear rolled down her cheek. "And there was no love with him. Nothing left to hold his spirit here on earth."

chapter ten

HALF THE PEOPLE THAT WORKED IN THE
courthouse probably knew about Cal Thomas and Yolanda but was
anyone telling? Did Nate think the affair between Cal Thomas and
Yolanda was relevant to the judge's murder? Had Yolanda lied to me
and Cal was the one who'd broken it off? I could see the headline
now—LOVE SLAYING. I thought that if I were investigating the homicide I would certainly factor it in, yet Hector had told Yolanda about
the note to warn her, protect her. Done on a computer, not handwritten. No proof, then, that she'd written it.

Years ago Lee had been crazy about Cal, then later he had Yolanda and she had . . . Willy? The person she'd called and then lied
about calling? Like Craig and I—everything nice, everything good,
well mostly anyway, then bam! What were relationships between the
sexes anyway? *Turning to poison while the bee mouth sips.* They
weren't even friendships. Nothing.

Freed of tourists on a Tuesday night, Main Street was empty. The
once dusty buildings where copper miners had done their business,
now refurbished and painted San Francisco colors, were quiet. Night-
lights burned in the shops that catered only to the tourists, selling
antiques and collectibles—mining artifacts, sepia photographs of miners, paintings of cowboys and Indians—souvenirs of the town as it
had once been and was no longer. And as the last of the mining
families died off, real estate prices were skyrocketing, the houses

sold to people from the cities, urban refugees, like me.

I thought of Lee. *"She left everything behind to marry the judge,"* Sylvia had said. *"She left her whole life. I don't understand why a person would do that."* And Nate, the carpetbagger, new to Cochise County, hot on a story probably everyone knew and no one wanted to talk about.

But none of us seemed to live anymore where we had grown up; we moved to other people's places, made souvenirs of their history. We all lived in ghost towns.

It was nine o'clock when I got home. The Santa Fe house across the street was dark. Next door, my neighbor Lourdes's new pet, Honey Pie, a hideous bad-tempered shar-pei, yapped and yapped, signaling that no one was home to anyone who cared.

"Dumb dog," I hissed. "Ugly too."

Yap yap yap.

Inside the answering machine was blinking but when I played it I only got two hang-ups. I carried the phone into the living room and slumped down into the recliner. It had been what? Saturday afternoon, Saturday night, all day Sunday, I recited in my mind, Sunday night, all day Monday, all day Tuesday and no word from Craig. We usually spoke on the phone nearly every night. Surely it was him calling.

Unless it was Nate.

Pretty nervy of him to go see Yolanda. I only had her word that she'd broken it off with the judge. Maybe she'd written the note as a veiled threat of blackmail. Maybe . . .

The phone rang. Right next to it, I jumped, but I let it ring three times before I picked up.

"Hello?"

"Hello?" someone said, a young girl's voice. "Chloe? I hope you weren't in bed. I called earlier but you weren't home."

"It's fine," I said airily. "I just got in. Who's this?"

"We've never met. My name's Nola."

"Nola! Of course, Nate's *girlfriend*," I said, with more sincerity. "What's up?"

"I know you two are good friends. I was wondering if you'd seen him lately?"

"I saw him Monday just after five. He was going to interview someone."

"Yesterday. Oh. He was supposed to come to my house for dinner tonight at six, but he hasn't shown up."

"No."

"I mean, he says things like he's a little rat, but he's not really. I don't think so, anyway. But now I'm worried that . . ." She stopped.

"That what?" I felt the sudden coldness of my hands on the receiver. I swallowed.

"Has he ever mentioned anyone else? You know."

"Oh," I said. "Like a girlfriend. No, just you. Have you tried calling him?"

"Well . . ." Nola hesitated. "Actually I didn't. *He's* the one who hasn't shown. He owes *me* the apology."

"Right on," I said, regressing to the sixties.

"Wait! I think I hear him now. Chloe! *Please, please,* don't tell him I called."

"No way," I said.

"Bye," she said.

We hung up. *Men,* I thought, thinking of Craig. I put on some music, old Graham Parsons, loud, to stop myself from thinking so much. I went into the spare bedroom where the ironing board was set up. Big Foot had been using my pile of ironing for a bed. I ironed a gray-and-black striped silk blouse for tomorrow, running masking tape over it to pick up the cat hairs. Then I did a pair of black rayon pants. They were full cut so I ironed them with a crease to take out some of the fullness. The music made it easy, restful to be ironing.

In a rush, I set down the iron, went back to the living room and dialed Craig's number before I had time to think about what I was doing. Shameless.

It rang and rang but no one, not even his answering machine, picked up. He was almost always home when I called him after nine. And maybe he was home now, listening to the phone ring, waiting me out.

Frustrated, I began an elaborate rationalization: a kind of meditation on time. Mornings, afternoons, evenings, nights, days, weeks, months, years; meaningless divisions that seemed to prevent me from doing anything because it was always too early or too late. But the reality was I could act any time I wanted to.

"Fuck this," I said out loud. I grabbed my purse, car keys and headed out the door.

I drove the fifteen mile stretch to the dirt road to Craig's in twelve minutes. He lived a mile down. I drove twenty-five miles an hour till I passed the one house before his, halfway there. Then I cut my lights and slowed, creeping along, straining to see the house, but a stand of tamarisk blocked my view until I was right up beside it. The driveway was empty.

I pulled in just far enough to be clear of the road, killed the engine. Was that a light at the front, behind the sunflowers? I rolled down my window. No, just the waning moon, winking off the glass, painting the house, the once bright sunflowers, silver-gray.

The lights were all off except for the office where a night-light burned. I took the flashlight out of my glove compartment, got out and walked softly to the office. The night-light was strong enough to see that the manure had been swept up, everything looked as usual except for the coffeepot, missing from its burner. Craig drank coffee day and night, I'd have thought he would have replaced it right away.

Maybe he was at Wal-Mart in Sierra Vista right now, getting a new one. Where did he go at night, those nights, every other night at least, that he didn't see me? In spite of all the time we'd spent together, I didn't know.

I could shine the flashlight into the house, but what did I expect to see? What was I looking for? Here I was, uninvited and alone at a place where I'd always been welcome, like a ghost returning to haunt my own previous life. Except it looked different now, the desert willow and the Mexican sunflowers dimmed, waning moonlight dissolving all the boundaries.

If I waited long enough I might see Craig and Chloe come out the front door, laughing. Occupying that same space occupied by Lee and Cal Thomas, Jack Townsend and his first wife Mary, drinking, dancing, flirting, driving with a six-pack through the big empty county.

If you leave him a note, the voice in my head said, *it won't be like you're spying on him.* I could reach in my purse, take out my notepad, scribble *Craig, call me, I'm worried.* That would be the thing to do. But I didn't move. I stayed there, breathing in the cool air spiked with the prickly scent of plants going to seed, dying.

I stood that way for a long time, expectant, as if I might see the headlights from Craig's truck coming down the road any minute. He would jump out with presents for me.

Then the chill got to me and I walked back to my car, started it up, and drove down the empty dirt road out to the highway.

chapter eleven

"SO YOUR BOY'S FLOWN THE COOP," SAID
Detective Mark Flannery, from the door of my office.

I looked up, startled. I hadn't seen Mark since the night of the death notification when he'd shown up at my house with questions about Craig and the lawsuit and here he was again, his timing creepily impeccable.

He must have snuck past Gigi. No, Gigi was sick, some kind of flu. Marilu and two of the attorneys were also out. They all had the flu, the Melvin-Huber-on-the-warpath flu. I was all alone with the posters on the wall about domestic violence, the compensation claims, the brochures about victim's rights, child abuse, and death of a loved one.

"Who's that?" I said.

"Who? No. Your boy."

"My *boy*?" I said, but of course I knew perfectly well who he meant. I licked the envelope I'd just addressed, with a victim compensation claim form in it. For some stupid reason I thought of *Seinfeld*, of George Costanza's fiancée, dying after licking all those cheap envelopes George had bought for their wedding invitations.

"Your friend then, Craig," Mark said. He still had on his baseball cap and a red U of A Wildcats sweatshirt as if he were headed for a big game. His thick white running shoes made no sound as he came all the way into my office.

"What about him?" I threw the envelope at the wire mail basket and missed.

Mark bent down and picked it up. "It looks like he's left town."

I felt a little sick but I kept my face noncommittal. "If he did, surely he has a right to. Anyway," I said firmly, "you already asked me about him. You said it was no big deal, just grunt work, remember?"

Mark pulled a handkerchief from his pocket and blew his nose. "Damn allergies," he said. "I hate fall. Well, he picked a bad time to disappear."

"He didn't disappear," I said patiently. "I saw him on Saturday. I think you just keep missing him."

"Saturday was four days ago. You talked to him since?"

"He might have called. I haven't been home much, I've been very busy," I said without conviction.

"He's your boyfriend and you haven't seen or heard from him since Saturday?" He cocked his head. "You two have a fight?"

"Well," I said, giving up. "We kind of did."

"Yeah? What about?"

"He wanted to watch *Air Force One*," I lied, because it was none of Mark's business, "for the millionth time and I didn't, okay? We had words."

The golden retriever face softened. "You don't like Harrison Ford?"

"I like Russell Crowe better."

"Who?"

"Never mind. Look, maybe he went camping or something, to stew about it." It was a great thought and it might even be true. "When I hear from him, I'll tell him to get in touch, okay?" I paused. "Mark, I can't believe you're actually pursuing this."

He shrugged. "Something to do," he said and walked out as silently as he had come.

The phone rang. I picked up. "Victim Witness!"

"Lee Thomas for you," said whoever it was subbing for Gigi.

"Lee?" I said. "This is Chloe."

"Yes, hello." Her voice was so faint I wondered how she'd gotten up the strength to dial the number. Yet Jack Townsend a.k.a. Buffalo Bill had said she had guts, wasn't afraid of anything. I wanted to shout over the phone, "Lee, wake up!"

"How are you doing?" I asked.

"Fine, thank you. I want to apologize for not being home, when I asked you to come over."

"Someone else was looking for you too," I said. "Buffalo Bill." Jeez. As soon as I said it I could have bit my tongue. "I'm sorry. I meant—"

"Jack Townsend," said Lee. "He told me he ran into you. Literally. 'Buffalo Bill.' How strange you should call him that. Cal used to, all the time."

"No kidding."

"Yes. I think Jack rather liked it." She tried a laugh, but it didn't quite work.

"Lee," I said, "it's okay to be upset. It's *okay.*"

There was a pause, silence. It seemed to last forever. Had I committed a faux pas against the well-bred?

Then she spoke. "Could you come to the house? I won't forget this time."

"Of course. When?"

"Tomorrow? Any time? There really is something I need to talk to you about."

Where was Craig anyway? Even the cops couldn't find him. I stopped in at the post office on my way home from work to check my mail. At ten in the morning when the mail is all out, the benches in front are full of retirees, young people, the unemployed and unemployable. Now they were empty and inside the fluorescent lights shone off the expanse of gray-blue linoleum, the little numbered boxes.

Maybe Craig *had* left town and there'd be a letter, a poem, waiting in my box. I opened it, threw three Victoria's Secret catalogs into the trash can and was left with one postcard.

Hi, Chloe, it's so beautiful here it takes your breath away, but don't worry I'm still breathing!! Love, Danny.

Postmarked Billings, Montana. Too much. I turned the postcard over and stared at the view of snowcapped mountains, far far away, horribly sublime.

I drove home. Craig was right, so was Nate. Danny was all grown-up. But so was Craig. Who cared?

Not me, I was disengaged. I began to fix dinner, watching my hands dump a bag of salad into a bowl. They seemed like someone else's. I wasn't hungry. My eye fell on Hal's tasteful wooden spice rack, stocked with all kinds of exotic spices. I'd never used them. The bottles were covered with greasy dust. Tension tightened my neck muscles. I tried a little deep breathing, which didn't help.

I went into the living room and aimlessly surfed the TV, landing on *Animal Vet* where they were hoisting up a large horse with pulleys, in preparation to giving him a hip replacement. There was a knock on my kitchen door, so forceful I sat bolt upright. My heart beat faster. Oh, no. Not *Craig.*

I clicked the TV off and peeked surreptitiously out the kitchen window. Standing in the carport, hand raised to knock again, was a young woman with bobbed dark hair, in a black mini T-shirt, olive cargo pants, enormous black shoes. I opened the door.

"Chloe?" Her face was a hectic pink and she breathed heavily, hyperventilating, as if she'd run over from Sierra Vista. Her green eyes, vivid next to the pink, seemed on the verge of tears. God, not a victim. Not *now.* How did she find me? My neck muscles tightened even more.

"Yes," I said reluctantly.

"I'm Nate's girlfriend, Nola, nice to meet you," she said in a rush. Her hand darted out as if to shake mine, darted back.

"Nola," I said guiltily. "My goodness. Please, come in." She seemed impossibly young, maybe sixteen, but Nate had said she was twenty. A dancer or something.

She clomped past me in the big black shoes, into the kitchen. Five-feet-five or so, not much over a hundred pounds but she radiated so much nervous drama, she filled up all the space. It was exhausting. Bipolar, I thought nervously, a manic phase?

"I have to talk to someone," she said. "Nate never showed up, that wasn't him that I heard. I've called him four times. His car's not there. I just checked. I called the paper. They haven't seen him since Monday and he had a story due about a play rehearsal—he never turned it in." She paused to take a breath. "He *always* turns stuff in."

I rubbed my neck.

"And that's not all," she went on relentlessly. "I went to the Tombstone Cafe—he has coffee there just about every morning—but he hasn't been there since Monday either." Her voice rose. "And the worst, the totally worst part is that I keep thinking—oh, good, he didn't stand me up, he's just . . . *dead.*" She began to giggle hysterically.

"Nola, you know Nate. There's all kinds of places he could be," I said patiently, thinking of none. "Calm down, okay? Would you like a glass of water?"

"Not really." She giggled again. "Maybe. Sure."

Compared to her, I was the calm one, but I seemed to have contracted her breathing problem and my hands shook as I filled a glass of water and gave it to her. Then I filled one for myself.

"Thanks." She drained the glass and went on. "I know he was working on this really big story but he wouldn't tell me anything about it. He reads these books, *The Executioner's Song, In Cold Blood, The Stranger Beside Me?* Where people go and interview murderers? You said he had an interview on Monday? You know what he told me his big dream is? To talk to a killer, to really get inside his head."

"He didn't say *that*," I protested. "He told me he was going to talk to someone who knew something."

"Well, a murderer would know something, wouldn't they?" she said with indisputable logic. She seemed calmer now that she had given all her worries to the nice victim advocate.

I'd warned him and warned him, but I couldn't believe he could really be missing—missing or worse. I wanted to cry. "Shit!" I said. I banged my fist on the counter. I still wanted to cry but violence was a good substitute. I banged it again. "That idiot! Well, it's his own fault."

Nola waited.

"Look," I said, "I have a lot of things on my mind, my brother seems to be screwing up, my boyfriend is God knows where and I'm not even sure if he is my boyfriend anyway. I'm really glad you're on top of this because it's too much for me right now."

"Your boyfriend?" said Nola, zooming in. "Craig? Oh no! Nate said he sounded so nice." Her voice rose. "He's missing *too*? You don't think—" Her eyes widened. She began to giggle again. "Maybe they ran off together!"

I felt a giggle coming on too. I blocked it. "I didn't say he was missing exactly and besides they don't even know each other. Just calm down."

"I am calm. Really. And I've got the key to Nate's apartment right here." Nola reached in her pocket and dangled it in front of me.

chapter twelve

THE MINER'S HOTEL WHERE NATE HAD A
room was a big grimy stucco building located up a long flight of crum-
bly cement steps behind the St. Elmo bar. We entered the dim lobby
where spotty wallpaper, faded to beige, peeled off the walls. A few
old gray men, ghostly with cigarette smoke, sat on couches in the
gloom, watching television and hacking up God knows what.

We climbed another flight of stairs, dull splintery wood. At the
top, we walked down a hall lit by a forty-watt bulb, to number nine.
"Who else lives here?" I asked. "Does Nate have any friends in the
building?"

"You saw the lobby," said Nola, unlocking the door. "Bunch of
dead guys. God!"

Inside the dark apartment, the street light made patterns on the
tan cloth shade that covered the only window. I hadn't seen a shade
like that in years. Nola fumbled, flicked on a light switch.

The apartment was spartan, painfully neat. One room, kitchen
lined up on the back wall, a bookcase, big *Pulp Fiction* poster above it.
By the window was a cheap desk whose oak veneer was peeling off.

"He doesn't even have a computer?" I said.

Nola rolled her eyes. "He had a clunky old four-eighty-six, but he
sold it. He has a notebook and does all his stories on the one at work."

The sagging single bed's brown top blanket was tucked in so tight
you could almost see the edges fraying from the strain. A black phone

and answering machine sat on the painted brown nightstand beside it. What were we looking for? I crossed the room and opened the door onto a tiny bathroom. I turned on the light—no blood spatters in the tub, on the sink, or the black-and-white tiled floor.

"His big backpack's still under the bed," said Nola, coming in behind me. She opened the white metal medicine cabinet. "Everything's here—razor, toothbrush. Not like he went on a trip."

"Still," I said. "They're not like us, they go places sometimes without taking anything."

"Not even us," said Nola. "It's so complicated. They're not all like that, but where are they, the ones who aren't?"

Was she asking *me*? In case she was, I went officiously back into the main room and opened the door of the only closet.

"I'll get the dresser!" Nola said.

I looked at a row of faded shirts, then the jackets, carefully arranged. He even hung up his jeans, his khakis.

"So many socks!" said Nola. She giggled. "Look at us! Going through all his stuff. He'd be so pissed!"

"We have to do it," I said firmly.

"We do!" said Nola.

I flipped through the shirts; bright aloha shirts, pleated tuxedo shirts, cream guayaberas, a fringed shirt with broncos bucking, the sombrero shirt. I held it out.

"He was wearing this when he talked to me," I said. "That means he came home afterwards. And it looks like . . ." I flipped through the jackets; a tweed, a denim, an ancient pinstripe that I'd seen him wear at a trial. "Wherever he is, he's wearing his madras jacket."

"His favorite." Nola gave a long shuddering breath.

I closed the door, feeling dizzy. "He hasn't lived in Cochise County that long. He told me his relatives all live in Ohio."

"He told me that too. His father died a few years ago and his mother's all alone in a big house. He worries about her. He really loves his mom. Maybe she got sick and he had to catch a plane right away."

"Ohio." I sat on the bed. "Did he say what town? I can't remember. God. Cleveland?"

"Maybe," Nola said without conviction.

"If some kind of emergency came up, someone would call him." I sat on the bed, by the answering machine. Five messages. I pushed play, the machine beeped, "Nine-thirty-three-Tuesday." "Nate, Ollie Menton here, I think you missed a deadline. You like your job? Give me a call."

"I told you!" said Nola. "Didn't I?"

"Nola," I said, "the first call is Tuesday. That means all the previous messages were erased. Did you call him *Monday* night, after you talked to me?"

"No."

Shit. I pushed play again, the rest were hang-ups. "Me, probably," said Nola.

I hit redial. "You have reached the offices of the *Sierra Vista Dispatch*. Our office hours are from eight to five—"

I hung up. "Shit. Just the paper."

Nola came up beside me and picked up the phone. "Star sixty-nine! To see who called him last."

"Very *good*," I said.

"Actually, it probably won't work. It'll just be me," said Nola, punching it in. "I called him . . . Wait, it's not me. It's not even local. Should I hit one to call the number?"

"*Yes.*"

After a while she hung up. "No answer and no machine," she said. "Pen. I'll write it down, while I still remember. I mean, it could just be a telemarketer." She sat down at the desk and pulled open the single drawer, found a pen, wrote on a Post-it and gave it to me. "We can try again later. I mean, you can. I don't want him to think I'm chasing after him, you know. I put my number down too, so you can tell me who it is."

I looked through the drawer. There were bills, and also Post-its, ballpoint pens, ballpoint pen caps, paper clips, rubber bands, a couple of blank yellow legal pads, matchbooks from local places: the Hitching Post, St. Elmo bar, Circle K. So many matchbooks and Nate didn't smoke.

"Nate's got marijuana stashed here?" I said. "If he does you better get rid of it."

"Come on," said Nola. "Fussy, fussy. I bet *you've* smoked it. My mom did. He doesn't have any marijuana." She looked abashed. "I checked when you were in the bathroom."

I took the bills out of their envelopes; they were the current ones for gas, water, electric, phone. I scanned the phone bill. "Just three long distance. A Tucson one and two in Cochise County. None to Ohio. But he'd probably call Ohio collect." I handed it to Nola. "Recognize any numbers?"

She looked it over and pointed to one of them. "There."

"That's St. David," I said. "Seventeen minutes. So whose is it?"

Nola smiled a little smug cat smile. "It's the one I just wrote down on the Post-it."

"That St. David number doesn't necessarily mean anything," I said. "He was already missing when they called." We stood outside at the top of the flight of steps that led down to the gulch where I'd parked my car. Clouds were thickening overhead, and it smelled like rain.

I looked at my watch. Nine-thirty. "Do you need a ride home?" I asked Nola.

She shook her head. "I live just up that way." She pointed. "What are we going to do?"

I had to go see Lee Thomas tomorrow. "Do you have a car?"

She nodded.

"Meet me outside the Sierra Vista sheriff substation, around eight-thirty. Okay? We could go together but I have something else to do there. We'll file a missing persons report."

"But why Sierra Vista?"

"That's where Hector Estrada works and he's the chief investigator in the judge's murder. If we're lucky he'll be around then."

"I'll bring a snapshot," said Nola.

"And, Nola? Try to be calm, okay?"

"Don't worry. The St. David's number, let's not tell the cops about that until we know what it is."

I looked at her curiously. "Why not?"

"It's ours."

We parted and I walked down the crumbling mismatched concrete steps to the gulch and my car. A couple of kids with backpacks were walking toward me, a young girl in a long black dress and a dark-skinned boy with rasta braids. Dudley was full of wandering kids, like it was still the sixties. The boy skipped along, singing, the girl carried a stack of papers. She gave me a beatific smile as I got in the car, and tucked a piece of paper under the windshield wiper. Probably an announcement for a poetry reading, or maybe an art opening.

It fluttered in the wind as I drove home worrying about Nate. I tried to remember just exactly what he'd said to me in the parking lot. *Land deals. The judge's family.* Whoever it was Nate had been planning to meet, he'd talked to them once before.

Postcards, sombreros receding. *"Say hi to Craig."*

But thinking about it got me nowhere, like everything I did lately. And Craig, he was gone from my life. I was back to where I'd been before we met. I'd been okay, I hadn't been unhappy. How had I managed that? I couldn't remember.

Under the windshield wiper, the piece of paper fluttered. I pulled into my driveway, got out, and took it from under the windshield wiper; it was slick in some parts, raspy like sandpaper in others. I carried it into the house to look at it in the light. It twinkled at me.

It was raspy from glitter sprinkled on glue over the label from a can of hot sauce, to form the words: *This is the key.*

I turned it over. The other side was blank. My phone rang then and I ran to answer it.

"Hi, sweetheart," said Craig. "I guess I need to tell you, I'm in Tucson at Mountain View Rehab. Where the hell have *you* been?"

chapter thirteen

WHAT? MY MOUTH FELT DRY. I NEEDED TO
sit. I carried the phone to the couch, its dragging long cord catching
the answering machine and knocking it onto the floor. I left it there.

"Chloe?" Craig said. "You still there?"

"Yes. Just a second." I sat down on the couch and took a deep
breath as relief, mingled with regret, flooded over me. Regret? For
what? Did I really like suffering that much? Then it registered. What
he'd actually said. "What do you mean, where have *I* been?" I said.
"Mountain View *Rehab*? What? For your back?"

"It's related."

"It's bothering you that badly?"

"I . . ." He hesitated. "There's a lot of things I wanted to tell you
Saturday. But you drove away. I called you the rest of the day Saturday, Saturday night too. Your machine was off. I checked myself in
on Sunday."

"Of course my machine was off. And why shouldn't I drive away?
After the way you acted," I said heatedly. "Silly me, getting upset
about you throwing bags of manure around. I bet that did your *back*
a lot of good."

"I'm trying to explain." Craig sighed. "Are we still having a fight?"

"And all these things are going on, scary things and you're not
around." I wanted to punish him. It was all so ordinary now, almost
banal.

"*Scary* things? Like what?"

But I couldn't talk to him about Nate. "Nothing," I said. I took a deep breath to calm myself down.

"We're still having a fight."

"We?" I stretched out on the couch, plumped a pillow under my head to better enjoy my moral superiority. "What did I do?"

"Nothing. Jeez, Chloe. I'm sorry I blew up like that, I'm sorry. I could feel it coming on and I couldn't stop it."

"But why? Why was it even coming on?"

"It's a long story. God." He sighed again. "Sometimes I feel like I'm on a railroad track, there's a freight train coming and all I have to do is step off. But I don't."

"Jeez," I said.

"It didn't have anything to do with you."

"But I was there," I said hotly. "I was the person affected by it."

"At first I actually thought it was your fault, 'cause you were bugging me—"

"Craig!" I said.

"It wasn't. I know, I know. It's so fucking hard to explain over the phone and I'm only supposed to talk for five minutes." He laughed. "Flame knew, she fucking *knew*. I thought she was going to bust me and I didn't want you to know yet. I was going to tell you after we had a good time. But you . . . No. It wasn't you."

"So are they giving you physical therapy or something?"

"It's not that kind of rehab. I'd have thought with your job you'd know about Mountain View. It's for addictions."

"*Addictions?*"

"I'm addicted to Percodans. That's why I was so crazy, I was taking all those Percodans . . ." He paused. "They started interfering with my antidepressants."

"Your *antidepressants?*"

"Zoloft."

My living room seemed to shift around me. How truly hideous the brown recliner was. Zoloft? I hadn't had a clue. I saw for the first time how trusting I'd been. "You never told me you were taking antidepressants."

"We were having fun. We were happy. It felt like a normal life. It's been years since I had a normal life. I didn't want to wreck it."

I swallowed hard. *Years since he'd had a normal life?* "I wouldn't have cared," I said. "You couldn't even trust me?"

"You hate all that therapy stuff. Twelve-step. It's overdone. Remember?"

"Craig!" I could feel my face getting red. "I don't. I mean I just hate it personally, for me. I—"

"It's okay," he cut in. "It's just the way you are. I've only got one more minute. You can come visit me next Sunday, three to five. Now listen, I need a favor. Could you go to my place, key's under a rock by the office door, and mail me all the black T-shirts you can find, and inside the greenhouse is a pot with strawberry plants in it, take those to Flame. And put a message on my machine, I forgot. I was all agitated about you. Say I'll be back in two and a half weeks. I gotta go."

"Where do I mail the T-shirts?" I said. "I don't even know where Mountain View is, how can I visit?"

"Call 555-7203, that's the office and get the address. Okay? Okay, Chloe?" His voice started to fade, as if swallowed up by the hundred mile distance.

"Listen, I want everything to be honest," I said loudly. "Can you hear me? Honesty. From now on."

His voice came back then, louder than before. "That's what I love about you, Chloe, you're so normal. You're so . . ."

His voice drifted off again.

"What?" I shouted. "I'm so *what?*"

"Easy to fool," he said, or did he?, and hung up.

Easy to fool? Had he really said easy to fool? I wasn't sure. I scribbled the number on a Post-it by the answering machine, then I sat back down on the recliner and stared at nothing for a few minutes.

"That's why I never worry. When you worry you don't have time for the things that really matter, like remembering the way the Flamingos sang 'I Only Have Eyes for You.'"

"Craig, you shit!" I said out loud. "Damnit!" I threw the phone as hard as I could at the brown recliner. It hit one hideous arm, bounced off, hit the hardwood floor, bounced again.

I went outside and to the porch, hoping the chill would clear my head. By now there was thick cloud cover and rain had begun to fall in spotty drops. All this, I thought angrily, on top of this stuff about Danny, about Nate. Nate-Danny, Danny-Nate, they were jumbled up together in the same lump of anxiety.

Now my anger felt like a block of ice, lodged in the center of my body, melting into my bloodstream. I'd never questioned Craig in the ways lovers do, never glanced through his mail, gone through his pockets, opened his medicine cabinet to check out the contents.

I'd saved that for Nate.

Well, it was different.

I wasn't normal. I was an idiot.

I shivered. The rain was gusting in on me, and suddenly I was appalled. Why couldn't I feel more supportive? What right did I have to be angry? Craig had been deteriorating right before my eyes, and I was so encased in my own little bubble, I didn't even see him. Plus Craig wasn't my first screwed up boyfriend. There was Logan, back in New York, still a drunk right now probably and there was that lawyer who was in A.A. If I'd known more about Craig I certainly wouldn't have . . . *Oh, yeah?* But I didn't feel like a life inventory right now so I went back inside and went to bed, falling asleep almost instantly.

At three in the morning, I woke up. *Nate's dead.* I should have listened to him, from the start, at the cafe. We were friends and I didn't even know what town his mother lived in, in Ohio. I hadn't really listen to Craig either. My God, did I ever listen to anybody?

I lay awake, listening now to the spotty rain hitting my tin roof and dripping off the eaves. It had a furtive sound to it, the spotty rain, like floorboards creaking, as though someone had entered my house, and was creeping stealthily from room to room.

chapter fourteen

WHERE WAS NOLA? EIGHT-FORTY-SIX BY MY
watch and she hadn't shown up. I'd told Hector everything I knew.
The rain had stopped and the wind had come up again parting the
clouds as I stood with him outside the Sierra Vista sheriff's substation,
located in a nearly new complex of pale brick county buildings, landscaped with gravel, ocotillo, and bird of paradise.

"So what are you going to do?" I asked him.

For a moment, he stared past me as though absorbed in something over my shoulder, though there was nothing there but the
Health Department building. "What can I do," he said finally. "You tell
me he's doing a story about the judge, but you don't know what it is.
He was going to interview someone but you don't know who."

His charcoal-gray shirt and gray and white tweedy pants set off
his salt-and-pepper hair and mustache perfectly. And his gray suede
shoes; surely they weren't just plain old Hush Puppies. Maybe they
were Bruno Maglis.

He fingered his mustache. "You said something about a snapshot?"

"His girlfriend's supposed to bring one. Nola." I looked at my
watch. Eight-fifty. Where was she?

"I'll put him on the computer. He gets stopped anywhere in the
country they'll get him."

"That's *all*?"

"Chloe, Chloe," he said sadly. "I got people coming out of the woodwork with information, not just you. I'll get a deputy to do some checking, how's that?" He looked at his watch. "Where's the girlfriend with the picture? I don't have all day."

An old blue Volvo pulled into the parking lot.

"Here she is," I said in relief.

We watched as Nola wound down the window and opened the door from the outside. She got out, holding a big manila envelope, and walked over to us. She wore a long black-and-white apron dress with a little white T-shirt and clogs.

"Hector Estrada, Nola—" I paused. I didn't have a clue what her last name was.

"Nola Collins! I'm very pleased to meet you!" she said, extending her hand to Hector. I was impressed, she had manners. She opened the envelope. "I brought this," she said. "I worked it up this morning, that's why I'm a little late. It's a flyer."

We looked at the flyer. HAVE YOU SEEN THIS MAN? in big letters over a snapshot of Nate, taken outside somewhere, looking young and bemused and innocent. Hector looked at Nola. Her bobbed hair was shiny, with little red highlights and there were pearls in her ears. She looked like a darling refugee from a nice Catholic girls' school.

Hector smiled.

"I need phone numbers to put on the flyer. I didn't want to use mine in case . . ." Her voice trailed off.

"Come inside," said Hector magnanimously. "We'll see what we can do. I'll want a statement too. You don't need to stick around, Chloe."

Maybe I should go to the paper, talk to Ollie Menton, I was thinking, as I pulled into Craig's driveway. I had to go see Lee Thomas later too but I wanted to do this first. I got out of the car. In the yard, the Mexican sunflowers were drooping, their seed heads heavy with moisture. I found the key under the rock and unlocked the door to the house.

Inside it smelled musty, like an attic full of old books. Craig had enough of them, in bookcases all along one wall. Dust motes danced in the watery sun that shone through the east windows. It shone on the cracked leather of the big club chair and on the maroon velour throw over Craig's ancient couch, the couch where we'd sat so recently, last Saturday morning drinking coffee before going to Flame and Roy's.

The cups were still there, next to a stack of seed catalogs and videos, my copy of *Kiss Me Deadly,* old ending, Craig's *Chinatown* and Altman's *The Long Goodbye.* We'd rented *L.A. Confidential* the weekend before last and had an L.A. noir film festival. When was it Craig had planned to tell me he was checking into rehab? After we had a good time. We had had good times watching L.A. noir, hadn't we, or maybe it was just me who had a good time while Craig silently suffered.

I wasn't so angry anymore. This was just a setback. Eclipsed by Nate's disappearance, it was sad, but hardly tragic. I could handle the Zoloft, the rehab.

I went into the bedroom, where not quite as recently Craig and I had slept in his bed. Sex was fine, sex was great but what I missed right now was the dance we performed late at night, in chilly weather, turning in unison in our sleep, seeking out new ways of fitting together.

Now the bed was made, the red-and-green striped Mexican blanket he used as a bedspread, smoothed out. He always made the bed, as soon as he got up, without fail, an experienced bachelor.

On the shade of the lamp on the bedside table, a lamp from his childhood, a horse reared up, the cowboy on it waved his hat at me. Next to the lamp a book lay face down, *No Mercy—A Journey to the Heart of the Congo.* "One of the best books I've ever read!" Craig had told me Sunday before last, with characteristic enthusiasm. He was only halfway through and he hadn't even taken it with him.

He kept his T-shirts in the top drawer of his dresser. I opened it, found three black ones, pulled them out.

I still had to put a message on his machine. The phone was in a little room he used as a study, on top of a filing cabinet. I went in, sat down on his desk chair, and fiddled with the machine, figuring it out, then put on the message.

Then I looked around. He dealt with business on a computer in his office off the greenhouse. This room was tinier than his office; here he wrote poems, letters, longhand or on the old Olivetti on the desk.

Everything he wrote here was personal, locked away in a four-drawer filing cabinet. On impulse, I picked up the phone, pushed the redial button and heard the quick tattoo of a number being dialed.

"Hi, this is 555-2132. At the sound of the beep, you know what to do." A woman's voice, what a class-conscious radical old flame once called a sorority girl voice, my voice, me, Chloe. Miss Chloe, Craig liked to call me sometimes. The last person he'd called before he checked into rehab. I smiled. Being the last person someone called before they checked into rehab—that was modern romance for you.

Suddenly I felt calm, ready to handle whatever came my way.

I got the key from the hook in the kitchen and went outside to the greenhouse to find the strawberry plants. Inside it smelled of manure and rich damp soil. There, just as suddenly my calm left me. The stand of seed packets Craig had sent whirling only days ago with its colored pictures of pansies, phlox, California poppies and black-seeded Simpson seemed garishly bright.

Pain stabbed my chest. I ignored it. I knew it for what it was, just anxiety. What if Nate was dead? How are you going to handle that, Miss Chloe?

"Here's a cuppa, Flame, oh Flame, oh Flame of my heart." Roy smiled his big toothy smile and set the cups of tea down in front of her and me on the cracked oilcloth strewn with cherries in the steamy kitchen. He wore a dark red wool crewneck sweater, full of moth holes. "Chamomile!"

Flame sipped. "Delicious!" To me she said, "No senior moments all morning. I really think it's the heat that brings them on."

"That makes sense," I said politely.

"One of the Kennedy boys will be looking after Craig's greenhouse, they live a couple of miles away." Flame pushed up the sleeves of her striped Guatemalan blouse that she wore under an old man's overalls. There were brown spots all over her arms. "Fred senior was one of Craig's students years ago."

Roy swiped at the table with a dishrag, then went to the sink and began dunking dishes.

"You knew Craig when he was a teacher?" I asked.

"That's how we met. Right after Roy and I moved here, and we were building the studio, we were pretty broke. I did some substitute teaching. Actually I met Linda first."

"Linda? That was his wife?"

Flame nodded, pulling the long rope of faded hair over her shoulder. It was braided with black yarn, like the yarn in the God's eyes that dotted the walls. "She taught third grade. They had us to dinner from time to time."

"That house!" said Roy with malicious delight.

"The house," said Flame. "Yes. It was rented but she wanted to buy. Everything was spotless, everything matched. She even had little crocheted covers for the toaster and all the Kleenex boxes." She turned her teacup around in her hands, nails blunt and cracked from the drying effects of clay.

Roy looked gleeful. "Tell her about the curtains!"

Flame said, "She kept the curtains drawn all the time, so the sun wouldn't fade the upholstery. She was way too bourgeois for Craig."

"No, she doesn't sound right for Craig at all," I said.

"Well, they got divorced ten years ago, about the time Craig decided to quit teaching and become a landscaper." Flame smiled with pleasure. "Linda didn't like the smell of manure."

"What happened to her?"

"Moved to California, married a man who could give her a nice house and some kids. Craig was heartbroken for a while, he always takes everything so hard. Has no sense of moderation."

"No, he doesn't," I said. "He really doesn't."

"He's a good man!" Roy said vehemently.

"He *is* a good man," said Flame. "After all, life's about as exciting as it gets if you have no sense of moderation." She looked at me with her eyes of two colors. "If that's what you want."

Was she asking me if I did? I looked at Roy, setting dishes in the drainer. I looked at the rows of bowls and cups and pitchers on the counter and then down at the cracked oilcloth. "Oh, Flame," I said. "I have no idea what I want."

"Well then there you are. Just sit tight and watch and wait. Let what you really want come to you. There's no rush."

But suddenly I was feeling urgent. Sitting here with Flame, every muscle in my neck and shoulders was tensed and ready for something. I didn't know what.

"Don't let him railroad you," Flame said. "You have to withstand him. Linda could never do that."

Roy picked up a dish towel. "Melissa sure could."

"Who *is* Melissa?" I asked.

"He hasn't told you, has he," said Flame.

"No."

Flame made a loop of her braid, put it on her head, let it fall, like a young girl. "Roy," she said. "There's a bowl in my studio, I think Chloe would like to see it, blue with green roses? Could you go look for it?"

Roy dropped the dish towel and headed for the door.

"Melissa Price," Flame said, after he left. "I almost thought we would lose Craig over her. They were close for about a year. He wanted to marry her."

"And she didn't want to?"

"Oh, there's no telling, what she would have wanted . . . Everything just blew apart, she was never the same after she got raped."

My mouth fell open. "Oh."

"Melissa was very independent, lived by herself in a little house near Highway Ninety-two. A man broke in. He had a gun and he used the gun to rape her." Flame closed her eyes. "They caught him, his last name was the same as ours, Harvey, no relation but it gave me the creeps. Allen, no, Elton. Elton Harvey. I don't know what happened after that. I don't follow the news and for a while Craig stopped talking to anyone."

"So, they broke up over it," I said sadly.

She shook her head. "They might have in the end, but she—well, she took too many pills one night. She'd been prescribed various things, you know, and she'd been drinking a lot. They didn't mix with the alcohol. She was drinking pretty heavily." Flame paused. "Craig did too, back then."

I stared down at the cherries on the oilcloth.

"It was this time of year, almost exactly," Flame went on. "That's why I was worried about Craig. Anniversaries are the hardest time. Everything smells the same, looks the same. Feels the same."

Under the crackles in the oilcloth the cherries looked round and ripe and absurd.

"Girlfriend after girlfriend he's had," Flame went on, "but it never works out. He always does something. I think it must be his way of being faithful. Maybe I shouldn't be telling you all this, but it might help you understand. He's seemed happier since he met you."

I walked out to my car. The red marigolds by the porch were fading, but the wind chimes—brass bells, glass, and old silverware—clanked and tinkled. Over by Flame's studio, Roy stood staring at me, a bowl in his hands.

"Hey!" he said.

I walked over. It was warming up fast but in spite of the red sweater with moth holes, he was shivering. I looked at the bowl, green roses drowning under an azure glaze. "It's beautiful," I said.

"Everything she does is." He looked puzzled, sad. "I can't find her. She's not in her studio. Where'd she go?"

"She's inside. In the kitchen." I took his arm, led him to the porch, watched as he limped up the steps to the door. At the door, he paused, turned to look at me.

"Go on," I said reassuringly. "She's in there."

He turned back to the door. "Flame!" he called, as he opened it. "Flame, oh Flame, oh Flame of my heart?"

chapter fifteen

MY HANDS DIDN'T START TO SHAKE TILL I
was a couple of miles away. I held the steering wheel tight to stop
them. *St. John's Wort.* Maybe I should pick some up, next time I was
at the food co-op. I swallowed but the lump in my throat wouldn't go
down. I drove slowly, because I had to go see Lee Thomas next and
I needed to be calm for a judge's wife.

When I got to Lee's I saw that someone had pulled up some of
the weeds from the gravel at the low stone house. The rain had refreshed the roses, but already the heat was coming back. I knocked
on the terra-cotta colored door, and waited.

No one was answering. Had Lee forgotten again? Damnit. I stood
still, listening, and heard voices from somewhere behind the house.
I saw a path next to the garage and followed it round to the back.
The mountains rose steep close behind the house, but long ago a
bulldozer must have sculptured out the yard. It was surprisingly large,
to have been so utterly concealed, a patchy lawn, a fraying badminton
net stretched across one end, and over to the right, the swimming
pool: concrete, with blue and white Mexican tile around the edges,
water afloat with dead bugs. Next to the pool were two blue and
white cushioned lounge chairs, beyond that a wrought-iron gazebo,
and inside the gazebo two women.

One was Sylvia Montano, the young woman I'd met in the kitchen
the night of the death notification. She had on jeans and a white

thermal tee, her black hair still in a thick braid down her back. I knew now she'd been devastated when her *nana* died and was "unstable." Yolanda had told me she'd gotten her the job here. Did Lee know that? Did Lee even know about Yolanda?

The other woman was Gladys Alexander in long white pants and a silk blouse printed with green and purple triangles, like those Pucci blouses people wore in the sixties that were coming back now.

My tan Aerosoles had made no noise and neither of them looked my way or seemed to notice I was there. As I approached, Gladys half stood up, shaking one hand back and forth. She let go and dice spewed out.

"Hah!" she said.

"Oh no." Sylvia held her head in her hands. "You did it again, Mrs. Alexander. You are really something."

"Hugh Peabody played me three straight days and nights," Gladys said, "and never beat me once. Oh, he was crazy for me. He was a Harvard man, you know, and he drove down from Boston every weekend, just so I could beat him at backgammon." She cackled. "Too, too killing."

"Hugh Peabody? Isn't that your first husband?" asked Sylvia. "Mrs. Thomas's father?"

I stopped.

Gladys's snorted like a horse. "We won't talk about that. My motto has always been 'life goes on.'" She paused. "Corney understands that, she's just like me."

I walked around the pool, up to the gazebo. "Excuse me," I said. Sylvia looked up. "Oh," she said. "Hello."

Gladys's eyes flicked off me without interest. Pearls that looked old and real gleamed against her scrawny neck. "I never should have married him in the first place." She picked up a whiskey bottle from the table and poured herself a shot. "He drank day and night." She brightened. "Night and day." She began to hum.

"What was it you wanted?" Sylvia said to me.

Gladys downed the whiskey in one swallow, then picked up a burning cigarette from an ashtray and took a long drag. Probably nothing would kill her. Only the good die young. "Who is this person?" she asked Sylvia.

"I'm Chloe Newcombe," I said directly to Gladys. "Lee called earlier and asked me to stop by. I knocked on the front door but no one answered. Chloe Newcombe, from Victim Witness." I paused. "With the County Attorney's office. I was here the other night."

For a second Gladys stared at me. I realized it was the first time she'd looked me in the eyes. Hers were blue, and for a batty old woman, disquietingly alert. I blinked.

Then she picked up a handful of backgammon chips and began to arrange them on the board. "One more game," she said, as if I weren't there.

I looked at Sylvia.

"Mrs. Thomas should be back soon," Sylvia said apologetically. "She and Justin went to the store. In fact, I thought I heard the car just a minute ago. You could go see."

I walked back past the pool toward the side of the house.

"Night and day," Gladys belted out behind me. Her voice was deep and whiskey husky. "You are the one!"

Lee Thomas came round the side of the house, with a bag of groceries in her arms. Justin, in a Charles Barkley T-shirt, trailed behind with another bag.

"What on earth—!" Lee said. She wore the same scuffed fuchsia ballet flats, jeans, a white cotton camp shirt. Her hair, still lank, was tied back with a pink ribbon. In the outdoor light her tired cameo face was crisscrossed with fine lines.

"She's singing, Mrs. Thomas," said Sylvia, her voice seeming to subtly mock Lee. "Isn't she good?"

"Mummy," Lee said, "it's hardly the time . . ." She noticed me suddenly. "Oh!" She looked harried. "Oh, God, I forgot again. I'm so sorry."

Justin looked embarrassed. "Mom forgets everything." Why wasn't he in school? His face was pale, peaked. Maybe he was sick. He set the groceries down and plopped onto a chaise longue. "No one knows why. She just does."

"Justin," shouted Gladys. "Come sit by Gammy!"

"No," said Justin.

"Justin . . ." Lee began, but changed her mind and sat down on the chaise next to him. She closed her eyes.

"Justin," Sylvia finished for her, "how can you be so rude?"

"Gammy loves you, Justin," said Gladys.

"Justin doesn't love Gammy," he said. He pulled the neck of his T-shirt up over his mouth so the words came out thickly. "She doesn't care that somebody killed Dad, she's glad."

"You should never speak like that to your grandmother," said Sylvia indignantly. "One day you'll be sorry."

They were so busy being dysfunctional, nobody seemed to care that I was there. Dysfunctional, the word Nate had used. How had he known, just rumor? Or had he talked to one of them, showed up inappropriately as he had at Yolanda's?

Gladys touched Sylvia's arm. "Did I tell you about my career as a singing debutante? It was at the Stork Club, lots of the girls that came out that year were doing it, that skinny Gray girl—it was a hoot."

But Sylvia was still looking at Justin. "It's not right." Her voice was fierce.

Justin pulled his T-shirt back down and began to thump the striped cover of the cushion with his tennis shoes. "She's the one that's not right." *Thump. Thump.* "Anyone can tell that but you, Sylvia. She tells you these dumb stories and you eat them up. You know where she belongs, don't you?"

"Please," said Lee faintly. "I don't want to listen to this." She opened her eyes and looked over at me. "I'm sorry . . ." she began.

"The old age home!" shouted Justin. "That's where Dad was going to send her! The old age home!"

Sylvia stood abruptly. The backgammon board slipped off the table, spilling chips onto the ground. She clenched her fists, glaring at Justin.

He glared right back at her. "He was going to lock her up! Throw away the key to the old age home!"

Lee looked at me. "Maybe . . ." She tried again for a complete sentence but failed.

Sylvia shouted, "I think it's time you went inside, Justin, I really do, and no dinner for you tonight either!"

"I don't have to do what you say, Sylvia," Justin shouted back.

"You're just a *servant.*"

Lee put her hands to her head. "I can't . . ."

"Maybe I should leave," I said to her.

"Yes. I'm really sorry." The corners of her mouth turned up, in imitation of a smile. "So nice to see you," she said, automatically relapsing into the stylized debutante talk of old money. She had all the reality of a hologram, seemingly held in the grip of overwhelming fatigue, trapped, while chaos reigned all around her.

Then she stood up. "I'll walk you to your car."

Lee stooped, tugged at a weed in the gravel, her movements, compared to how she had been out by the pool, remarkably decisive. "I wanted to ask a favor of you. I don't know who to ask. It concerns my daughter, Cornelia. I thought you might be able to help."

Several sentences completed without hesitation. Away from the others, Lee was suddenly different, more focused.

"Yes?" I said.

"I have to get in touch with her." Her eyes shifted toward the house and back to me. "I can't even be sure she knows about Cal."

"Surely, she knows by now."

"She's so, so *disdainful* about certain things, she may not even watch television or read a newspaper. And she won't answer her phone or even get an answering machine."

Not like Willy. Willy had an answering machine.

"She lives in Tucson," Lee said. "I wondered maybe . . ."

"You want me to go to Tucson and talk to her, is that what you're saying?"

We reached my car.

"Talk to her, yes," said Lee. She wrapped her arms around her body. "She needs to come home now. Tell her that." Her voice rose. "Tell her to please come home."

"Lee," I said, as gently as I could. "She's over eighteen?"

"Twenty-one."

"Not a minor anymore. I don't mean to sound harsh, but she has a right not to see her family if that's what she wants. I can't force her to do anything."

"Does that mean you'll go talk to her?"

"If you think she'll be willing to talk to me," I hedged.

Lee glanced at the house again, as if her mother might be inside now, peering malevolently through one of the many windows. "If she won't, could you at least, give her this?"

She pulled a white envelope out of her front jeans pocket. "It has her address on it, it's in the university area. I need to know she got it, I . . . I don't want it coming back here." She thrust the envelope toward me. "Please?"

I took it.

"So you will?" she asked.

"Yes, but I can't make any promises about the outcome."

Lee's gray eyes were wistful. "She's supposed to be going to the U of A, studying art." For a second, her eyes brightened. "She's a gifted photographer. She's been in several shows and even won some awards."

"That's great," I said. "You must be proud of her."

"Yes." Her gray eyes clouded. "She doesn't keep in touch, I'm not even sure she's still doing it. You'll let me know right away if you find her?"

"Yes," I said. I got in my car.

"Don't leave a message, all right? Messages don't always find their way." She looked back at the house and shrugged. "It would be best if you talk to me in person."

"What's Cornelia so mad about?" I asked suddenly.

For a moment Lee didn't answer. "She's like me," she said finally. "Unforgiving."

Unforgiving of what?

"Lee," I said. "One more thing. I was wondering, have you talked to any reporters?"

"No." She sighed. "I wouldn't. Several have tried. Sylvia screens the calls."

"But before this all happened, maybe. Someone called Nate Pendergast with the *Sierra Vista Dispatch*?"

Nothing flickered in her eyes. "I haven't talked to any reporters in years," she said.

"I'll be in touch," I said.

As I drove off down the drive, in my rearview mirror I could see her still standing there, arms wrapped around her body as if warding off a hurricane. Inside herself, she probably was. It takes a lot of energy to fight off your own emotions.

chapter sixteen

"NATE?" IN THE LITTLE CUBICLE THAT WAS
his office, Ollie Menton, number one reporter for the *Sierra Vista
Dispatch*, caressed his beard. "We're not too happy about old Nate
around here right now."

"Why not?" I asked.

He took off the wire-rimmed glasses, revealing bushy black eyebrows that met in the middle. "He missed the deadline for a story,
for one." He polished the glasses on his navy blue polo shirt. "Guess
he was just too busy hanging around the courthouse."

I said nothing but Ollie looked at me accusingly. "It was the
Buena High School play dress rehearsal. Guess that kind of stuff isn't
important to *Nate,* not Pulitzer material. But what about those kids?
Working hard every day after school and no story in the paper." Ollie
picked up a pencil and jabbed it at me. "Hey? What about them?
They don't *count?*"

"I didn't—" I began, but he cut me off.

"Nate doesn't realize you have to pay some dues. He thinks he
can start off at the top. He thinks—"

"Ollie, *listen,*" I said. "You're probably right. But that's not the
point. He's vanished. No one's seen him since Monday."

Ollie gave a hearty laugh, his gold molars glinting at me. "Vanished. Come on. He just went off somewhere to pout, probably."

"Without telling anyone?"

"Sure, without telling anyone. That's part of being young and restless."

"Well, I've filed a missing person report. His girlfriend is worried too."

"So?" He looked exasperated. "She's a *girlfriend*. That's what she's for, kind of like Mom. Think about it, am I right?"

"In a way," I began, "but—"

"Look," Ollie interrupted. "This is between you and me—Nate had a fight with the editor Monday. Someone, I'm not at liberty to say who, complained he was interviewing people about the Judge Thomas murder."

"Like who?" I said. "Who was he interviewing?"

"It doesn't matter who. They didn't say anyway. Nate thinks he can go talk to anyone he wants to, ask them any damn question that comes to mind. This isn't *20/20,* this is a small-town newspaper. Here we treat people with *respect.*"

"Who complained, Ollie?"

"Respect," Ollie pontificated, ignoring my question. He banged his fist on the desk. "If we had more of that in this country, instead of a bunch of gossip-mongering media sharks, we wouldn't be in the mess we're in today. If his girlfriend's so worried why don't you tell her probably Nate got pissed and took off."

"Who complained?"

"Hector Estrada."

"Oh," I said, which meant it was probably about Nate talking to Yolanda. For just a second I wondered if it had been wise, putting Nola together with Hector. "Look, what if something actually happened to him? Could you maybe look at the stories he's been working on, please? Anything—"

"To explain his absence?" Ollie snorted. "I already looked at what he's been working on, thank you, because I'm the one that had to finish the play rehearsal story. That was half done plus the one on the city animal shelter—that came out already and that was about it."

"But if he were talking to people about the judge's murder, wouldn't there be at least some notes—"

"There was diddly shit, Chloe. Probably has them with him in his notebook from which I have never seen him part."

"One of the things he was researching," I said, "was some quasi-legal land deals, involving Judge Thomas."

Ollie raised his eyebrows. "That Jack Townsend shit?"

Jack Townsend. Last known person to see Cal Thomas before he was murdered. I had an image, smooth Buffalo Bill, nearly running into me in his red rental car, all concerned about Lee. "Jack Townsend was in on them too?"

"Jack Townsend's in on everything." Ollie shook his head slowly from side to side with fake wonder. "Nate, Nate, Nate. I showed him my file and he—You know anything about those deals?"

"No."

He looked at his watch. "Come on, I'll buy you a cup of coffee."

The coffee shop down from the *Dispatch* offices was practically empty. Plastic ferns and philodendrons hung in the plate glass windows, the beige walls had prints of New England seascapes. We sat in a green vinyl booth near the back.

"These land deals," said Ollie. "They're kind of legal pyramid scams. You buy a whole bunch of land at maybe three hundred an acre, subdivide it, sell that for a thousand or so an acre, the person who buys it subdivides it again."

He picked up his danish, iced and studded with almonds, took a huge bite.

"So? That's a scam?"

Ollie swiped at the icing that clung to his beard. "It's when the parcels get small the scam begins. The big thing is the water—you only get so much, it's all there in the fine print. So if your buyer subdivides his lot into say, four, only one of the lots in the new subdivisions gets the water."

"But how can they get away with that?" I asked.

"You lie by omission. You tell the buyer you have water going to your lots and hope he doesn't check too carefully. That's why you need a hotshot like Jack Townsend fronting for you. He charms the pants off the buyer and they don't do the research. They trust him, the poor fools."

"Wow," I said. "So why shouldn't Nate be interested? It sounds like an awfully good story to me."

"It was, once."

"Once?"

"It's old, way out of date. I started working here eleven, twelve years ago, and I thought it was a good story back then too. I even interviewed some old guy and his wife way down at the bottom of the pyramid. They took me out to their land. We had to hike to get to it, no utilities, couldn't drill for water, beautiful piece of property for a picnic. Editor liked it, but he took me aside. 'We can't use this,' he said, 'half the bigwigs in Cochise County are involved in this in some way.' "

"So you killed it?"

"Damn right I did." Ollie paused. "Don't look at me like that."

"Like what?"

"I liked it here. Back then we had a brand-new house, our first baby on the way. I didn't just drop it, I kept a file updated, thinking at some point I would use it with some other paper, get a foot in the door. That's what I showed Nate. The ungrateful little shit."

"Well, if you weren't going to use it . . ."

He snorted. "It doesn't matter anymore. It's old eighties stuff, there are new rules and regulations now, people can't get away with it anymore. The system eventually takes care of itself. That's what Nate doesn't understand. There're so many regulations now, you'd have to get in, get out so fast you'd be a blur. Take the money and run. Move to Barbados. That's not Jack Townsend's style."

"So what was he doing in Cochise County, the night he had dinner with the judge?"

"The guy's from around here. He and Cal Thomas were old friends."

"Ollie, listen, all we know about what went on is what Jack Townsend says. Maybe he's got a new scam," I said. "Someone else fronting for him."

Ollie swallowed the last bite of danish and wiped his fingers on a napkin. "I'm sure he does. But not in Cochise County." He stood up. "Nate's so interested, he should move to Phoenix, get a job with *New Times,* some liberal rag like that." He laughed, molars glinting. "He should anyway, because he probably doesn't have a job here anymore. You tell him that, next time you see him."

I drove home. So maybe it wasn't land deals, or it had started that way and progressed somewhere else. Did it involve the judge's family somehow? Lee or Cornelia? In my kitchen, I stared at the address on the envelope Lee had given me, maybe answers to my questions were inside. But I wouldn't look.

I still knew people in New York, on the North Shore but farther out than where the old money lived. But still. Roxanne Steinberg, she and her daughter were former clients of mine. I found her number in my address book.

"Roxanne," I said, after making sure everyone at the Steinberg house, especially Didi, was copecetic. "You grew up on Long Island, didn't you? Does the name Peabody mean anything to you?"

Roxanne snorted delicately. "Sure. It's one of those Wasp names. *Social Register.* Piping Rock. That crowd. I never keep track of those people."

"But did you ever know any of them?"

"Chloe, repeat after me, my last name. What is it?"

"Steinberg," I said.

"And my maiden name was Cohen. So there you have it, in a nutshell. Who cares about those people anymore? So inbred half of them are idiots."

"This would be a while ago," I prompted. "When you were a teenager. A Hugh Peabody?"

"*Hugh Peabody.* Oh. Well. Yes. That was all over the papers, they made a big deal out of it."

"*What* was all over the newspapers?"

"He killed himself. Carbon monoxide, in his garage. Sometime between Christmas and New Year's. It was awful because the daughter found him. She was around my age so it stuck in my mind."

Zap. *Lee* had found him.

"Remarkable," I said to Roxanne, "what you can remember when you're not even keeping track?"

Her voice sharpened. "Why do you want to know about all this? Are they opening up the case again? Don't tell me!" Her voice was triumphant. "Hugh Peabody was murdered!"

"Roxanne, get hold of yourself," I said. "I'm out here in Arizona. What would that have to do with me?"

I hung up, thinking no wonder Lee had flashed back to her father that night. But it wasn't information that would help me find Nate.

I still had the phone number Nola and I had gotten at Nate's when we'd pushed star sixty-nine, written on a Post-it. I dug through my purse, found it, and dialed the St. David number.

"Hello," said a woman's voice, cautious.

"Hello," I said. "Who's this?"

There was a pause. "Who's *this*?" she said suspiciously. "I believe you called me. Before you start I don't have time for telemarketers."

"I'm not a telemarketer," I said. "Maybe I dialed wrong. I'm calling 555-5380."

"Okay. You got the number right." Her voice was impatient. "So who the hell are you calling?"

"I'm looking for a friend of mine. His name is Nate. Nate Pendergast."

There was a long silence. Had she hung up on me? "Hello?" I said.

"Yes?"

"Nate Pendergast. Do you know him?"

There was another silence. This time I could hear breathing. *"Who?"* she said finally.

I looked at the phone bill again; sure enough he'd talked for seventeen minutes. And gotten a call from that number after he'd disappeared. "Nate Pen-der-gast," I said loudly and distinctly. "I'm sorry to bother you, he's an old friend. I need to get in touch with him. It's kind of important. Maybe he called someone else in the household."

"There is no one else in the household."

"Maybe you had a houseguest until recently?"

"No." She snorted. "Give me a break. I already told you I don't know anyone by that name."

"Look," I said in frustration. "I know he called there. He talked for a while."

"Oh. Well. I'm just nuts, I guess. People call me and I don't even remember talking to them. Pardon me while I go drool."

"And I know that you called him," I said to the dial tone.

The woman on the phone had to be lying and I hadn't even gotten her name, but I had an old reverse phone directory, I'd snitched it at work when they were throwing it out.

The number Nate had called was listed, at least in 1996, as E. Brownwell, 300 Sunrise, in St. David. E. Nate had never mentioned any Elizabeth, Ellen, Evelyn, Eulalia, Evangeline. She'd sounded mature, a grown-up. Why would she lie? I could stop by there tomorrow on my way to Tucson to see Cornelia. It couldn't hurt.

chapter seventeen

THE SUN WAS SHINING AS I SLOWED DOWN
into St. David's, passed the big white Church of the Latter-day Saints
on my left, Grandma Goodman's grocery store coming up on my right.
The town was ablaze with trees, more trees than any other place in
Cochise County, as if this Mormon farming community had received
some special dispensation from God regarding rainfall.

I hadn't been sleeping well, but I felt remarkably energetic, hyped
up even, as if I'd been slipped a few grains of methamphetamine in
my morning coffee. I stopped at Grandma Goodman's. A thirtyish
pleasant looking woman with short brown hair and a big shiny nose
was behind the cash register.

"Good morning!" she sang out. "And how are you today?"

"Grand," I said, heading down a narrow crowded aisle to the
cooler. "Beautiful weather we're having."

"And it may go on to Christmas!" said the woman.

"It may go on all winter," I said. "And into the spring!"

"Yes!" she said.

"We may not even have a hot summer," I said.

"Well," said the woman carefully. "I've never seen *that* happen."

I plunked a carton of orange juice down on the counter. "Could
you tell me where Sunrise is?"

"Sunrise, it's just off the main road on the left, as you're leaving
town."

Sunrise was gilded with gold autumn leaves, but the houses were a widely spaced sporadic mix of cinder blocks and trailers lining the unpaved road. I couldn't see a number anywhere.

An elderly woman in a flowered housedress, running shoes, and stockings rolled down around her ankles sat out on a lounge chair in front of a tan double-wide. I slowed, wound down my window. "Excuse me. Where's three hundred?"

"Down the road aways, honey, just about where it ends. Big white lump of a place."

I drove on, careful with the ruts. The trees faded away, then the houses, so there was nothing left but desert. Then when the road seemed about to peter out entirely, I came to a house set back on a dirt driveway. It *was* a big white lump, a straw bale house, actually made from bales of straw and stuccoed over. There was a FOR SALE sign in front, Myrna Blodgett, relator. Fantastic. It gave me a reason for being there. Judging from the way Ellen-Eileen-Eulalia Brownwell had sounded on the phone she might not welcome casual visitors.

A high wooden fence that looked new blocked my view of the back, but the front yard was dirt. E. Brownwell wasn't a gardener. Rabbit brush grew along the driveway sending out clouds of fluff, drifts of it had settled on a sea-foam green eighties Toyota parked in front.

I parked behind it and got out. People who lived at the end of long dirt roads usually knew when you arrived, long before you knocked on their door. Someone was there, judging from the Toyota, and probably watching me.

Then a gate opened in the high fence and a woman in her forties came through, holding a hammer, a blue bandanna tied around her forehead. She wore a navy sweatshirt, jeans, and had a nail in her mouth.

"This house is for sale?" I asked.

Close up, she had a broad snub nose, and eyes so improbably

green, she must have been wearing contact lenses. She took the nail out of her mouth.

"That Blodgett woman! The dingbat from hell. All syrupy-sweet but she gets her way. I *told* her to have people call first. What? I'm not supposed to have a life now?"

"I'm sorry," I said, eyes on the hammer. "I was just driving around and I noticed the sign. The house looked interesting. Are you Mrs. Brownwell?"

She sighed, dropped the hammer and left it lying in the dirt. "There isn't any Mrs. Brownwell," she said with phony patience. "My name is Poppy Walker. Brownwell's the guy who's letting me live here. I'm just the house-sitter, so don't ask me a bunch of straw bale shit. The backyard's all fenced in or will be when I finish the damn fence. You don't need to see it 'cause there's nothing there but a bunch of dirt, weeds, and a damn barbecue grill."

"Oh," I said.

"Come on." She sighed. "I'll show you the inside."

At the door she paused. "The town's full of Mormons, not too friendly to the spiritually uninclined, and some craftspeople, not too friendly either unless you're just like them. Also people growing marijuana, or so I hear."

"I guess you're just dying to leave this house," I said.

She snorted and opened the door. The living room was large, sparsely furnished with a couple of futons, and surprisingly beautiful: the flooring old brick, the white stucco walls softly rounded. In one corner was a work table and an easel, sideways to me, on a plastic drop cloth.

"Nice room," I said. "You're a painter?"

"I'm on sabbatical from my job, to see if I am. So far I don't think so. I teach eighth grade." She took off her bandanna, revealing mashed colorless hair. She ran her fingers through it and said suddenly. "How's Hal?"

"Hal?" I looked at her, stunned. Hal, my brother's lover, Hal who had willed me my house, Hal who had been dead for years. It was the last thing I'd expected. My head felt suddenly light. It made no sense. "Hal," I said again stupidly. "How could you know *Hal*?"

She smiled. "I don't. I just have caller I.D. You're not here to buy a house. You're the person who called me yesterday."

I'd never changed Hal's phone into my name, it was kind of a protection. Considering what I'd gone through in the last few days, I'd been holding up remarkably well, and now Hal's name came up out of the distant past and shattered my defenses. My mouth was dry, my head so light I thought I might faint. I sat down abruptly on a futon.

"Are you all right?" Poppy said.

I bent over, let the blood rush to my head.

"Wow. Sorry." Her voice was contrite. "Can I get you a glass of water?"

I nodded and closed my eyes.

Had I had breakfast this morning? I couldn't remember. My super hyped-up energy had left me all at once, as if it had never been mine at all. The white walls of the room seemed to vibrate softly as if they were breathing. I should take some time off, get some rest, and eat properly. How could I do all that?

I took a deep breath, which helped, and looked around me. From here I could see one of Poppy's paintings, propped against a wall. It was incredible. A mass of muddy drab blotches, it was probably the worst painting I'd ever seen. There was not one redeeming feature. For some reason, seeing such a lousy painting made me feel a lot more confident.

Poppy returned with a glass of water. "You feeling any better?" she asked.

"I'm okay," I said, draining the glass.

Poppy looked concerned; her toughness, I could see now, was all on the outside. "I didn't mean to upset you. Who is he, your husband?"

"He was a good friend." I took a deep breath. "He's been dead for a while. He left me his house and the phone's still in his name."

"You never told me yours," she said.

"Chloe. Chloe Newcombe."

"Chloe Newcombe." Poppy plopped herself down on the other futon. "Well, why didn't you tell me right anyway? We could have saved ourselves a lot of bullshit."

"I don't understand."

"Nate said you were okay."

"Then you do know him."

She nodded. "I met him when he was doing a story on straw bale houses. We got along."

Surely, surely she and Nate weren't . . . As if she read my mind, she laughed. "God, I'm twice his age. It's nothing romantic. Nate's . . . oh, I don't know, he's a good kid." She made a face. "You don't teach eighth grade unless you like kids, you know? And sometimes you meet people that you feel like you already know. I guess we both kind of felt that way. And it's lonely here in St. David."

"I need to talk to him," I said. "Have you seen him? No one knows where he is."

Poppy looked alarmed. "What do you mean, no one knows where he is?"

"No one's seen him since Monday."

Poppy clenched her fists. "That little shit! I told him to be careful, goddamnit!"

I couldn't help but smile.

"Poppy," I said, "when did you see him last?"

"Sunday. He was here. He drove over from some ghost town near Tombstone where he was researching a story."

"Windy City."

"Right. He said, he actually *said* to me, with that little smirk he has, 'lots of people are going to be mad at me pretty soon.' That's why I didn't tell you anything on the phone. I thought maybe you were one of those people who's mad at him."

"But did you ask him why?"

"No."

"Weren't you curious?"

"Of course, I was. I . . . I don't keep up with the local news but I knew he was investigating something about a judge getting murdered so I said, 'Hey, Nate, maybe you should be careful.' "

"Poppy, did he tell you anything about his investigation?"

"Not much. Except, wait—this old guy he talked to in Windy City—"

"B. W."

"Yes. B.W. Actually now that I think about it what he said was, 'I talked to B.W. and lots of people are going to be mad at me.' "

B.W. had told him something? All B.W. had done was find the body.

"God, Chloe," said Poppy, "you don't think . . ."

"I don't know what to think. Did he say anything on Sunday, about going away for a while?"

"No. Why would he go away? He was really excited about this story." She wrung her hands. "Oh, hell! It makes me so mad, boiling mad!"

She got up and walked over to the wall where her painting was propped. "I didn't really take him seriously. Nate exaggerates things." She kicked at the easel. "Damnit!" She looked over at me. "Listen, you call me, when he shows up and tell him to get in touch. I need to know that he's okay."

"I will," I said.

Poppy leaned over, turned the painting so it faced the wall and said, her back to me, "And call me if he's not okay too. I can take it, I just need to know. You promise?"

chapter eighteen

IN TUCSON IT WAS WINDY BUT WARM. STU-
dents thronged the crosswalks in shorts, T-shirts, backpacks—scruffy
and improbably young. I turned onto La Cholla, a small side street
and found a parking place several houses down from 310, the address
on the envelope Lee had given me. I got out, feeling ancient in my
black jeans and short-sleeved black sweater.

The houses were large; once this street must have been middle
class and prosperous. Edged with palm trees and red birds of paradise, it still had a shabby charm. Three-ten was a two-story stucco,
casement windows, red tile roof, set close to the street. The front
door seemed to be sealed up, an arrow pointing round the side. I
walked down the asphalt driveway to the back. A sculpture made of
rusted car parts stood next to an orange tree full of ripening fruit.
The yard behind was large. A fat black cat sunned itself on a patio
paved with broken pottery in bright colors, and on the wall that separated the yard from the next one over, someone had painted a mural
of low-rider cars being blessed by the Virgin of Guadalupe.

"Hi there!" called a female voice. "Looking for someone?"

I turned. A young woman, in tight black Spandex bike shorts, a
lime green sweatshirt, and little round glasses, was pushing a bicycle
up the driveway. Her blond hair stuck up in little spikes and around
her neck was a leather thong with a plastic skull. Despite the skull,
behind the glasses her sky blue eyes were wide and guileless.

"Yes," I said. "Cornelia Thomas. Does she still live here?"

"Corney? Of course. There." She pointed to a separate small adobe building at the back. "We call it the carriage house. But she's not here now. Hold on a minute while I chain my bike. I've had two stolen already."

"You know when she'll be back?" I asked as she hooked a chain to the wheel and then around the orange tree.

"No idea at all. She's out of town." She looked at me with interest. "Are you some sort of gallery person or something?"

"No," I said. "Is she that good?"

She rolled her eyes. "Are you kidding? She's the best. You've never seen her work?"

"Photography, right?"

She nodded. "I'm mostly mixed media myself. People are scornful about photographers, but she definitely surpasses the genre. She and Marcos, who did that mural, are the stars here. We're all art students." She lowered her voice. "But Corney's better than Marcos. He'd kill me if he heard me say that, but it's true."

"I really need to find her," I said.

Suddenly she looked stricken. "God! I'm blabbing away, and it just occurred to me. Her family. You're a family member?"

I shook my head. "My name's Chloe Newcombe. I'm with Victim Witness in Cochise County. You're a friend of Corney's?"

"Yes. Ginny. Ginny Taylor." She looked distressed. "Victim Witness. You've come about her dad, then? We heard it on the news. Her phone's been ringing and ringing, but her door's padlocked and no one has the key. She's been gone since before . . . it happened. Mostly the places she goes are pretty isolated." Her eyes widened. "She might not even have heard!"

"Then someone has to tell her," I said. "You don't have any idea where she is?"

"Actually, she wrote it down, I didn't really look, I was on my way out when she came up to my room. I have it somewhere."

* * *

Inside, the big house smelled of Pinesol, patchouli, and just faintly under it all, a hint of marijuana.

"Ginny," I said. "I was wondering. Did a reporter ever come to Tucson and talk to Corney?"

"A reporter? I don't think so."

"His name's Nate. Nate Pendergast."

"Coming up!" Ginny called in warning as we ascended the steps to the second floor. She turned to me at the top. "I don't think so. It doesn't ring *any* bells."

The walls were papered in a yellowed print of flower bouquets and from somewhere Beck sang insouciantly.

"I'm not supposed to give out her address to anyone," Ginny whispered as she unlocked the first door on the left. "*Especially* family, but under the circumstances . . . Can you imagine, hating your family that much? I call mine twice a week."

Inside, sunlight poured through front casement windows filled with potted red geraniums. Over a large sagging couch covered with a brightly striped blanket hung a collage: a delirious mix of pastel colored string mingled with costume jewelry, sequins, and luscious thick squibbles of paint.

"That's mine," she said when she saw me looking. "For what it's worth. All sweetness and light. Disgusting, isn't it?"

"No," I protested. "It's nice."

"Nice." She made a face. "That's me all right. All I can say is don't come from a happy family if you want to make art."

Ginny's skin was clear, rosy with health. Behind her little round glasses, her blue eyes were young and still dreamy enough to see unhappiness as romantic. "I'll probably just end up teaching art to first graders." She sighed. "Now where did I put that address?"

She walked over to a desk in one corner, pulled open a drawer and then another. "Got it." She glanced at the slip of paper then handed it to me. "She doesn't have a real address because she sleeps in her van to save money."

I looked at the unlined paper. All it said was *Corney, c/o the*

Bowie Cafe, Bowie. "Then she's in Cochise County," I said. "What's she doing in Bowie?"

"Cochise County is where she takes most of her photographs."

"But why Bowie?" I knew where it was, though I'd never been there, way up north in the middle of nowhere, near the New Mexico border.

"Bowie makes sense," said Ginny. "The motels. I guess they're really ancient and she wants to capture all the old stuff before it's gone forever." She brightened. "I've got three of her photographs. They're in another room. Want to see?"

The three photographs hung on the wall in a line, all black-and-white, eight-by-ten, matted and in cheap aluminum frames.

"These are the early ones," said Ginny. "Her breakthrough stuff."

"Breakthrough?"

"She started off doing the usual—nudes, sunsets. They were nothing much: pretty, kind of dutiful though she's always had a good sense of composition. But she learned her craft and then a couple of years ago I guess she got a vision and there she was, tools sharpened and ready, and she came up with these. They were the show's centerpiece, she displayed them like a triptych. She calls them 'Three Silent Screams.' "

"Oh?"

"Don't ask," said Ginny. "Corney hates interpretation and she never wants to explain."

I stared at the first photograph, of a frame house, oddly constructed with two peaks in the roof like an "M." Paint was visibly peeling off the boards, the windows were pointed shards of glass. One wooden step led up to where a door would be, but the door was gone, just a rectangle of darkness. A rubber baby doll lay at the top of the step, at the rectangle, head first as though emerging.

"Being born," said Ginny wisely. "Though I wouldn't say that to Corney."

The second one was also of a house: small, adobe, and clearly abandoned. A door hung from one hinge and where windows had been were only two vacant black holes. In the dirt yard, next to a dying desert willow, the rubber baby doll lay face down and above, the clouds seemed to streak away as if desperate to depart.

Ginny sighed. "They're so sad. So much feeling. The way she gets the light, I think. This next is the saddest of all. It's the first one she did."

This time there was no house at all. Where some sort of building had once been, two adobe walls formed a triangle and thorny weeds grew all around, prickly poppies, devil's claw. The black-and-white of the photograph was glaringly sharp, each detail etched with riveting precision. The doll lay face up this time, spread eagled, vacant eyes staring at the sky.

Behind the doll on one of the adobe walls someone had spray-painted in white letters: FUCK YOU TOO, WYATT EARP.

"What's wrong?" asked Ginny.

"Nothing," I said.

Whatever Corney's vision had been, it seemed to include precognition. I'd stood there recently among the grasshoppers with an old man named B. W. Watkins and looked down at the dark stain in the desert where Corney's father's life had seeped away in Windy City. I had to go to Bowie right away and talk to Corney.

chapter   nineteen

BOWIE WAS TWO HOURS AWAY FROM DUD-
ley. The next day I drove into the town around three, under an overcast sky. It was a tiny town, but once it had been bigger, a convenient
stopping place for tourists until the interstate freeway system wiped
it off the tourist map. The motels, Desert Springs, Palm Courts,
Mountain Vista were mostly stucco, with red-tile roofs, built in the
1940s, stranded in another time. Bermuda grass poked up through
the cement walks that led to the miniature cabins, tall palm trees
leaned desolately over cracked swimming pools.

The motels of Bowie seemed to float in the chill of the milky
afternoon light.

The Bowie Cafe was in the middle of town on the main drag,
another stucco building with a slanting tile roof and the ghosts of two
gas pumps out front. I pushed open the door: inside it was hot—
steam blurred the big plate glass window—and nearly empty, just a
young cowboy in one of the red vinyl booths and two old guys in feed
store caps at the long counter. Behind it, her back to me, a waitress
fiddled with a coffeepot.

The young cowboy glanced over, the two old guys set down their
coffee cups simultaneously, looked at me in unison, then looked stu-
diously away.

I sat at the end of the counter next to a plastic dome that covered
half a lemon meringue pie, stiff with corn starch. The waitress turned

then, saw me. She was gray haired, about six feet tall, in jeans, cowboy boots, and a man's faded blue work shirt.

"Hi, hon," she said, smiling. "Be with you in just a minute."

"Hey, Randa?" called the young cowboy. "I been thinking on them chili relleños. Manny doing the cooking still?"

Randa put her hands on her hips. "He got in a little trouble, Sonny. He's back across the line. We're out of 'em anyway. Lunch crowd ate 'em."

"Got to go to McDonald's now, I guess," said one of the old men. They both guffawed loudly.

Randa strode down the counter toward me, carrying a coffeepot. She wore silver and turquoise earrings with silver feather dangles, silver and turquoise rings on most of her fingers.

"Just coffee," I said, adding by way of conversation, "There's a McDonald's in town?"

She grinned. Her face was broad, handsome in a way that made me think an ancestor must have met up with a good-looking Apache. "Closest McDonald's over in Willcox, twenty-five miles. That's just their idea of a joke." She reached down and brought up a cup, filled it and pushed it toward me.

"Those motels," I said. "They're really neat."

Randa's mouth fell open in disbelief. "You really think so? Should of seen 'em years ago, don't nobody stay in 'em now but Mexican field workers. Come in to harvest the pistachios, one room for ten of 'em, get drunk, tear the place apart."

"I've got a friend here," I said. "A photographer. She's taking pictures of them. The only address I have is care of this cafe. Cornelia Thomas?"

Randa nodded. "Sure. Takes most of her meals here."

"You know where she is now?"

She glanced over at the young cowboy. "You should ask Sonny there. He knows her pretty good, don't you, Sonny?"

"Sure do!" He paused. "Well, I mean . . . kind of sort of . . . I guess."

Sonny was fair-haired, blue-eyed, with one of those eager cocky faces you just know is headed for trouble sooner or later. He looked at me with interest. "You're a friend of Corney's, no kidding?"

"I've got a letter for her," I said fudging the question.

"She took a whole bunch of pictures of me the other day!"

"Really?" I said.

He sat up so proud in the booth, his chest seemed to double in size. "Had me lying down at the bottom of an empty old swimming pool, I swear she did!"

"Now why did she do that?" asked Randa.

"Hell if I know, but Dwight Yoakam made that movie over in Willcox, four, five years ago, was it? *Red Rock West!* I went over to watch and I'll be damned if ol' Dwight's not getting bald! And I got me a full head of hair! You just wait, Randa! One of these days, Hollywood'll be calling!"

"You better hope," said Randa, "you don't find yourself a job soon."

"Do you know where I can find Corney?" I asked Sonny.

He scratched his chin. "She stays at the Palm Court, sometimes, but mostly just camps out. Got an old gray Dodge van, U of A parking sticker on the bumper. You drive around, look for that and the camera. She'll be set up somewhere, guarantee you."

"Great," I said, finishing my coffee. "Thanks a lot."

"You tell Corney I said hi!" Sonny called after me.

I drove slowly back down the main drag, but saw no gray Dodge van with a U of A bumper sticker in front of the Palm Court or the Mountain Vista or the Desert Springs. I passed the fire station on my left, on my right the Bowie Mercantile whose window had a big hand-lettered sign saying *Pistachios,* a line of orange pumpkins, and strings of chilis, their red vibrant in the dusky afternoon light.

Little streets led off from the main one, but seemed to peter out. Then at the very end where the main street petered out too, I came upon a gray Dodge van, U of A bumper sticker, parked in front of the Blue Oasis Motel.

No one had stayed at the Blue Oasis in years. A neon sign, half the glass tubing gone, B UE O S S, hung crookedly from a tall post. The door to the tiny blue stucco office was covered with a sheet of plywood. I parked behind the van and got out. Blue cabins similar to the office formed a half circle, obscuring what would probably be a courtyard.

I saw no one.

I stepped over the chain that blocked the entrance to the courtyard and heard a woman's voice, clear, authoritative.

"*Bueno. Muy, muy bueno.*"

I came around and saw a pool was in the center, half the turquoise tile gone, prickly poppies growing through the cracks. Yuccas, white flowers gone to dry seedpod grew everywhere. At the far end, in front of one of the blue cabins, a Hispanic woman in a long white dress sat on a rusty cast-iron chair. Her dense blue-black hair hung in two thick braids and around her neck she had a heavy silver crucifix. She was smoking a cigar.

The woman saw me, suddenly. She dropped the cigar and smiled, her teeth flashing white. Then she coughed. And coughed again.

"*¿Rosalia, que pasa?*" someone said, the same voice I'd heard before. A woman came out from behind a yucca, tall, slender, dressed in a long black skirt, boots, tan buckskin fringed vest. Her back was to me.

Rosalia shrugged, leaned down and picked up the cigar. She rubbed it out slowly on the cement, leaving a trail of ash. She coughed again, and said something rapidly in Spanish, gesturing over at me.

The woman turned then and saw me. Young, with Lee Thomas's face, all over again, only bolder, less refined. "For Christ's sake," she said in exasperation. "Who the hell—"

"Sorry," I said.

"No more cigar," said Rosalia, patting her chest.

"Shit," said the young woman. "*Sí, sí, cigarro no más.*" Resigned, she reached into her skirt pocket and pulled out a cigarette, lit it with a silver and turquoise lighter. "Well, the mood's wrecked now anyway. It's okay, Rosalia. *Finito. Gracias, muchas gracias.*"

The woman stood up, rubbing her back. *"Ai,"* she winced.

The young woman handed her a folded up bill. *"¿Mañana, sí?"*

"Sí, sí," said Rosalia nodding, pocketing the money and walking off.

The woman I assumed was Cornelia turned to me. "So, who are you?"

"Chloe Newcombe," I said. "I'm a victim advocate with the County Attorney's office."

She took a drag on her cigarette. "Why am I not surprised?"

"You *are* Cornelia Thomas?"

"Yes." She stared at me.

"Maybe we could sit down?"

She blew out a long stream of smoke. "So you can break the news about my father? Don't bother, I already know."

chapter twenty

"HAVE THEY CAUGHT THE PERP?" HER FACE
was a calm mask, it told me nothing.

"No," I said. "If there's even a suspect, they're not telling."

"Who's handling the investigation?"

"Hector Estrada."

"The bullfighter." Corney smiled. "I used to call him the bullfighter, 'cause he has such slick moves."

She was so controlled and self-possessed. I had twenty-some
years on her, but I felt like a kid in comparison. She sat down on the
edge of the crumbling cement fountain. "So why isn't Hector here,
instead of you?"

"I guess he doesn't consider you part of his investigation. I'm here
because your mother asked me to find you." I sat in Rosalia's iron
chair. "How did you find out about your father?" On impulse, before
she could answer, I took a stab. "Did Nate tell you?"

"Nate? Who's Nate?"

"He's a reporter for the *Sierra Vista Dispatch*. I thought maybe
he'd talked to you."

"A reporter?" She shuddered. "I wouldn't talk to a reporter. This
kid told me." She laughed. "A cowboy. Sonny."

"Sonny? I met him. At the cafe."

"He's always at the cafe. That's how I met him too." Cornelia's
face softened. "He looks like some local yokel, but he actually went

off to college for a couple of years. Then he comes back here and doesn't know what to do with himself. We're kind of drinking buddies, so when he heard it on the news—they do have television here, believe it or not—he came to the van and told me."

What a way to find out, I thought.

As if she read my mind, she said, "Better him than most people I know and besides he brought along a six-pack." She leaned down, stubbed out her cigarette.

I reached into my purse and took out the envelope Lee had given me, got up, and handed it to her. "This is for you," I said apologetically. "From your mother."

She glanced at it and shoved it down into her skirt pocket.

"Cornelia, she'd like to see you. She wants you to come home."

She looked away from me, chipped at the crumbling cement with her fingernail. "It was bad enough before and now Gladys is there too. Riding everybody. She and Daddy . . . oh well." She glanced in my direction. "You're standing there looking so self-righteous. Would *you* want to go home?"

I sat back down. "Corney," I said, as a kind of revenge for the self-righteous bit, "who is Willy?"

"You don't know?"

"No."

"Then I'm not going to tell you. My mother deserves her privacy."

For a moment there was a silence. "Sorry," I said. "Don't kill the messenger, okay?" I didn't want to push it. I stared past her shoulder, at the camera on a heavy tripod half hidden by a yucca plant. I was trained not to lecture. Victims were supposed to take responsibility on their own, it was called empowerment. I hated words like "empowerment."

Cornelia tossed her head. "Shit. All I did for years was think about my family and I do not do that anymore. I've had it! I've quit!"

"It's your call," I said. "Really."

"It's her own fault. She could have saved herself but no, she stood by and let things get worse and worse. She should have divorced him—" She stopped abruptly and took a deep breath. "But I have to admit I do worry about Justin." She sighed. "At least I have some good memories. What does he have? Poor kid. He was so little when everything started to fall apart. But what can I do? I mean—" She lit another cigarette.

"How old were *you* when everything fell apart?"

"Sixteen."

"Ouch," I said. "That's a hard time too."

"Daddy was up for reelection. Usually it would be a shoo-in but that year he had a serious contender, Phil Harris, an attorney over in Sierra Vista. Phil was spending a lot of money." She paused, looking at the end of her cigarette.

"But he won."

"Yeah, he did. I've been going over and over stuff in my mind ever since I heard he was . . ." She shuddered.

"Over and over stuff?" I said. "That's not good."

"Over and over. *God.* I'm *sick* of it."

She was up here with no one but Sonny to talk to, itching to confide, I could feel it. "You can tell me if you like," I said. "I mean, I'm bound by confidentiality."

Corney blew out a stream of smoke. "It's just another sad story. You've probably heard a million of them."

I leaned back in the cast-iron chair and for a second seemed to see the motel in some old-fashioned advertisement: the pool full of glittering blue water, cabins spruced up, a family checked in on vacation—Mom and Dad settled in their chairs, Mom knitting, Dad smoking a pipe. Dick and Jane and baby Sally cavorting in the pool. A family as a family used to be, before a million sad stories.

"A drop in the bucket," I said. "In one ear and out the other."

"I was pretty wild in high school," said Cornelia, "living down being a judge's daughter, you know? One Saturday I went out to the desert with a bunch of high school kids and this older guy. Anyway the long and short of it is that the kids started leaving and after a while I was alone with this guy. He had some Wild Turkey and I was a little drunk. Actually pretty drunk and . . . well, the guy raped me. Afterwards I ran off into the desert, and he yelled for me to come back and then finally he left too."

I winced. "I'm sorry."

She looked amused. "Don't be. I've told enough counselors about it, it's kind of lost it's impact."

"Did they catch him? Was he charged?"

She screwed up her face. "I'm getting to that. I walked down the road until I came to a house and called home. My mother and Justin had gone back east for a week so Daddy was the only one there. He drove out and got me."

"Your mother," I said. "She was involved with the Rape Crisis Center. Is that what got her started?"

"No. She was already involved when it happened. That's the irony. Think about it—because of her, I knew everything you were supposed to do. I wanted to go straight to the hospital so they could do the rape kit. I knew they could get the guy, because he was over eighteen and even if he said it was consensual, just having sex with a minor was illegal. I wasn't afraid. I was angry."

She looked angry now. She lit a cigarette off the stub of the one she had going. "Daddy said no." Her voice rose. "He said it wouldn't look good. A judge's sixteen-year-old daughter, drunk. *Like it was my fault*. He worked on me and worked on me all the way home. This can be our secret, he said, there's no reason to let your mother in on this, it will upset her too much. I'll take care of it. I was crazy about my father, back then." She paused and added, "I thought he must have something up his sleeve that he wasn't telling me, some way to get the guy no matter what."

"And did he?"

She snorted. "Shit. All he had up his sleeve was the election coming up."

"Your name wouldn't have been in the papers," I said. "And even if it went to trial, the election would have been long over by then."

"Don't you see? Everyone in the courthouse would know, his little courthouse *family*. They all worshiped him. Being a judge was all he ever wanted, it was more important than his real family. That's what my mother said, when I told her."

"So you did tell her."

"Of course. She was my mother. She got me into counseling. She was so mad at Daddy she told him she wouldn't campaign for him ever again. They stopped speaking. I thought she should just get a divorce, why live with someone you're not speaking to, but she didn't and that made me furious so finally everyone stopped speaking to everyone else."

"How awful," I said.

"Isn't it? Everything kind of accelerated, like we were on this train out of control and no one could stop it."

"But, Cornelia," I said, "you can stop it now. Your mother sent me to find you. I'll be seeing her again. What should I tell her?"

"Not where I am," she said. Suddenly she looked tired, defeated. "Oh, I don't know. Tell her I'm safe. Tell her I'm thinking of her. Maybe . . . give Justin a hug from me."

She stood up and walked over to her tripod and began to dismantle it. Her back was to me. I couldn't see her face.

"I'm not on the train anymore," she said. "I jumped off a long time ago. I've got my photography now. I don't need anything else."

The spikes of the yucca were sharp as knives, the thorny edges barbed. The light had faded, taking any warmth with it. I pushed down the sleeves of my sweater. Ginny's words. *"Her breakthrough."*

"I've seen some of your work," I said. "Ginny showed me. The ones with the doll. They're very good. The rape, where was it?"

She scowled. "What difference does it make?"

"It happened in Windy City, didn't it?"

The tripod clattered to the ground. "Who cares where it happened?" she said. "Daddy's being murdered had nothing, *nothing* to do with me. Or with my mother, if that's what you're thinking. You're clueless, you didn't understand diddly squat and I've wasted half the afternoon talking to you. I don't know why. Now why don't you just leave?"

chapter twenty-one

THE LIGHT WAS AN EERIE ORANGE ON THE cornfields as I drove home the back way. There was something about the chill of fall in the evening, a sad gray beneath the bright colors of leaves, that was primeval and called up endings, not just our personal dying but death itself, the death of everything.

So the judge had been murdered on the same spot where his daughter had been raped, years before. Corney hadn't told me his name, the rapist's. What was it? I had to go see Craig tomorrow at Mountain View Rehab. Craig's old girlfriend Melissa had been raped too. What was the name of her rapist? Flame had told me. Elton. Elton Harvey.

I shivered, it was so cold in the car and the heater didn't work. *Don't think.* It wasn't the same kind of thing, the same kind of rape. I was clearly exhausted.

By the time I drove over the Divide, through the Mule Pass tunnel and into Dudley, it was dark. The town was strangely alive, more people out than usual, but I hardly glanced at them. The energy it took to keep from thinking was making my whole body ache, as if the thoughts were a virus I couldn't shake.

I pulled into my driveway. Standing in the carport, her back to me, was a woman with long dark hair and a strange looking hat. She turned: She was hideous with a red grinning face and big hook nose studded with warts.

I got out to the sound of Honey Pie, yapping herself into a frenzy. Next to the woman, a small ghost shouted, "Trick or treat!"

Halloween. My heart slowed back down. All those pumpkins in Bowie and it hadn't even occurred to me. Life was passing me by. Honey Pie yapped on.

"Shut up!" I shouted automatically. "I'm sorry," I said to the witch and ghost. "I don't have anything. Try next door." I pointed to Lourdes's house.

Inside it was dark. I yelped as Big Foot moved against my legs. Halloween. As a kid I'd gone trick-or-treating with my brothers James and Danny. Danny the brat would always have a hidden bar of soap and if James and I didn't watch him, he'd draw on people's car windows. We'd come home afterward and James would read Edgar Allen Poe out loud, with a flashlight in the dark. "Ullalume" was his favorite.

> *The skies they were ashen and sober;*
> *The leaves they were crisped and sere—*
> *The leaves they were withering and sere:*

I hadn't had another postcard from Danny since the day Nola stopped by. What was he doing for Halloween?

I kept the lights off except in the bathroom where I took a shower, put on black jeans, a dark olive chenille turtleneck, and short black boots with two-inch heels.

> *It was hard by the dim lake of Auber,*
> *in the misty-mid-region-of-Weir:*

I intoned to the mirror to keep my thoughts at bay, stretching out the words as I applied eyeliner, blusher. Boy, that Edgar Allen had rhythm all right. Somewhere in my bookcase was the exact same book James had read from, but I had not a kernel of candy corn, much less a Hershey bar or a Snickers. I couldn't stay home to look for it.

I got in the car and drove to the garage of a man I knew. He restored cars. The lights were on, a big old-fashioned car parked in front. I didn't recognize it. I knocked, walked in.

WANTED: A GOOD WOMAN WHO CAN CLEAN AND COOK FISH, DIG WORMS, SEW AND WHO OWNS A GOOD FISHING BOAT AND MOTOR. PLEASE ENCLOSE PHOTO OF BOAT AND MOTOR.

The sign that hung on the wall in Brody's shop had been there for as long as I'd known him. The garage smelled the way it always had, old grease combined with the prickle of gasoline. Even the radio was turned as always to KWKOOL FM, Oldies but Goodies.

Sonny and Cher were singing "I've Got You, Babe" as if in Brody's shop Cher would never be a superstar, Sonny would never go to the House of Representatives and ski into a tree. And everyone I loved was still alive.

"Hey there, stranger." Brody grinned, a smear of black grease on his forehead. "Where you been so long?"

Once we'd been lovers. We'd had nothing in common, fought all the time. I don't know why seeing him made me feel happy, but it did. With his blue eyes and rough sandy hair, jeans and sweatshirt, he looked like one of those baseball players who should have retired long ago but still stand there on the pitcher's mound, throwing balls into the dusk.

"Hither and yon," I said. "What about you?"

"Here and there." He slammed down the hood of the black '47 Mercury, dotted with silver Bondo, with a bang. He'd been working on the Mercury for as long as I'd known him. He pulled a rag out of his back pocket and wiped his hands. "I got a new car."

"No kidding."

"Yep. Parked in front. A new old car. 'Fifty-nine Buick LeSabre."

I didn't know a Ford from a Buick from a Chevy, even after all the time I'd known Brody. "Good!" I said.

"Darn tootin'." Brody smirked. "It was a great deal."

"Are you busy?" I asked.

" 'Bout to stop and clean up."

"Don't forget your face," I said. I rubbed my forehead. "You've got grease right here."

I moved aside a bunch of *Hemmings Motor News, Hot Rod* magazines, and torn-out pieces from the classifieds of good car buys circled in red and sat down on the old Chevy seat Brody used for a couch. Waiting for him to come back, I felt my whole body relax, muscles I hadn't even known were tense, softening up.

"So what's up?" said Brody returning.

"Danny left the Buddhist colony, he's running around in Montana somewhere." Brody knew Danny, from the time Danny had visited here, when Hal, our brother's lover was living here, still alive. In fact, it was because of Danny that I knew Brody.

"No kidding." Brody chuckled. "Montana, huh. That devil. Good for him."

I sighed. "Maybe we could take a ride," I said. "In your new old car."

The tail fins of the 1959 Buick LeSabre were mottled with rust but still jaunty. The interior was two-tone, vinyl and cloth in burgundy and cream. The Buick insignia was stamped into the vinyl on the doors.

"Pretty cool, huh?" said Brody. "Got eighty-twenty loop pile carpeting. Power brakes, power steering."

"Um," I said. "Nice." The heater worked so well, my brain felt feverish. "Down in the dank tarn of Auber," I recited. "In the ghoul haunted woodland of Weir."

"What?"

"It's from a poem my brother used to read on Halloween."

"Yeah? What's it about?"

"Actually I'm not sure," I said. "Maybe just about the sound of words." I wished I'd looked for James's book, I could have brought it. "Edgar Allan Poe."

" 'The Tell-Tale Heart,' " Brody said. "We read that in high school."

"You and everyone else." I took off my boots and tucked my feet up under me as we sailed like a cabin cruiser in gentle waters down the two-lane blacktop. I closed my eyes. "Tell me a story," I said to stop "Ullalume" from running around in my head.

For a moment Brody thought. Then, "Trick pigeons," he said.

"What? Trick pigeons?"

"There's two kinds. You got your rollers and your tumblers. Now your rollers, they'll be flying along and out of nowhere, they'll turn over, like a Two-oh-six Cessna doing barrel rolls."

"Really," I said. "How do you know about trick pigeons anyway?"

"They're part of a show in the wildlife section of the zoo. In San Diego."

"Oh," I said. "And what about your tumblers?"

"Your tumblers?" Brody laughed. "Well, your tumblers will be flying along nice and straight like they know where they're going?"

"Um-hum."

"And then—right in midair—they'll plunge. Drop maybe fifteen, twenty feet."

"No kidding." I opened my eyes. "Then what happens?"

"Everyone claps, I guess."

"I mean, do they hit the ground?"

" 'Course not. Where's your faith? They're trick pigeons."

We drove along in silence for a while. Outside, clouds covered the moon, the stars. Nothing to see anyway but a bunch of leaves, crisped and sere.

Brody cleared his throat. "Well, I figure there has to be a guy in here somewhere. Last I heard you were seeing that gardener, what's-his-name."

"Craig."

"So how's Craig?"

"He checked himself into an insane asylum," I said. You could say anything to Brody, he had no sense of political correctness.

"Jesus Christ," said Brody. "You mean they still have those?"

"Actually it's rehab," I said.

"Rehab. That's not such a big deal."

"But I thought he was really together. I thought he knew what he was doing."

"None of us do," Brody said. "You just noticed?"

I shivered. "Brody, sometimes I'm really scared."

"Not 'cause of the rehab, I hope," Brody said. "Back when I was drinking, I knew a hundred guys went to rehab."

"I guess it's just finding out he wasn't as together as I thought."

"Nobody's perfect. Don't be so hard on him, give the poor guy a break."

"You're right," I said. "I'll be okay in the morning."

It was nearly midnight when I got home. No tricksters had smeared my windows with soap or vandalized my house. What had happened to tricks? Regular kids didn't play tricks anymore, not unless they wanted to be charged with criminal damage and put into juvie. I flicked on the lights, looked through a couple of bookcases until I found James's copy of Edgar Allan Poe and turned to "Ullalume."

Long. I skimmed, then near the end where the poet is talking to Psyche I read out loud to myself:

> And I said: "What is written, sweet sister,
> On the door of this legended tomb?"
> She replied: "Ullalume—Ullalume—
> Tis the vault of thy lost Ullalume!"

Suddenly I saw past the rhythm to what the poem was about. Little chills ran up my back, but I kept on.

> Then my heart it grew ashen and sober
> As the leaves that were crisped and sere—
> As the leaves that were withering and sere.
> And I cried: It was surely October

On this very night of last year
That I journeyed—I journeyed down here!

On this very night of last year. It was a poem about an anniversary. What was it Flame had said about Melissa's death—it was this time of year almost exactly? Anniversaries are the hardest time, she'd said. No wonder the poem had been haunting me. Cal Thomas had been murdered close to or maybe even, for all I knew, on the exact date of Melissa's death.

chapter twenty-two

EXPECT A MIRACLE SAID THE SIGN AS I
drove up the tastefully landscaped curving driveway to Mountain
View. I'd blocked out thoughts of Craig for a while now, but here they
were unavoidable. Should I ask him about Melissa? Surely it was too
big an issue not to discuss; it even seemed to me, that had he talked
about it, he might not even be here. In jail at Mountain View ReHab.

Beside me, on the seat was the packet they'd sent me in the mail.
No books, no music, no shorts with less than a seven-inch inseam,
no weapons. It didn't actually say no weapons, but I kept flashing
back to twenty-some years ago in Michigan, when I went to visit my
brother Danny in prison.

He'd gotten busted for marijuana possession in the wrong state
at the wrong time and had served nine months of a two-year sentence. He was only nineteen and his prison haircut made his ears
stick out. Except for his eyes, he looked about twelve. Each time I
went to see him, he looked paler and thinner.

Afterward it was a four-hour drive back to college through a win-
tery landscape, the black exclamation line of telephone poles along
the road sticking up through snow and once, there was no road at
all, just a sheet of white. It seemed to me to be the landscape of all
my visits to Danny. They stole my brother, just a wise-ass bratty kid,
and sent him back nine months later: cagier, more knowing, not quite
Danny anymore.

I pulled into the Mountain View parking lot, got out, and walked down the brick path past the fuchsia bougainvillea, the waxy white flowering spikes of aloe. I pushed open the glass door. Inside was all muted shades of terra-cotta, peach, and turquoise with big watercolors of desert scenes. A pleasant New Agey woman with big ethnic earrings, looked me up on the guest list, went through my purse and made me sign a paper saying I wouldn't reveal the identity of any of the patients.

Then she handed me a name tag to fill out. "Visiting hours are three to six." She smiled. "Craig will be out in a minute."

I ducked into the restroom, more peach and terra-cotta. Had Craig gone to court with Melissa? Cochise County had been slow to use victim advocates; I was the first. There would have been no one there, except a distracted prosecutor, to explain things. I combed my hair, put on blusher, refreshed my eyeliner. The lighting was bright but without shadows, flattering. Here I was at the Mountain View Rehab Center and, despite the locked knots of muscles at the base of my neck and along my shoulder blades, I looked to be in the peak of health.

What kind of sentence had Elton Harvey gotten? Who had the prosecutor been? But I couldn't just fire questions at him.

My hands were clean, but I washed them anyway. Dried them carefully, staring down at the paper towel as if to memorize the dotted pattern embossed on the pale beige. It was so pleasant in this tasteful restroom, I could have lingered for hours, but I took a deep breath from my diaphragm, something I'd learned in some long ago yoga class, and opened the restroom door.

Craig was standing, his back to me, out in the waiting room. He wore jeans and his French-blue, knit shirt. My heart started going *thump thump* as if something alien were trapped in my rib cage, trying to get out. My boots with two-inch heels made no sound on the carpeting.

"Hey," I said when I was a couple of feet away.

Craig turned. "Chloe!" He smiled. A nice Zoloft smile with no kinky edges; beatific.

We hugged. He smelled freshly washed with some expensive herbal soap; obviously he hadn't done a lick of work in days. He wasn't Danny and this wasn't a prison.

"I really missed you," he said.

I rested my head on his French-blue knit shoulder. My heart slowed down to where it scarcely beat at all. "I missed you too," I said.

"You didn't take your book," I said. "*Journey to the Heart of the Congo.*"

"You can't bring books in here," said Craig. "You can only read books on their list."

What kind of fascist place was this? I opened my mouth to comment, closed it.

Low white clouds drifted slowly across the mountains behind Mountain View Rehab, like clouds might in a haiku poem. Craig and I sat outside in an enclosed patio at a wrought-iron table, sipping lemonade sweetened with fructose. Down a few tables out of earshot were other patients with visiting families, people with good haircuts in casual, expensive-looking clothes.

"Pretty fancy place," I said.

"Expensive as hell. Lucky when I quit teaching I kept up on the insurance." Craig squinted in the light. I wondered if they'd confiscated his sunglasses. "What have you been doing?"

I watched a pink cloud relinquish one mountain, go on to the next. How could I tell him anything? Or ask him anything either. It was implicit in the surroundings. "Running around too much," I said. "Work has gotten pretty crazy." I paused. "But what about you?"

"My back pain's almost gone," he said.

"Really?"

"It got so bad because I was fighting it instead of letting it go. That's the secret to life—just let things go."

"That makes sense." I rubbed my neck and tried to keep the skepticism out of my voice. "How do you do that exactly?"

"Let God and let be."

Slogans. "Um." I kept my face expressionless. I hoped they were doing more for Craig than giving him some slogans. I assumed they sat around in groups and talked. Talked and talked. Did Craig go on and on about Melissa?

"Twelve-step stuff." He looked apologetic. "All it is, really, is a mental attitude. I wish I could tell you all the stuff we've been doing, what I've been learning about myself."

"You *can't*?"

He shook his head distractedly. "All I can say is everyone here is great. I've always liked this place."

"Always?" I said alertly.

He ducked his head. His face looked somehow bare, vulnerable, not Craig's face anymore. "I was here before."

"You were? When?"

"Four or five years ago. I went through some heavy duty stuff and I almost lost it."

"Oh?" I prompted.

Craig stared past me.

I sat very still, holding my breath. Across the patio was a tree: bright yellow, unreal, like the mountains and the clouds and me and Craig.

"Maybe . . ." he paused.

"Maybe?"

"Maybe some time I'll tell you about it. It's a long story."

Even though I already knew some of it, it wasn't the same as him telling me. I should ask him to tell me now, but I couldn't. I was sure of him one moment, full of doubt the next. I was the one who was unreal; an imposter, possibly even a betrayer.

"I took Flame and Roy the strawberry plants," I said to change the subject.

"How's Roy?"

"Good one minute, terrible the next."

"When I first knew them," said Craig, "they used to ride together all over the county, miles and miles."

"Ride," I said. "They had horses?"

"Bicycles."

Bicycles. Someone had ridden a bike to Windy City. *Forget that stuff.* The lightness came back to my head, but I ignored it. By now I was so used to living on an emotional edge, it seemed like simple reality.

Craig laughed. "They had these old Schwinns that belonged in a museum. They'd pile everything into the baskets."

Everything meaning what? Guns? But it was ridiculous. My voice was outside myself. I heard it ask, "What happened to the bikes?"

"God knows." He stood up. "Let's take a tour. You're staying for dinner, aren't you?"

"Sure," said my voice.

We had mesquite-broiled steaks, potatoes, sour cream, and salad, sitting out on the patio again to get away from the hordes of other patients and their families and their good haircuts and expensive clothes.

"Listen," said Craig. "I know this is weird for you. All this twelve-step stuff. I know you think it's all New Age bullshit."

"I never said that. I don't know that much about it."

"But you're blocking me, I can feel it. I think there's a lot of bullshit here too sometimes, but I don't have a choice and besides it works."

"It's fine," I said.

"I'll be out in two more weeks, the last week is family week. Families and significant others come for the week. My mom's not coming."

"Why not?"

"She'd have to fly from Oregon. It's too hard on her. My dad had a big drinking problem and she doesn't need any more grief in her life."

"You haven't even told her you're here, have you?" I said.

"No, I haven't."

"So if you don't tell people things," my voice rose, "it's like they never happened?"

"I told you. I'm doing the best I can. Okay? I thought—if you could get the time off—I'd like you to come, even if it's just for two or three days. Then you could really see what this is all about."

Maybe it was the haiku clouds, but suddenly I had a little satori: everything was imaginary—the judge's murder, Nate's disappearance—all imaginary, something I'd made up to get away from this new Craig. For a second, I clung to Nate like a life preserver; I had to find him first, before anything else, didn't I?

"I could probably get some time off," I said. "I'll try."

"Here," said Craig. He leaned over the table, put something small and fuzzy in my hand, folded my fingers over it.

I opened my hand. A tiny purple teddy bear lay against my palm. "What's this?" I asked.

"It's a symbol," said Craig. "You can get them in the bookstore."

"What kind of symbol?"

"My inner child."

"What?"

He looked abashed. "Take it with a grain of salt."

I put Craig's inner child carefully in my purse. My heart was pounding again the way it had earlier, trying to escape from my rib cage, trying to escape from all this serious, responsible stuff.

He grinned. "You don't fool me, Miss Chloe." When he grinned he looked like Craig again. "This isn't your cup of tea at all, is it."

I said suddenly, before I thought, "When you get out are we still going to go see movies, and rent videos, have film festivals?" My voice shook. I was appalled at my own superficiality. "Like we used to?"

"Why the hell not? For God's sake it's not like I just had a lobotomy."

Actually it seemed to me it was, kind of. Here Nate was missing and Craig, who'd never even met him, didn't like him. And now he'd fixed it where I couldn't talk to him about anything, didn't even know if I could *trust* him.

"Jesus, Chloe. You're *crying*?"

I sniffed. "No, I am not."

chapter twenty-three

NATE STARED BACK AT ME FROM THE BUL-
letin board in the break room at the County Attorney's office. HAVE
YOU SEEN THIS MAN? God, Nola was diligent. I'd passed about five of
her posters on telephone poles on my way to work. It was Monday
and I'd spent all morning in court. There was another poster on the
bulletin board outside the post office, when I ran in at lunch, and one
outside the Circle K when I stopped to get gas.

Now back at work, I spent a couple of hours in court and at three,
I called Lee.

Sylvia answered. "Mrs. Thomas isn't here right now," she said,
her voice vacuous with politeness.

"That's all right," I said. "I wanted to stop by a little later and
talk to her. Can you tell me when she'll be there?"

"Not today."

"She won't be home later? Is she out of town?"

"Tomorrow," she said doubtfully. "Maybe tomorrow."

"You don't know? Listen," I said patiently, "Mrs. Thomas *wants*
to talk to me. It's important."

"I can take a message," said Sylvia, in a robot voice.

"No."

"Excuse me," she said. "I have to go now."

It wasn't busy at work. I'd planned to leave early to go see Lee.
I drummed my fingers on the desk. Craig had been at the back of my

mind all day, his inner child in my purse. I picked up a Post-it pad and pencil and walked back to the main office where the legal secretaries were. Tension hung thick in the room, palpable as cigarette smoke. Marilu was sitting bolt upright at her desk. When she saw me she put a finger to her lips.

"What's—" I began but she shook her head.

"Shh." She tilted her head in the direction of Melvin's office. "Listen."

The door was closed. I heard a muffled drone, then a louder exclamation, the muffled drone again, another drone louder. A bang.

I raised my eyebrows.

"Melvin's hitting his desk," Marilu whispered.

"Who's he talking to?" I whispered back.

"Hector Estrada." She looked at her watch. "He's been in there for almost an hour."

As if on cue, the door to the office opened. Hector strode out, Melvin behind him.

"Marilu!" said Melvin.

"Yessir!"

"I'm leaving for the day."

"Yessir!"

We watched as Melvin and Hector strode out the back door.

"Who can work?" said Marilu. "At least you showed up. A bunch of people are out today."

"More flu?"

"Flu, elective surgery, whatever." She grinned. "Gigi actually made it in, to her eternal regret. But the last, the very last, person I'd want to be right now is Hector Estrada. And he and Melvin used to be so tight. It was 'cause of Melvin he made detective."

"Is this all about the judge?"

"What else?" She swung her chair round to her computer and sighed. "Back to work. Oh, by the way, some guy called you when you were in court and Gigi routed him back to me instead of taking a message 'cause he said he would be leaving town and he wanted your home phone number." She paused. "I didn't give it to him."

"Good," I said. "Who was it?"

"He wouldn't say. He said he ran into your car and he wanted to make sure it was okay. Does that ring a bell?"

"Jack Townsend."

Marilu raised her eyebrows. "That was *Jack Townsend*? He ran into your car?"

"It's a long story."

I went to the Rolodexes and found the one with the old cases in it, flipped through the names of defendants, alphabetized, until I got to the H's. Hernandez, Hopewell. I backtracked. Harvey. Elton. Two of them. Two? One was for drug charges, and aha, sexual assault. I wrote the criminal report number on a Post-it.

"Can you give me the key to the storeroom?" I asked Marilu. "Got to research an old case."

Marilu opened her desk and took out a key. "How's Lee Thomas doing?" She dangled it just out of reach.

"Not so good really," I said. "It might help if they had a suspect."

She handed me the key.

The storeroom was beyond the library. Inside, big brown accordion files were piled everywhere, on the floor, stacked high on utility shelves, and only roughly in order of case number. But if things were even minimally in order it looked like the Elton Harvey file would be on top of one of the utility shelves. I moved a stack of boxes, old homicide cases, then found a library stool, dragged it over and stood on it. Reaching up, I yelped and almost fell over backward as a large cockroach ran over my hands.

Not that anybody cared that I was here, everyone was too intent on their own lives to notice what other people were doing. My nervousness was hyper-guilt, a kind of offspring of hypervigilance and had to do with snooping into Craig's life behind his back.

Standing on tiptoe, I rifled through the brown accordion files until I finally found the one with Elton Harvey's case number on it near the end. I pulled it down, sat on the library stool, and took out the disclosure file. Just a peek, I told myself, was all I wanted.

I flipped to the back, where the investigation started and saw a name I recognized. Mark Flannery. Lead investigator. Suddenly my hands were a little trembly. I flipped back to the front. Division Two. *Cal Thomas had been the judge.*

"Chloe?"

I jumped.

"Sorry." Marilu stood in the doorway. "He's here. Jack Townsend."

I put the disclosure file back in the accordion file, stood up, tucked the whole thing under my arm.

I heard Gigi laughing as I walked down the hall to the reception area. It was a happy laugh, relaxed and tinkly. "Mr. Townsend," she was saying, "*really,* you're such a—" She stopped abruptly when she saw me. Her face was pink, animated. "*There* you are. Chloe, this gentleman wants to talk to you."

White mustache resplendent, Buffalo Bill was leaning over the wood divider that separated Gigi from the rest of the world, spiffy in a dark brown western suit with cream cording, white shirt, bolo tie, cowboy hat in hand. I wondered when was the last time he saw a horse.

I shifted the file from one arm to the other. "Hi," I said.

"Hello there!" said Jack, his astonishing blue eyes full of good will. "After you drove off, I started thinking, I never gave you my card. Sometimes these cars seem okay, then they get to acting up. And I have car insurance up the wazoo."

"It seems fine," I said cautiously. I didn't want to talk to Jack in front of Gigi. I wasn't sure I wanted to talk to him at all. From what I'd heard about him, he seemed to me to be subtle in ways I didn't know how to deal with. "Hold on a minute, I'm on my way out if you want to walk me to my car."

* * *

Outside, he put on his hat, carefully adjusting the brim. "You seen Lee since the day I saw you last?"

"Once."

"How's she doing?"

"Holding up," I said.

"Good." He smiled at me, his eyes crinkling. "I been worried about her ever since the day I saw her. And another thing—this investigation—I can't get old Melvin to talk to me and I even tried Hector Estrada, but he's never around. I wondered, you work here, maybe you could tell me how it's going."

"I'm just the victim advocate," I said. "They don't tell me anything either."

He stepped a tiny bit closer, so tall he had to bend his head to look at me. "You're good at your job, dedicated. I can tell, just by talking to you so briefly. We need more people like you." His voice was warm. "I know how it is, when you work some place. People talk, they let things slip. I'm just an old family friend." He made a gesture across his lip, zipping it up. "Discreet as hell."

"Gee, Mr. Townsend, I wish I could help you. All I know is no one's been charged."

"Not that I'd want you to tell me anything you shouldn't." He winked and reached in his breast pocket. "Anyway, here's my card, give me a call if there's anything you can tell me. I'd sure appreciate it."

I looked down at the card, rich cream, raised letters, expensive, *W. Jackson Townsend, Real Estate.*

"I can see you're busy." His eyes lingered on the file under my arm. "Taking work home with you and all. Call me if that car acts up too. Send me the bill."

"Thanks," I said. "I will."

I watched him walk to the red rental car, a wild surmise entering my mind. It had been so hard to think with his blue eyes trying to persuade me to tell him everything I knew about the judge's murder, not that I actually did know anything much. He opened the door.

"Oh, Mr. Townsend," I called.

"Jack," he said, with the big smile. "You make me feel like an old guy. Call me Jack."

"What does the 'W' stands for?"

He kept on smiling.

"Walter, Wallace, or maybe *William*?"

His smile broadened. "Honey, don't you know better than that?" He got in the car. "Someone gives you a card, first name just an initial, you don't ask."

Wilton, I thought as I watched him drive away. Wilberforce, Wilhelm. Lee had told me Cal used to call Jack Buffalo Bill just like I did. William.

Willy?

chapter twenty-four

I WAITED TILL AFTER I'D HAD DINNER AND
watched the news, then I set the file on the coffee table, and opened
it up, turning the pages until I found what I was looking for:

**INTERVIEW CONDUCTED BY DETECTIVE MARK FLANNERY WITH
MELISSA PRICE AT THE COCHISE COUNTY SHERIFF'S SIERRA
VISTA SUBSTATION**

Flannery: ... calmed down a bit so I'm just going to turn on the tape
recorder, if that's all right with you, Melissa?

Price: Yes.

Flannery: This is Mark Flannery talking with Melissa Price. Just go on
with what you were saying, Melissa.

Price: ... lights went out. They do that a lot during monsoon season.
I mean there wasn't a storm but I thought ... And my boyfriend was
coming over.

Flannery: Your boyfriend. That would be ...

Price: Craig. Craig MacDonald. Did you call him, someone said you
were going to call him.

Flannery: Sure, we're taking care of that. You were saying, the lights
went out.

Price: I was right in the middle of ... I was annoyed. Then I heard
someone at the door ... sure it was Craig. It was right when he was

supposed to...and I was angry because of the lights so I didn't look out the window first I just opened it...When I saw it wasn't Craig I ...he leaned against the door and pushed hard and (unintelligible). (pause)

Flannery: Melissa. You okay? You want take a break?

Price: No. He pushed...pushed me inside, then I could feel something against my head...he...he said it was a gun...
(pause)

Flannery: You're safe here, Melissa. Okay? Take a deep breath.

Price: I'm okay...just tired, really tired. He pushed me on the floor and then he stuck...stuck the gun up inside...my vagina.
(pause)

Flannery: Just the gun?

Price: What?

Flannery: I meant...not his penis.

Price: Just the gun.

Flannery: Do you know anything about guns, Melissa?

Price: Like?

Flannery: Kinds of guns.

Price: Some. I mean, I know how to shoot one.

Flannery: Any idea what kind of gun it might have been. A big gun?

Price: (unintelligible)

Flannery: Sure. Of course. I understand. (pause) What about a voice? He say anything?

Price: (unintelligible)

Flannery: You'll have to speak up. The tape won't record that.

Price: ...pulled my hair...uh...so I would, you know, see the gun. And I don't know...breathed funny...(pause) Bitch. He said "bitch."

Flannery: Uh-huh. So you heard his voice? Think you'd recognize it if you heard it again?

Price: Not really. (pause) But he sounded funny. Like a frog.

Flannery: A frog?

Price: I think he was . . . disguising his voice.

Flannery: Oh.

Price: He hit me with the gun too. He did it a couple of times. There's all these . . . See?

Flannery: Right. Yes. Melissa, there's no doubt in my mind that someone did something very bad to you. Now if you can bear with me, try to relax, we're trying to find out who did it. So we can catch—uh—put him away.

Price: (unintelligible)

Flannery: So he won't do it to someone else. (pause) Disguised his voice. This Craig? Your boyfriend? Is it possible—you said it was dark . . .

Price: No.

Flannery: No. Any idea at all who? Someone you've seen around maybe? Someone mad at you?

Price: It's hard for me to . . . think . . . right now. Could we . . . do this later? I could get some sleep.

Flannery: You might remember better when it's still fresh. Take a couple deep breaths. If you want to take a little break . . .

Price: No. (pause) I told you, it was dark. Could I have a glass of water?

Flannery: Right there, beside you. (pause) Would you like to take a break?

Price: It's okay. Let's just get it over with.

Flannery: I know it was dark. But you might have seen more than you realize. We've got some photographs here, if you'd take a look at them. (pause)

Price: Who are these guys?

Flannery: Just a bunch of guys. Some have records for sexual assault, or other stuff. Others are just . . . you know . . . guys.

Price: Guys.

Flannery: I notice your hand . . . uh . . . kind of . . . wavering there. Take your time. We want you to be sure.

Price: Okay. It was dark. I'm really tired.

Flannery: Just go through all the pictures, okay?
(pause)

Price: (unintelligible)

Flannery: You need to speak up. We're taping this.

Price: This one. He looks . . . familiar.

Flannery: Familiar. You mean someone you know?

Price: (unintelligible) It might be him . . . uh . . . yeah.

Flannery: But you're not sure? You're nodding. The tape won't pick that up.

Price: Sorry. No. I think it's him.

Flannery: You're positive?

Price: No. I mean, yes. It's him. Sorry. Does he have a record . . . uh . . . I mean, for sexual assault?

Flannery: It doesn't matter. You identified him. Let the record show that the victim has positively identified Elton Harvey as her assailant.

Some crimes you don't want to think about, you skim over the details, keep your emotions, your worst fears out. She'd positively identified Elton Harvey. In a state of extreme trauma and fatigue. I bet the defense attorney picked some holes in that one.

I flipped to the next page and my stomach lurched. Pictures, Polaroid snaps of Melissa. Her hair was short, dark blond, the flash had whited out her features. My rival, Melissa, glassy-eyed, face blank with shock, marred with dark bruises, posing for the camera in what must have been one of the worst moments of her life. She'd done nothing to me, she was entirely innocent and not only that, she was dead. I was here now looking voyeuristically, when she had no means of defending herself. Abruptly, I felt terrible shame.

I turned the page again to make myself stop looking at her and came cross a Xerox of a piece of paper, spidery writing scrawled across the page, labeled.

Page From Notebook Belonging to Elton Harvey
So here's the Joker's ultimate fantasy as far as women go. Women, chicks, broads, I could get dirty here but I won't (ha, ha). Ladies? Not too many of them. My ultimate fantasy, the JOKER'S (haha) ultimate fantasy is to DO IT TO HER WITH A GUN!!!!! My trusty twenty-two. Do what? MAKE LOVE!!!!! Scared but excited too. BOTH of us!!! Riding high on an ultimate FANTASY TRIP!!!!!

Yuck, I thought but at least they got him. The page from the notebook was how they got the sick fuck, as Mark Flannery would probably call him. You could pick holes in Melissa's I.D. but the lowlife scum of the earth wrote it all down. And what did the lowlife scum of the earth get? I turned to the front, to the last minute entry, Notice of Intent to Appeal. The defense always appealed. Except this wasn't the defense, and it wasn't an intent to appeal. What?

I read the minute entry carefully. For the charges of breaking and entering, kidnapping, aggravated assault with a deadly weapon, and sexual assault he'd been found not guilty on all counts.

Jesus Christ.

Who was the prosecutor anyway? An idiot? B. Johns. Barney Johns. Barney wasn't a prosecutor anymore but he was supposed to be pretty good. So what had happened? If the interview was dubious, surely the page from the notebook was as damning as you could get. Could the defense possibly have made a case for it being consensual? How? But as a prosecutor once said to me, who knows what juries think.

Barney Johns lived over in Sunsites, on the Sunset Ranch Estates, everyone had kidded him about heading off into the sunset at his retirement party. I'd danced with Barney at his retirement party, he smelled like beer and he came down hard on my big toe and I'd limped for weeks afterward. He didn't know Craig was my boyfriend. He owed me.

"Chloe!" he said, jolly as ever, maybe even smelling of beer now as we spoke on the phone. "Sure I remember you. Wore black all the time, came from New York."

"That's me," I said.

"Guess you got yourselves a hell of a commotion at the County Attorney's with Cal Thomas getting himself murdered." He laughed. "Mel must be shitting bricks."

"And no suspects. We're all lying low," I said. "Listen, Barney, I've been studying up on some old cases. Victim Witness is researching rape, kind of a victimology study and I came across this one where you were the prosecutor. Cal Thomas was the judge. Elton Harvey? A sexual assault?"

He snorted. "Sure. Goddamn. Just thinking about it still gets me mad. Elton Harvey. It wasn't his first sexual assault either. Pure unadulterated scum."

"Acquitted on all counts. How—"

Barney went on as if I hadn't spoken. "He got off on that one, but he went away on some methamphetamine charges. Another lowlife up in Florence stuck a sharpened spoon in him, goodbye Elton. The Lord moves in mysterious ways."

"Sometimes," I said. "But how did he get *off*?"

"Directed verdict."

"*What?*"

"Cal Thomas directed the verdict, not enough evidence. Cal, he hated listening to those rape cases and he liked directed verdicts. Unusual when you think about it."

"But why? I was looking at the file. They had that note he wrote, that looked good, even if the I.D. didn't."

"Yeah, Flannery kind of blew it on the I.D. 'cause he already had the note. It was the strongest piece of evidence they had. They never found any kind of gun. That dumb shit Elton had the note on him, in a drug log, a week before he raped Miss Price, and the log got confiscated before shit for brains even did it."

Big Foot appeared at the French doors, his mouth opened in a soundless meow. I ignored him.

"And?" I said.

"The main reason he got off is right there in the file, motion to suppress filed by the defense."

"Huh?"

"The motion was to suppress the note on the grounds the search warrant was for a drug log and that page wasn't technically part of the log." He paused. "Motion was just junk, legal shmegal. Except it worked because Cal granted it."

"He granted the motion to suppress the note?"

"Cal could be a little rigid. And, God, he hated to be overturned on appeal. And of course without the note, it kind of blew the whole thing. I consider it one of the bigger mistakes of his career. Cal was squeamish, like I said, he hated rape cases. Gentleman Cal. Besides, no matter what Cal did wrong, it always just slid off him like water."

Jesus Christ.

I thanked Barney and hung up. Directed verdicts were fairly rare, yet Cal Thomas had directed the verdict in Craig's lawsuit too. No wonder Mark was interested in finding Craig. Insult added to injury. But Melissa's rape was *five years ago* so wouldn't the time for any vengeance be long past? No one would wait that long, would they? No one, except possibly someone who'd been on antidepressants all that time, on antidepressants until maybe a month ago, when the Percodans began to interfere with the Zoloft.

What bothered me the most was the memory of Nate and me at the Tombstone Cafe. He would have told me everything, back then, had it not been for the damn tour bus and me being in such a hurry. Of course, he'd have had to work up to it. What was the last thing he'd said to me?

"Say hi to Craig."

Craig didn't like Nate, sight unseen. Maybe Nate and Craig *had* met. Maybe Nate had talked to him about Melissa. But Craig had nothing to do with Nate's disappearance. I'd talked to Nate on Monday and Craig checked into rehab on Sunday. At least Craig *said* he checked into rehab Sunday. But he hadn't actually called me until after Nate disappeared.

chapter twenty-five

EARLY THE NEXT MORNING, I PULLED IN BY Craig's greenhouse and got out. The sun made long shadows of the sunflowers. There was a chill in the air. I found the key under the rock and unlocked the door to the house. All night, thoughts like ants, like borer bees had swarmed my brain as over and over I relived the sight of Craig, out of control, throwing bags of manure.

First thing in the morning I'd called Mountain View, but, no ma'am, we can't violate patient confidentiality.

"Say hi to Craig."

I started in the bedroom, picked up *No Mercy—A Journey to the Heart of the Congo*, held it upside down and shook it but nothing fluttered out. I opened and closed bureau drawers, went through the two closets, searched in the pockets of jeans, shorts, shirts, and jackets. Then I moved to the living room and went through piles of magazines, books, newspapers; pulled up the seat cushions and felt around underneath. Explored the kitchen drawers and cabinets, and then finally went into his study.

I tugged at all the drawers of the four-drawer filing cabinet but they stayed stubbornly locked. I sat down on his office chair. Despite the fact that I'd had no sleep last night, I was once again full of energy, so much energy I could hardly keep up. I leaned over, pressed redial on the phone, listened to my own voice, eerie with chipper brightness.

"Hi, this is 555-2132. At the sound of the beep, you know what to do."

I was the last person he'd called but who was the last one to call him. Star sixty-nine.

I pressed the buttons.

"Mountain View!" said a another chipper voice.

I hung up. There was just one drawer in the desk. Suddenly I was struck by the resemblance to what I was doing now and what Nola and I had done at Nate's. With the prescience of youth Nola had known what to do right away. *Find out all their secrets.* I opened the drawer. Poor Nola. I'd forgotten to call her about my meeting with Poppy.

There were bills and receipts and torn-out articles of interest from magazines and newspapers but no key to the filing cabinet. The ancient tan paper that lined the drawer was cracked and split. I pulled at it and underneath found a piece of yellow, lined paper, folded into a square.

I unfolded it. A poem. Old, ink faded, paper creases deep. *"To Melissa."* Not a whole poem, part of one, the first four lines crossed out, only the last line readable: *"You were the dark rose that fades in the sun."*

I poked my head round the edge of the half-open door to the studio. "Flame?"

She was at her work table, painting a bowl. When I said her name she paused in midstroke. Under her blue-and-red striped apron she wore a purple gauze Indian blouse, both garments dulled with clay dust. "Chloe." She didn't look surprised. "Come on in."

"I wanted to talk to you," I said.

"Well, pull up a chair. The green one's good." She frowned at my black jeans. "Better dust it off first."

I walked across the floor, chalky with clay, powdering my black suede shoes. I pulled the green chair over, dusted it off and sat down.

"I worried after you left." With a flick of her wrist, Flame painted the four petals of a poppy on the bowl. "Thinking I should have left it to Craig, to tell you about Melissa."

"No," I said. "I needed to know. At work yesterday I found her file. I mean Elton Harvey's. I read it."

Flame nodded. She put down her brush and rested her chin on her hand, looking at me directly with her green and blue eyes and said very seriously, "And was it helpful to you? The file?"

I didn't exactly understand the question. My mind froze. Clay dust had settled on Flame's face, getting into the wrinkles. How relaxing it must be to get old, I thought irrelevantly, to do without the blusher, the eyeliner, the control top pantyhose.

I wasn't sure how to go on. "It was pretty upsetting," I said.

"This may not make much sense to you," said Flame, "but it's not what actually happened that matters. It's how Craig perceives it."

"How Craig . . . ?" I stared at her. I hadn't even told her why I'd come, hadn't gotten to the bad part, and she was making these irrelevant statements.

"I can see you're upset. What I mean to say is, I think if I were you, I'd ask him about it directly."

I said, "I just need to talk about this. It's really important. You're on Craig's side, so I thought it would be okay to tell you." I paused. "That judge, the one who was just murdered?"

"What about him?" Flame picked up her brush again, swished it in water, dipped it in black paint.

I told her about the notebook, about Cal Thomas granting the motion to suppress, the directed verdict, about Mark Flannery coming to see me. Then I told her about Nate, our talk at the cafe, his disappearance.

"And?" said Flame.

"Don't you see? That must be what he was going to tell me."

"Well, now," Flame said, "you can't be sure, can you? And first things first. Maybe with the detective it really was just about the lawsuit." With a flick of her wrist, she put four black spots at the center of the poppy. "Besides," she said, "even if he is investigating Craig, what do you think he could possibly find?"

"That's what scares me."

"Chloe," she said, "it was five years ago. You're not thinking. Craig was checked in to rehab when your friend disappeared."

"He says he was."

Flame wiped her forehead with the back of her hand. Her voice was patient. "I've known Craig for years. Impulsive, yes. Has a temper. But he's certainly not a killer. Do *you* think he is?"

"I don't know who he is," I said.

"Okay, that's what scares you. You've found out he's not quite who you thought. We all find that out sooner or later about the people we think we love. If we decide to keep going after that, that's when real love starts."

"But . . ." I said, muscles around my shoulder blades already beginning to knot up. "I mean . . ." I felt my face getting pink.

"Forget about Melissa," Flame said gently. "I shouldn't have told you. I think you need to look at what's really between you and Craig, not make up false obstacles."

She was right, I told myself as I drove away. The sky was a flat cool blue, sunflowers lined the blacktop and every couple of miles, road-kill. I would proceed with my life and forget about Craig until he was out of rehab. I would talk to Lee Thomas. And there was B.W. Poppy had said that Nate had talked to him and B.W. had apparently told him something that would make a lot of people mad.

Maybe Craig was, at this very moment, sitting in group with a bunch of supportive people, confessing. I would be allowed to visit him in prison and our relationship, all secrets vanquished, would reach a new high.

No, Flame was right. Surely she was right.

chapter twenty-six

SYLVIA MONTANO, IN NAVY BLUE SWEATS, A
bright red scarf round her hair, stood beside a pile of weeds and drew
an old rusted rake toward her, leaving a long ridged path in the
gravel. When I pulled in, she didn't look up. Still holding the rake,
she bent down, pulled up a weed and threw it into the pile.

"Hello?" I said through my open window.

She raised her eyes. "Sometimes I'm ashamed," she said. "No one
seems to care. Mrs. Thomas could afford to hire a gardener."

Her eyes startled me. They were leaden, empty. "Is she in?" I
asked.

Sylvia looked down at the rake as if she'd forgotten what it was
for. Then she dropped it and looked reluctantly back at me. "Who?"

"Mrs. Thomas. Sylvia," I added, worried, "Are you okay?"

"She's not here," she said ignoring my question.

"Will she be back soon? I need to talk to her."

"She won't be back all day. She went to Tucson." Her mouth
snapped shut.

"Is that where she was yesterday too? In Tucson?" I paused.
"Maybe seeing her friend Willy?"

She looked thoughtful. "Mrs. Alexander said to her, when she
was leaving, 'Willy won't help you, haven't you figured that out yet?'
But Mrs. Thomas never *listens*. Anyway, I don't care what Mrs. Thomas does. I don't *pry*."

Sylvia stared past my car at nothing. "I can take a message," she said after a moment.

"Just tell her I was here. That I'll come back tomorrow."

"Okay." She picked up the rake. Her skin seemed colorless today, against it the red scarf garishly bright.

"Sylvia," I said again. "Are you sure you're all right?"

But she walked away, pulling the rake behind her without answering.

"*You're the only one I can trust, the only one.*"

"*Willy won't help you, haven't you figured that out yet?*"

In Tombstone, tourists milled along the boardwalk on Allan Street, in the tourist uniform of shorts, running shoes and T-shirts, ambling along slowly with the gait of cows grazing in a pasture. I walked with them, past the Bird Cage Theater, the Bovis Tombstone Bead Company, and then on a corner was a little rusty looking shop, a big gaudy sign in front saying B.W. COLLECTIBLES. I went inside. The room was tiny; dark wood walls hung with rusted bits and pieces of Western tack, a long counter that filled most of the space, displaying more objects under glass and most everything seemed to be in various shades of rust and decay. The place appeared to be empty.

"Hello?" I called. "Anyone here? B.W.?"

"Hang on!" said a voice.

I hung on for what seemed like several minutes. Then there was a little ping and a moment later B.W. emerged from the back holding a Styrofoam plate with food on it. He had on a red cowboy shirt that looked too big for him, festooned with white fringe and pearl studs. Even in the dim light I could see all his wrinkles.

"Just fixin' me a little lunch," he said. "Wife makes me one of them super burritos every mornin'; I just nuke it in the microwave. What can I do for you, young lady?"

"We met before," I said. "At Windy City."

"Windy City, well, sure," he said without a trace of recognition. "If you're interested in ghost towns, I got a bunch of ghost town stuff.

Real stuff. Everything I got here is real in fact, none of your 'Made in Taiwan' for the tourist trade."

He hefted the super burrito, held it aloft. I could smell tomatoes, beans, cumin, oregano, and longed for lunch.

He winked. "This is a little place I run in my retirement or I'd be flat broke. Most folks don't know what's real and what's not and what's more, you know what? They don't even care." He took a big bite, chomping down with vigor as if it were an uncaring tourist.

"B.W." I said. "Sunday before last, remember? At Windy City? A reporter came by and talked to you. Nate Pendergast?"

"Nate Pendergast." His face brightened. "Good golly. Sure, I remember him. We talked a long time."

"Did he come back to see you again?"

"Naw. Just that once. How's that little wife of his doing?"

"That little wife," I repeated.

"Well, she sounded pretty sick. And that damn newspaper, saying they'd fire him, if he didn't come up with a whiz bang story. I tell you the world's gone cold. Cold and everyone talkin' about the old days, the gun fighters, how dangerous it all was, but you know what? Folks stuck by each other back then, they had their values."

Not Nate, I thought, Nate was absolutely shameless.

"B.W." I said. "Nate's in some trouble."

He set down the burrito. His eyes, sheathed in pads of wrinkles, came alive. "A good boy. Liked him. What kind of trouble?"

"He's missing," I said.

"Missing?" He scratched his head. "Hot damn. With his wife sick and all?"

"She's fine now. No one's seen him since the day after he talked to you. It may be connected to the story he was working on, the whiz bang story."

B.W. looked thoughtful. He picked up the burrito, set it down. "Nah," he said.

" 'Nah' what?"

"I don't think he'd do that."

"What?"

"Talk about the particulars. I told him to keep his mouth shut about them. It was just to give him a head start on doing his own investigating. 'Cause that sheriff's detective was gonna hold it back. In a murder investigation, the less people know the better, he said to me, then certain people, if you know what I mean, he said, don't go running."

"The detective," I said. "Hector Estrada?"

He nodded. "Gave me his card, said to call him personally, not to speak to anyone but him, if I remembered anything else. Thinks a lot of himself. Acted like I was gettin' senile or on the sauce maybe, when I told him what I seen. But I'm not and I weren't." He scowled. "Kind of got to me. Just 'cause I'm old and got a shit load of wrinkles don't mean I can't see what's in front of me. That was partly why I told your friend. Well, hello there!"

I turned. A family had entered the shop. Man, wife, two little girls. Didn't kids go to school anymore?

"How you folks doin' today?" B.W. asked heartily. "Handsome family. You want real collectibles you come to the right place cause every da-rn thing I got here is one hundred percent authentic."

"Mommy," whined one of the little girls, in shorts and a T-shirt emblazoned with an Indian head in full color. "Everything here is *dirty*."

"Melanie, hush."

"We were looking for a good restaurant," said the man.

"Right down the street, Bella's Delights. Best in the west!"

B.W. winked at me after they left. "Bella's my wife's sister. She don't know shit from shinola, comes to cookin'. But hell, she needs the business. And these tourists, they don't know the difference anyway. They won't be back, right?"

"What was it you saw?" I asked. "That you told Nate?"

"Well. It was a woman. Passed her on the road that very night the judge was killed, 'bout eleven, eleven-thirty."

"No kidding!" I said.

He nodded. "Old Hector says, could you identify 'er if you saw 'er again? Hell no, I said, I barely saw 'er the first time. But soon's I saw them bicycle tracks, I remembered. Swear to God, for a second I thought it was a ghost—wasn't wearing them Spandex things these cyclists usually wear nowadays—she had on a long dress, old-fashioned like, real long hair too, all down her back, dark hair. Pedaling along like it was the most usual thing in the world, to be out in the middle of nowhere, nearly midnight on a bicycle."

Could it have been Yolanda, with the beautiful long dark hair? Yolanda, the judge's clerk-mistress, who'd broken it off, weeks before he'd been murdered. Or so she said.

chapter twenty-seven

"ANDA ONE ANDA TWO ANDA THREE AND
turn," shouted a woman's voice inside Googie's Gym over LL Cool J,
singing about *doin' it, doin' it, doin' it good.* "Anda one anda two
anda three anda . . ."

It was approximately six-ten. On the brick wall of the alley outside the gym hung one of Nola's posters. HAVE YOU SEEN THIS MAN?
Nate, bemused and innocent. I sat down on a bench under a shedding
cancer tree to wait till Yolanda Sanchez got done with her five to six-
fifteen workout.

Probably a dumb thing to do, talking to Yolanda, possibly even
dangerous, but I was too concerned about Nate to care. Besides I'd
thought about it and I had a theory.

After a while, women, flushed, exuberant, in a wide variety of
workout clothes ranging from gray sweats to purple Spandex filed
out of the gym. Encased in their little world of good muscle tone and
hyped-up energy, no one noticed pale and probably flabby me. Just
when I was wondering if Yolanda had gone out some other exit, she
appeared, carrying a navy Adidas gym bag. She had on black Spandex
bike shorts, big workout shoes, a tiny cropped gray halter top, and a
headband that matched the top.

"Yolanda," I hissed.

She stopped. "Chloe? What are you doing here?"

"Do you have a minute? I wanted to talk to you."

"Oh," she said. "Okay." She sat on the bench beside me, putting the gym bag down in front of her. "What about?" What a big healthy girl she was, well muscled, no fat that I could see anywhere.

"The reporter?" I said. "Nate Pendergast, remember you said he came to see you?"

"Yes." Yolanda sighed, suddenly looking tired. "Your friend, with the funny glasses and the old clothes." She propped her feet on the gym bag. I saw a tiny purple vein just where the bike shorts ended a few inches above the knee. The light was fading, but it appeared she'd tried to cover the vein with that waterproof cover-up stuff. "What about him?"

"Didn't you notice the poster?" I asked. "There. Right behind you."

She turned, looked. "Oh. I never notice posters. They're always for things I don't want to go to." She looked confused. "He's missing?"

"He's been missing for a whole week now. I'm really worried about him."

"Oh?" Yolanda tugged at her headband. "These things, they always give me a headache." She pulled it off. "I'm sorry," she said politely. "But he'll probably turn up. I don't really know him, I mean he hangs around the courthouse, but I only really talked to him that one time."

"What was it you talked about?"

"I thought he would come right out, ask about me and Cal. But no. It was all how did the staff feel, how were they taking it. But then he asked me how would I feel if I'd been *raped* and Cal was the judge at the trial. So rude, so sneaky. Really, I know he's your friend, but . . . I told him 'I think you better leave now.' " She sighed again. "It was so obvious what he was getting at."

"What was that?"

"For heaven's sake. To get to me. To get me angry so I'd say things about me and Cal, of course. Besides why would there be a trial? Cal was my *lover*. He would have . . . I don't know, he would have . . . oh, killed him." She shrugged. "Or gotten someone else to."

Her careless naiveté astounded me. As if murder was just a run of the mill way to deal with certain circumstances. Or maybe I was the one who was naive.

"Maybe Nate just wanted your opinion," I said. "I mean you were the judge's clerk. A lot of people thought Cal Thomas was weak on sexual assault cases."

Yolanda tossed her head. "He always treated me like a queen. But—oh, I guess he didn't. It's like a dream now, me and Cal, a bad dream, seeing him up there in his robes, so important, always wondering, will he leave his wife? When it was only really this old man. An old man with a good job, so rare in Cochise County."

"I was wondering if you'd called Nate, set up another meeting."

"No." She shrugged and began to wrap the headband round her fingers. "Why would I do that? The first was bad enough."

"I don't know." Just like Nate, I wanted to provoke her, get her riled up, because she seemed like the kind of person, who, riled up, would spill the beans. "Maybe you wanted to explain to him why you were out riding a bicycle at Windy City, the night Cal was killed."

Yolanda's face turned white. She sat very still, and small beads of sweat appeared on her forehead. "What are you talking about?"

"Maybe you were supposed to meet Cal, but someone else got there first?"

She raised her hands and covered her face. "Hector!"

"*Hector* got there first?"

"I missed Hector. When I was in high school, he used to always protect me. All the boys treated me with respect, they knew if they didn't, they'd have to answer to Hector. Chloe, he was my very best friend."

"*Really,*" I said. Hector was Yolanda's very best friend? Wow, no wonder he'd told her more than he should have.

"Then," she went on, "he came to my house, three years ago when he found out about me and Cal. His face was so red but his eyes were like ice. He shouted at me, called me *putana*. 'He's just using you. He's a thief,' he said, 'robbing you of your good name.' " Her eyes blurred. "After that he wouldn't speak to me, even at family gatherings. Everyone noticed. It was so *embarrassing.*"

"Hector was there, at Windy City?" I said. Was she saying Hector Estrada had killed the judge, in a jealous rage?

Through her fingers, Yolanda said, "How could he? He promised. He *promised* me . . . Oh God." She paused. "What was the question?"

"You *saw* Hector there?"

"Where? At Windy City? Of course not." She lowered her hands. "He promised it wouldn't come out, about the woman on the bicycle. 'Don't worry,' he said, 'nobody has to know.' And he went and told a *reporter.* I can't believe it. He still hates me after all."

"I never said Hector was the one—" I began guiltily but stopped. "So you *did* have a meeting with Cal. You went to Windy City and argued or something and you left. And after that . . ."

"After that?" Yolanda's eyes widened with scorn. "After what? There wasn't any *before.* Hector knows I wouldn't lie to him. But other people, if it came out, would think . . ." She stood up. "Don't you see? I already told you that once. That must be what they wanted. Whoever it was. To make it look like me." She stamped her foot.

"But it wasn't?"

"I *never* went to see Cal. I *never* wrote him a note. I was through with him. I was home that night, sound asleep. Since I broke it off, I sleep through the night now, not tossing and turning and wondering. At least I *did.* "

I looked at Yolanda, had a flash of her life, a sort of Helen of Troy of the courthouse, full of passion for the wrong man, not even noticing the ones who really loved her, Hector for one.

She clenched her fists. "I hate this place. I hate my job if I even have one anymore. I hate the courthouse. I hate Cochise County." She kicked the gym bag. "I'm going to move to Los Angeles. I have an uncle there, cousins. It's like heaven there, they all say so. So many jobs, so much to do. And good for Latinas now, not like it used to be. In Cochise County it's always the same. Well, people here can find somebody new to talk about, to fill up their little tiny empty lives!"

I didn't know what to think. Was she lying? And whether she was or not, did Hector believe her? And how far would he go to protect her? What if Nate *had* talked to him, like I'd urged him to, mentioned what B. W. had told him.

"Nola," I said, back at home, "it's Chloe."

"Chloe! Wow! Great! Did you find out who called Nate?"

"What?"

"You know, the star sixty-nine person."

"Oh. Sorry I didn't get back to you on that. I was swamped," I said. "It was Poppy. Poppy Walker. Has he ever mentioned her?"

"No," said Nola in a little voice. "Never." She sighed. "Shoot."

"Wait," I said, catching on. "Nola, she's my age. Just a friend. She doesn't know any more than we do. When you talked to Hector, how did that go?"

"It went fine, he was very nice. He really listened to me, even though I could tell I wasn't being helpful."

"No follow-up interview?"

"No. Why?"

"Just wondered," I said.

"Something was *funny* about Nate's apartment," said Nola.

"Oh? Like what?"

"I'll let you know when I figure it out."

"Please do. And me—not Hector. Okay?"

chapter twenty-eight

THE NEXT DAY WAS WINDY, TOSSING around the desert plants along Highway 80, screeching through the cracks where my car windows didn't close completely as I drove to Sierra Vista to see Lee Thomas. Again I pulled in the circular driveway, parked by the woody roses. They weren't blooming now; the last of the petals had been swept away by the wind, or more likely, by Sylvia. There were more ridges in the gravel and the old rusted rake leaned against the wall by the garage door. Already the piled leaves had begun to scatter and litter the gravel.

The old station wagon was nowhere in sight.

All the curtains were drawn on the windows and suddenly I wanted to giggle—here I was again at the House of Usher. I knocked on the painted door. It opened quickly as if someone had been standing just inside, waiting for my knock. Sylvia stood there, a big white towel draped over her head. Her face looked very clean, childish, vulnerable.

"Hello," she said. "What can I do for you?" Her voice was polite but she didn't ask me in, blocking the door as if I were someone making the rounds with a stack of pamphlets and good news from the Lord.

"I wanted to talk to Lee," I said. "Remember, yesterday? Did you tell her I stopped by?"

Her heavy black brows furrowed. "She's out."

"So when's she coming back?" I asked patiently.

"She's doing some errands. It's hard to say." She reached up and tucked in the ends of the towel. "Would you like me to take a message?"

Sure. "Look, Sylvia, she's the one who wants to talk to me. You need to tell her I was here." I looked at my watch, nearly noon. "I'll come back this afternoon."

"I'll tell her," said Sylvia, her eyes blank.

I wanted to break through her impenetrability, see her react honestly for once. "So how are you and Mrs. Alexander doing?" I asked her.

"We're well," she said primly.

"I know everyone didn't get along," I went on. "Sometimes that makes it even harder."

"What do you mean?"

"Unresolved issues, that kind of thing."

"It makes me sick," said Sylvia suddenly. "He had no respect for her. He treated her like she was nothing at all," her voice rose, "instead of a real lady, like my *nana* was."

Her lower lip trembled, the sunlight glittered in her eyes. Suddenly I was ashamed.

She blinked back the tears. "He . . . he threatened her. He said he'd put her in one of those long-term care places. You know Mrs. Alexander is perfectly capable of taking care of herself. But he would never have done that. He wouldn't dare. I don't think." She stopped, looking at me with her blank eyes.

"Sylvia! Who is that?" called a voice.

Sylvia turned her head. "It's Chloe Newcombe, Mrs. Alexander, you know, from . . ."

The voice came closer. "Of course, I know."

"She's looking for Mrs. Thomas. She's just leaving," said Sylvia.

"That's ridiculous. Where are your manners?"

"But . . ." Sylvia stepped back and there was Gladys Alexander. Her gray permed hair was slightly askew as if she'd just woken up. She had on a pale cream tunic today, trimmed in black, and she was smiling. Her smile enfolded me, confident in its ability to charm. I stared at her in astonishment. She seemed completely transformed. She held out her hand.

I took it.

"Chloe, my dear, how lovely to see you again. How are you?" Her hand was powdery dry, bony as a bird's claw, her rings cut into the flesh of my fingers. "Fine, thank you. How are you?" I managed.

She lowered her lashes modestly as if her own well being was not of the slightest importance. "Please, come in. I'm dying to have a chat. Sylvia, I'm sure Chloe would like something." She looked at me. "Coffee? Tea? A Coca-cola?"

"No, I'm fine." A chat? With Gladys Alexander? I stepped into the sautillo-tiled hall. "Thank you."

Gladys made shooing motions with her fingers at Sylvia as if she were a chicken. "Go, go."

Sylvia backed away, her face stoic.

Gladys took my arm and steered me into the living room. Pillows were scattered around as if someone had had a pillow fight. Some kind of ninja toy lay on the carpeting. Gladys kicked it to one side, and sat me on the couch.

"Let me just get my cigarettes," she said, walking over to the end table by the big armchair and picking up a tooled red leather cigarette case.

Nervously, I looked at the silver-framed photographs on the table beside me. Justin on a horse, a little younger, Lee by the swimming pool, Cornelia—But where was the judge? His photograph had been there before, the night we'd done the notification: a snapshot of him wearing a down jacket, cowboy hat. Now it was gone.

Gladys lit up a cigarette.

"Now." She sat beside me, so small and thin she scarcely made a dent in the cushions. She took a long greedy drag on the cigarette and looked me up and down. "Don't you look *chic* today."

It felt like an insult. I wasn't chic in the black T-shirt and sweats I could see now were getting threadbare. Her gaze was so intense I felt uncomfortable.

"A working woman," she went on. "We never worked, of course, but I tell Lee, all women work today, whether they need to or not. Lee will be thrilled you stopped by. And so sorry to miss you. She talks about you all the time."

"She does?" I said.

Gladys Alexander's lashes were thin, beaded with mascara, but her eyes were deep blue, almost purple, hypnotic. I realized she must have been stunning once. "I feel quite left out." She flicked her cigarette, fluttered her lashes. "Stuck on a shelf like some dreadful old kewpie doll. And of course Lee is so busy coping. But you must talk to me, tell me all about what's going on." She smiled again. "She sent you on some kind of errand, didn't she?"

"Lee asked me specifically to talk to her in person," I said.

Her smile dimmed slightly. "Well, I *am* her mother. You can tell me and I'll pass it all along to Lee, you needn't ever come back."

"I don't mind coming back," I said.

"My dear, really." Gladys stared at me as if she'd suddenly noticed a large pimple festering on the tip of my nose. "She's always *pleasant* but it's a strain on her, all sorts of people, coming in and out."

"I'm sorry." Why was I so nervous? I had every right to talk to Lee. "I really do think . . . I have to talk to her."

The old woman stayed utterly still but her eyes darkened. "All sorts. And no manners at all." Her eyes darkened even more. "Servants and shop-girl types."

"I should be going now." I stood up, roused to action by her sheer nastiness. "Could you tell your daughter I'll be back this afternoon? I know my way," I said brightly. "You needn't show me out."

If she weren't a little old lady who scarcely made a dent on the cushions I'd have sworn the darkness in her eyes was pure rage.

I walked out of the living room, my knees a little trembly, walked down the dusty hall and through the terra-cotta colored door. The sunshine exploded on my eyes. Leaves were strewn on the gravel. Out here, the wind had made the air fresh and clean.

I got into my car and drove back down the windy road. Just ahead, before the curve where I'd run into Jack Townsend, a woman trudged along, her back to me. All I could see was her long hair, held back with an elastic band. Dense, thick, so black it seemed to absorb the sunlight. She turned. It was Sylvia, though I scarcely recognized her. Her face was quivery, muscles working at odds with each other.

"What's wrong?" I asked worriedly.

She didn't answer, just stared, as if she didn't know who I was. But she hadn't always been this spacey. What was going on?

"Where are you going?" I persisted. "Do you need a ride somewhere?"

She blinked. "No!" she shouted.

She backed away, then ducked under a small mesquite tree by the road and began to run through the desert, stumbling on the rocks. For the first time I noticed something glittering in her hand.

I parked and went after her.

chapter twenty-nine

THE RED DESERT DIRT WAS LITTERED WITH big jagged rocks. I ducked under the same mesquite tree. Head down to negotiate the rocks, I lost sight of her.

I stopped. "Sylvia," I called. "Wait a minute! Could I talk to you?" A cluster of grackles in a live oak to my left came alive, their rusty voices raucous as a gang of kids on a city street corner. The wind gusted, bending the branches of the live oaks, the manzanita, the mesquite. I couldn't see her anywhere.

"Sylvia!" I called again.

She stepped out then, from behind a big creosote bush, about fifteen feet away. Fat black grackles rose in a whirr of heavy wings. She'd taken off the elastic band and her hair was loose, freshly washed and damp, falling around her face in long tendrils.

"Leave me alone!" she shouted.

I saw now what she had in her hand, a pair of orange handled scissors. What did she have them for? I stepped back a couple of feet. The wind gusted again, blowing hot dry dust in my face, blowing Sylvia's hair in her eyes. It was drying rapidly now. Good hair. Dark and shiny and thick. Long, so long. *Hair all the way down her back.* My God. Could it have been *Sylvia* on the bicycle? For a second everything went quiet around me.

"Sylvia!" I shouted over the wind, trying to make my voice sound neutral, debating whether or not, considering the scissors, I should just leave, get help. "Are you sure you don't want to talk?"

Sylvia spat dry dust and wiped her mouth. "You leave Mrs. Alexander alone," she shouted. "She's just a little old lady. She's had a hard life and now she needs some peace."

"*She* wanted to talk to me," I said as reasonably and patiently as I could, considering I was shouting. "Just like Mrs. Thomas wants to talk to me, Sylvia. I only come when I'm invited. I wasn't bothering her."

The wind died suddenly and it was calm. Now I could hear the desert soundtrack cicadas.

"I just want to help," I said. "I'm concerned about you, that's all. Something's wrong, Sylvia. What? I'm not your enemy. We can talk about it! Maybe I can help!"

Her face wobbled. She sniffed. "No one knows. No one really knows. No one wants to listen."

"Sylvia, I'll listen," I said urgently, my heart pounding with the thought of what she might be going to tell me.

She sniffed again.

"It's okay," I said.

For a moment there was a silence again, then, "My . . ." She brushed her hair off her face. "My *nana.*"

I was taken aback. "Your *nana*? What about her?"

Sylvia gulped. "I changed her sheets everyday, washed them myself, she was always fresh and clean. And her feet, her little feet, her toenails were perfect, like a girl's." A tear leaked out of the corner of her eye and slid down her cheek. "Even when she was dying, she was *beautiful.*"

"Oh, dear," I said.

"I watched her slipping away, she was like . . . like a *fish* that you try to catch in the water, I couldn't hold on to her, every day she went away a little further. At the end"—Sylvia's mouth twisted—"she . . . she didn't even recognize me."

"Oh, Sylvia," I said. "I'm so sorry. It must have been terrible."

A strand of hair stuck on her lip. She brushed it away. "This *hair,*" she said. "I hate it!"

She grabbed some and began to saw at it with the scissors.

"No!" I said. "Stop it!"

A big clump of hair fell to the ground. She grabbed another and sawed at that. I watched helplessly, afraid to go closer, till the ground was littered with long black hair. What was left of her hair stood up in short uneven lengths.

"There!" she said, shaking her head back and forth. Then she threw the scissors as far away as she could. They clattered over the rocks.

She looked at me with satisfaction. "I'd better get back to the house," she said calmly. "Mrs. Alexander will be needing me."

Mrs. Alexander took one look and sniffed. "*Not* becoming," she said. "I'll take you to my own hairdresser tomorrow."

"Sylvia," I said. "Why don't you go sit in the living room. I need to talk to Mrs. Alexander."

Sylvia left, not looking back.

"Mrs. Alexander—" I began.

"Mummy was furious at me when I cut my hair," she cut in. "Of course, she bobbed hers back in the twenties. We all cut our hair, we didn't want to look like schoolgirls. We—"

"Mrs. Alexander," I interrupted. "Can't you see that Sylvia might need some counseling?"

She ignored me. "I went to the hairdresser in the village, instead of going into the city, so Mummy was furious about that too. What was that girl's name?" She patted her sparse perm. "After she finished, there were great masses of my hair on the floor, natural blond hair the color of butter. Mummy said later the girl probably gathered it all up and sold it. Blond hair was at a premium, you know."

I positioned myself directly in front of her so she had to look at me.

"Mrs. Alexander," I said. "*Listen.* This has nothing to do with young rich girls rebelling and cutting their hair. Sylvia's spent most of her life helping other people and now she needs to start thinking about herself. She needs professional help. She's emotionally disturbed. Do you understand? I can give you some names of counselors if you like."

"Counselors," she said, scornfully. "Charlatans is what they are. That's not how we handled things. *We* were brought up to believe in self-control—will power—and a good hot bath."

My knees were shaky, I was so angry. I was so angry it was on the tip of my tongue to say, *"Is that what you told your husband before he went into the garage and asphyxiated himself? Take a good hot bath?"*

"Sylvia needs quite a bit more than that," I said.

In Gladys's blue eyes, for just a second, I seemed to see an unselfish thought swim to the surface. I watched it drown.

"Sylvia's *perfectly* all right," she said.

chapter thirty

I SAT IN A BOOTH AT DENNY'S NURSING A
BLT and watching the glitter of cars pass by out on Fry Boulevard.
I didn't want to go back to Lee's until she was more likely to be there.
I couldn't face Sylvia and Gladys alone. I gave up on the sandwich,
paid, got in my car, and drove to the next street over, to the Salvation
Army. There I found two black T-shirts totaling two dollars and
twenty-five cents. They would probably lose their moldy, sweet thrift
store smell once I washed them and would probably look good too,
once I cut out the shoulder pads.

Coming out, I saw that the sky had clouded over, the temperature
dropped a few degrees. And at that moment, it caught up with me.
The thought of Nate, who knew where, slipped through my busyness
and wrapped my heart with fear. An image, somehow even more
disquieting, of Sylvia, sawing at her hair. In my mind, the strands got
longer and longer, till they represented years and years of growth,
from childhood on, dropping onto the red rocks of the desert.

"Chloe," said Lee Thomas, dressed in a pink cashmere cardigan and
jeans. The cardigan was covered with little pills. She had large
pouches under her eyes, as though she'd recently been crying but
her hair was clean and freshly streaked with silvery highlights.

For a second I thought of Jack Townsend's seductive blue eyes as he'd handed me his card.

"I found Cornelia," I said.

"Oh!" She put her hand over her heart, took a step back, almost tripped on nothing. "I'm sorry," she said. "I didn't mean to keep you standing outside. Please, come in."

Inside, the tiled hall was cold underfoot. Lee lingered by a small cherrywood table, its surface powdery with dust. I wondered, was Sylvia just a companion to Mrs. Alexander? She certainly didn't do much housework.

"When?" said Lee.

"Friday afternoon."

I followed her into the living room where she sat on the couch and I across from her in the chintz-covered armchair. The curtains were open on the French doors to the back. I could see Justin outside by the swimming pool, one arm raised in the act of throwing a large rock into the water.

"You found Corney in Tucson?" Lee asked. She seemed calmer now.

I saw the splash as the rock hit the water. I tore my eyes away. Lee could see Justin too, from the couch but she didn't seem to notice what he was doing. "No," I said. "I really can't tell you where she is. She asked me not to and she's over eighteen. Lee—Justin—he's—"

"You told her about Cal?"

"She already knew." I glanced out at the pool but Justin had vanished. "Lee, she seemed like a strong, self-reliant person. Like she could handle it."

Lee made a face. "Yes, that's Corney. Did she say she would come home?"

"She said to tell you she'll be in touch when she's ready."

There was a silence. Outside, Justin reappeared, lugging another rock. Inside Lee sat, oblivious in her chilly living room. Willy. Tucson was midway between here and Phoenix, where Jack Townsend lived. Was he Willy?

She sighed and said, "Ready. What does she need to do—" She

stopped at the sound of the front door opening and Gladys Alexander's voice.

"Gladioli," she was saying. "Such hideous flowers, so vulgar. They belong at a shopkeeper's funeral."

She appeared in the doorway. She'd changed from her beige tunic to a brightly colored ski sweater, matching knit cap, as if ready for a weekend in Stowe, Vermont. "You're back again," she said to me. "You should mind your own business."

Sylvia came up behind her in a long black tunic sweater and jeans, chopped hair sticking up in little tufts.

"Mummy! Please," Lee said in exasperation. "I invited Chloe."

"We don't need outsiders here," Mrs. Alexander said.

"I was about to make cocoa," Sylvia broke in. Her face was flushed from the wind, her dark Indian skin even darker than usual. "Would you like some too, Miss Newcombe?" she added politely, as if we'd just met, as if I hadn't watched her hack off her hair in a frenzy of grief.

"No, thank you," I said. Where was Sylvia's room? I wondered, where did she sleep, hang her clothes, and did they include a long dress? Where did she keep things that were important to her, in this house where no one cared about her personal life? It would be interesting to spend a little time alone in her room.

Sylvia's eyes drifted off beyond me, then she gave a little gasp. "Mrs. Thomas! Justin's throwing rocks in the pool!" She hurried to the French doors, opened them. *"Justin!"*

It was absurd. It reminded me of a scene from the movie *Tampopo* where the dead woman continues to make dinner for her family.

"You've had *her* talk to Cornelia, haven't you," Gladys said to Lee. "You couldn't pull yourself together and go yourself? Of course not. Cornelia's more mine than she is yours. She's like me. You're just like your father." Her voice was scornful. "The Peabodys never could pull themselves together. They expect everyone else to do the coping for them. *Where is she?"*

"Mrs. Thomas," Sylvia said, "Justin's throwing big rocks into the pool!"

"Mummy, I don't *know,*" Lee said, ignoring Sylvia. Her face was pale and her fingers twitched nervously. She stood up, walked to the center of the room and stopped. She seemed to vanish. She took a breath. "I think . . ." Lee began and stopped, winded. "Chloe was about to leave," she said breathlessly.

I was? I would, gladly. The house so dusty and somehow unlived in, Lee's transformation back to a hologram, Justin, unnoticed with his rocks, Sylvia with her ruined hair—the whole scene gave me the creeps. It was like a stage setting, where people spoke their lines tonelessly while holding masks in front of their faces.

As I pulled into my carport a man came out of Bill's house next door. Black sunglasses, black pointy toed boots, hair combed down on his forehead and the collar of his white shirt turned up rakishly. He came down the steps, stopped close to my driveway and snapped his fingers.

"Hey, hey, hey, hey," he said.

I stared. "Bill? Is that you?"

"Roy Orbison." He grinned. "Karaoke night over in Sierra Vista at the Sin of Cortez. I'm trying out my new look. You've got a visitor by the way. She was here for at least an hour sitting on the floor of the carport so I told her, 'Why don't you go round and sit on the front porch.' She gave me this poster to hang up in the bar."

"Great."

I walked through the house and there was Nola in a tiny white T-shirt and black jeans, her feet propped up on the porch railing.

"What's up?" I said.

"I figured out what was so funny about Nate's apartment!"

"Oh?"

"There was nothing there."

"What are you talking about?"

"Think about it, Chloe. Remember the answering machine? Not a single message on it till Tuesday! Half the time it takes days for Nate to get around to erasing his messages. And we didn't find anything really except the phone bill and that was useless. No clues at all! I think someone got there before we did! Erased his messages, got rid of stuff!"

"God," I said. "You might be right."

"I went back to Nate's apartment and talked to all the tenants to see if they saw or heard anyone. But they're so—out of it. Then I went through his apartment, the kitchen cabinets, the closet, the wastebaskets, I crawled on the floor and looked underneath the bed, and I went through all of his pockets. I brought everything I found with me, except the used Kleenex." She held up a little plastic bag.

I sat on the other porch chair. "Let's see it."

She handed it over. "There isn't much."

I dumped everything into my lap: receipts, matchbooks, a black comb, a pen inscribed with *Arizona Bar Association Conference, Phoenix Marriott*.

"The receipts are just for gas from the Circle K," said Nola, "but still . . . and I saved the matchbooks that weren't local 'cause I remembered you looking at them in his drawer."

I turned the matchbooks over, one from Grandma Goodman's in St. David, one from the Blue Willow, a restaurant in Tucson, and one—"Wow," I said.

"What?" said Nola. "You found something? I did good?"

One from the Bowie Cafe, Bowie, Arizona. Corney had told me she didn't know him. Corney had lied to me.

"You did good," I said.

chapter thirty-one

EARLY THE NEXT MORNING I DROVE TO
Bowie again, the back way through the valley farmland. The sky was
still overcast, a dull silver-gray. The light intensified the burnt yellow
of the dying cornfields where crows scrabbled and flapped their enormous black wings.

When I got to Bowie I saw Corney's gray van with the U of A
sticker immediately, parked just down the street from the Bowie Cafe.
Inside, the cafe was half full, mostly groups of cowboys and Mexicans
in the booths. I didn't see Corney though. Randa was gone, a young
blond girl wearing a pale blue western shirt with pearl studs, hands
full of plates, was behind the counter.

"Annalee! More coffee!"

"Annalee, you forgot the damn salsa!"

"Hold on!" she shouted. "I'm going as fast as I can."

I sat at the counter to wait till she had things better under control. The pie under the plastic dome looked like apple crumb.

"Just coffee," I said when she made it over with the coffeepot.

She bent down, came up with a thick white mug.

"I was wondering," I asked as she filled my cup, "did a reporter
stop by here, maybe in the last month or so?"

She cocked her head. "A reporter? I don't think so." A small red
pimple on her cheek marred her otherwise flawless skin. She touched

it gingerly. She had silver rings on every finger of her hand. "I mean, what for?"

"I just wondered. He's a friend of mine."

"My mom might know. She's here more than I am."

"Randa?"

She nodded. "But she went to Tucson. She stuck me with all *this.*" She gestured. "Like I don't have a life."

Teenagers all talked the same now, learned everything from the TV.

"Actually I'm really looking for Corney, the photographer? Her van's parked out front."

"Corney. Sure. She went off with Sonny in his pickup to look at this old house he's been telling her about. Some guy was murdered there, about fifty years ago. Corney loves that kind of creepy stuff." She shuddered with delight, eyes gleaming. "She's a little crazy."

"How can I find them?"

"Well, keep going south about a mile out, straight, you can see it from the road, on the left. Look for Sonny's rusted-out old pickup. Ug-*lee.*"

A mile out, there it was, what was left of it, a gray wooden house set back in a field, Sonny's rusted-out old uglee pickup to one side. Skirting the field was a dirt road; I turned left onto it. It was overgrown, full of deep ruts, bisected by washes. Halfway there, at a particularly deep wash, I stopped. Maybe Sonny's pickup could make it but I didn't trust the Omni. I got out and walked the rest of the way.

One side of the house had caved in, prickly poppies growing in the jumble of silver-gray boards lying in the dirt. I saw no one, but heard voices. I walked around the side that was still intact and there were Sonny and Corney, half turned away, sitting on a couple of rocks.

". . . Satanists in this county than all of Tucson," Sonny was saying, " 'cause they're all Christians out here. You got to be a Christian—"

He noticed me then; his hand snaked down to his side and touched the rifle lying on the ground next to him.

"Don't shoot," I said.

"Hey!" He grinned cockily—handsome, young, self-confident. "I remember you."

Corney sighed. "My mother's back."

Sonny looked at me wide-eyed. "Your mother? This is your mom? You never told me—"

"In a manner of speaking," Corney said. "Sonny, why don't you take a walk?"

For a second Sonny looked out at the rocky prickly desert, so empty, then picked up the rifle, stood and walked away.

"Nate Pendergast," I said.

Corney lit a cigarette. She was wearing faded jeans, the same buckskin vest she'd worn the last time, a camera slung around her neck. "Who?"

"Nate Pendergast. A reporter for the *Sierra Vista Dispatch*?"

"I remember," she said. "You asked me about him the last time you were here."

"I know I did. Maybe he never told you his name. He's young, brown sort of crew cut, glasses, wears an earring."

"Sounds like half the guys I know." She looked disgusted. "Anyway I told you, I wouldn't talk to a reporter."

"Maybe you forgot," I prompted. "You see, his girlfriend found some matches from the Bowie Cafe in his room."

"So? Maybe he came looking for me. But he didn't find me, I promise you," Corney said. "Thank God."

I sat down on the rock next to her, deflated. "Shit," I said. "Oh, *shit.*"

"Look, maybe your friend got the matches from the truck stop on the I 10. Randa leaves some there from time to time, like advertising."

"Maybe," I said.

Out in the desert, Sonny walked tall, alert. He raised his rifle. *Bam.*

"Rabbits," said Corney. "A day can't go by, he doesn't shoot off that gun." She sighed. "I called my mother last night. She's very grateful to you."

"You did? How did it go?"

"Okay," she said shortly.

Fine. I'd done my job. We sat in silence. Out in the desert Sonny raised his rifle again, but he didn't shoot. On the ground between Corney and me, a blue-throated lizard did a pushup, then scurried up the broken wood steps and flashed up a window frame, vanished under a board. On sunny days the light would come in slanted, through the holes in the roof—the house would be filled with it and whatever murderous secrets it held would be exposed, negated, wiped out. I was sick of murders, dead ends, secrets.

"Corney," I said. "What about this friend of your mother's, Willy?"

"Oh, for Christ's sake!" She stood up and walked back a few steps, unslung her camera. *"Willy,"* she said. She aimed the camera at the house, looked through the viewfinder. Then she lowered the camera without taking a picture. "I can't believe she's still seeing him."

"Jack Townsend? Is that who Willy is?"

She stared at me. "Good God, no. My mother hates Jack Townsend."

"But I thought they were old friends."

"I guess they were, I think he got too crooked for her. In her own way she's very principled. But Willy . . . I always thought she could do better. Ned Flanders, that's who he always reminded me of. Ned Flanders from *The Simpsons*. Hey, diddly, diddly. If there's a positive thought to be found anywhere, Willy will find it." She looked at me. "You really don't know who he is?"

I shook my head.

Corney looked away. "We didn't talk about that the last time you were here, did we? She doesn't like people to talk about it. Gladys made her that way, ashamed."

I was confused. "She doesn't like people to talk about what?"

Corney held the camera up to her face. "My mother's sick," she said, from behind the camera.

"Sick?" I parroted.

"Sometimes she's okay, she goes up and down. I could tell by her voice when we talked last night, she's in one now or on the verge— major depressive episodes. They started a few years ago. It runs in her family; my grandfather killed himself when she was sixteen." Corney lowered the camera. "Willy's her psychiatrist."

"One day she lit up a room, the next she could barely get off the couch." How could I have been so stupid? All the signs were there, the genetic link, the abrupt dropping out, the exhaustion, the lack of grooming. I thought of Craig, how he'd fooled me too. I felt a little sick.

She stared. "But you've spent time with her. You couldn't tell?"

"I wasn't paying attention," I said.

Corney sighed, looked though her camera again, then put it down. "She had her first episode, around the time I told her about the rape. I think it was a precipitating factor."

I sat up straight on my rock. I wasn't going to let her get away with that. "Come on, Corney."

She shrugged. "Just thought I'd mention it."

"It wasn't your fault you were raped and you needed to tell your mother. Some things aren't anyone's fault, they just happen. It would have happened sooner or later. It's genetic. Your grandfather killed himself."

"Oh shit, I know all that," said Corney. "I've worked it out, okay?" She sighed. "The thing is I love her, she was so great before, the greatest person. And now I can't stand to be around her for more than ten minutes; it's like I catch it too. And I can't help her. She goes off into another world and there has never been anything I could do to help."

"What about medication?" I said, thinking of Craig. "Prozac, Zoloft . . ."

"It works, then it doesn't. They switch her around."

It works and then it doesn't. Oh, great.

Corney sighed. "I'm like *her,*" she said. "Gladys, I mean. I hate it, but it's true. I'll shut people out if I have to . . . and speaking of

Gladys, when I talked to my mother she said Gladys had a dizzy spell, late yesterday afternoon. So she's taking her to the doctor in Tucson today. So that's one more reason she needs me." She reached up and around and removed the camera from around her neck. "I'm going home tomorrow."

"Good," I said.

"What's good about it?" Her voice rose. "I'm sick, I'm so sick of it all!" She held the camera high over her head. "I guess I won't be needing this anymore."

Out in the desert I saw Sonny stop, look back. "Corney?" he shouted. He strode across the desert toward us. "Corney, what the hell you doing!"

"I'll just give it all up! Who cares anyway?" She began to twirl the camera by its strap. "I'll just go home and take care of my mother for the rest of her life! And her mother too! Her horrible mother!"

"Stop that!" Sonny reached the yard, dropped his rifle, caught the camera just after Corney let it fly. "It's all bullshit, Corney and you damn well know it. You go see your mother, like you *should*, she's your *mom*, then you're coming back here and taking more pictures. If you don't, I'm coming to get you. I'll take you away if I have to shoot the whole damn family!"

I was thrilled. *"Keep him,"* I wanted to say.

Corney's face collapsed. She began to giggle.

Sonny glared at me. "And you. Every time you show, she goes and gets all riled up. You go away now, leave her alone."

I did.

chapter thirty-two

WHEN I GOT BACK HOME, NOLA'S BLUE
Volvo was parked in the driveway. I pulled in behind it. Nola stood
by my kitchen door doing a little dance, in black tee and cargo pants.

"Chloe! Where were you? I've been calling you and calling you
and calling you, then I just came over."

"What? Nate's back?"

"No."

I gave a little gulp. "Then . . . what?"

"I found his car!"

"Where?" I said.

"Out in the desert! A couple of miles off Highway Ninety-two—
this woman called me. Really irate, you know, said I had no right to
abandon my car and she was going to call the police and report it
and I was like, wow, lady, my car's right here, what are you talking
about?"

"Nola," I said nervously, picking up on her mania as usual. "Get
to the point."

"Well, then I thought, oh my God, because Nate's car is registered
in my name, it used to be mine, then I got the Volvo which is like
newer, and getting the title changed was such a hassle—"

"Anyway," I said.

"Anyway, so she told me how to get there. Her kids go horseback riding and they saw it. They didn't tell her right away. It's been there for *days*."

I felt sick. "For *days*?"

"All this time we've been looking, I guess. I called Hector." She said his name like it was someone she knew well, someone she went to high school with. What else had she told Hector? "I had to, Chloe. But he wasn't there, so I left a message. I'm going out there now. Are you coming?"

"Of course. I'll follow you."

The sky was still overcast, luminous, the desert dirt a deep almost cadmium red where Nola turned off Highway 92 down a dirt road. With absolute clarity I could see Nate's shirt printed with sombreros and postcards of Mexico, but his face, his face seemed to recede, I couldn't get a good look at it. I couldn't think of one good reason why his car would be abandoned out in the desert.

Sunflowers, six feet high, and goldenrod lined the road. Nola rounded a curve and there it was: Nate's car. His '56 turquoise and white Chevy, the FOR SALE sign still in the back window, parked in front of yet another old frame house. The back left tire was completely flat. I pulled in just behind Nola and we both got out.

"I *told* him he needed air in that tire," I said inanely.

"He must've had a flat," Nola said in a little voice, "and he had to walk out to the highway to hitchhike."

"That would be days ago."

"He's so irresponsible."

But we couldn't just stand there like two biddies clucking. We walked over together and peered inside the car. The turquoise and white vinyl seating was shredded, the floor matting so worn away you could see the ground under the gas pedal. A Circle K Styrofoam coffee cup, on its side, lid still on, and a copy of the *Sierra Vista Dispatch* lay on the passenger seat.

I squinted at the date. "Sunday before last."

"Chloe! I hate this!" Her voice rose. "I'm getting the creeps."

"We have to be calm," I said in a shaky voice.

"It's not locked," said Nola. "That woman had to have opened the glove compartment to get the registration." She started to open the driver side door.

"Wait," I said. "Don't touch anything."

"That's right—fingerprints! I wasn't—" Nola blinked a couple of times. "And that woman probably left some there." She shivered. "Where could he go without a car?"

"I guess we should . . . let's look around," I said reluctantly.

The porch of the old house sagged, paint was visibly peeling off the boards, the windows were pointed shards of glass. A vague sense of déjà vu nagged at me, or something like it. The desert stretched away on either side, long ago overgrazed to desolation, dotted with mesquite and pepper grass clear to the far mountains: empty desert, flat, without secrets.

We walked around to the back of the house, to the same vista.

"Could he be living here?" I said.

"Nate!" shouted Nola. "Hey, Nate!"

We came back around and went up the steps. The door was gone. Inside we were immediately hit with the rank smell of feces.

"Gross me *out!*" said Nola, holding her nose.

Glass and cigarette butts were strewn around the dirty, possibly beige, linoleum floor. At the far end was what must have been a kitchen, pipes jutting out where appliances had been yanked. A filthy dark green sleeping bag, ripped, down feathers leaking out, was bunched on top of a stained mattress in the middle of the room, beside it a used condom.

I looked at Nola. "Could he have been hiding out here?"

"*Please,*" said Nola. "No way. Not like this. He's too fastidious."

She walked across the room, peered through a door. "Nothing," she said.

"Don't touch anything," I warned.

"Are you kidding?"

I went down a hall off the kitchen, where the smell was strongest, found a bathroom, no sink, just the toilet, reeking, clogged with I didn't want to know what. A scorpion skittered away.

"Let's get out of here," whimpered Nola from the front room.

We walked back outside to the gray luminous sky.

"It's worse now than it was before," said Nola. "Isn't it? I mean, he can't have gone any place in his car." Her voice was plaintive. She sat down abruptly on the bottom porch step.

"He could have met somebody here," I said. "Gone off with them. Damnit, we drove over that road, we could have messed up some tire prints, we should have—"

Nola yelped. "Oh my God! *Chloe!*"

"What?"

"The trunk! Chloe, what if he's . . . ?"

Nausea tickled the back of my throat. "Nola, forget it."

"We have to open the trunk." She jumped up and started toward the car.

Very reluctantly I stood up too. "We can't. We need the key. You don't have a key, do you?"

"Wait." She went to the back wheel, bent and came up triumphantly with a hide-a-key box. "Still there!" She took out the key. "Here."

I backed away. "No, you."

She screwed up her face, as if the light were suddenly too bright. "That's not fair. He's just your friend. He's my boyfriend."

"You're right. Okay. I'm sorry." I took the key, but I stayed where I was. The gray of the sky seemed to enter my bones, filling me with grayness too.

"Go *on,*" said Nola. Her voice trembled. "It's just as hard for me."

"In a minute."

"If Hector were here, he could do it." Nola looked down the road. "I told them to tell him it was urgent."

I took a deep breath.

"There isn't any smell," said Nola suddenly. "The car's been here for days." She began to giggle. "I mean . . . if he's . . ." The giggles came out in little hiccups. "If he's . . . in there . . ." She bent over, racked with laughter, she laughed and laughed, her face bright red, tears coming out of her eyes. "If he's . . . in there," she gasped, "it would *stink*."

I began to laugh too, I couldn't help myself, the thought of Nate's body, rotting in the trunk while two banshee, hyena women stood around and laughed was too hilarious. I laughed and laughed, until I was empty inside.

Then I walked to the back of the car, inserted the key in the lock and popped the trunk. Other than a jack and a can of Inflatatire, it was empty. Nola sat down heavily on the ground.

From down the road a sheriff deputy's car came slowly toward us.

"Hector," Nola said.

Hector was inside. Nola and I sat and watched as Deputy Ken of Ken and Barbie paced the nearby desert. We hadn't thought to pace the desert to look for Nate's body in the dry washes. I was feeling antsy, restless.

"I think I'll leave," I said. I didn't have it in me to just sit and wait for some horrible discovery.

"I'm staying," Nola said.

"Call me then. If anything . . ."

"I *will*."

I went to my car, got in, and backed to turn. I hadn't really looked at the house except close up; I'd been too distracted by Nate's car. Now I could see it whole. A frame house, oddly constructed, with two peaks in the roof like an "M." Paint visibly peeling off the boards, the windows pointed shards of glass. One wooden step led up to where the door would be, but the door was gone, just a rectangle of darkness . . .

Little goose bumps rose along my arms. The only thing missing was the rubber baby doll at the top of the step, just at the rectangle, head first as though emerging, everything else was the same, even the eerie luminous gray sky just like the sky in the black-and-white photograph of Corney's, the one I had seen in her friend Ginny's apartment.

I turned off the ignition and jumped out of the car. "Hector!" I yelled. "Hector!"

"What?" said Nola as Hector appeared at the doorway.

"Is this an emergency?" he said. The biggest flirt, maybe in Cochise County, his face now seemed drained of animation, dark circles lined his eyes. He looked like he hadn't had a good night's sleep since Cal Thomas's body was discovered.

I faltered. "Not . . . exactly."

"Then talk to me later, Chloe. Okay? I don't want to lose my focus."

chapter thirty-three

IT COULDN'T BE A COINCIDENCE. NOW
there a clear link between Nate's disappearance and the judge's murder. And whoever was responsible knew Corney's photographs. What a story it would make if the press got hold of it. Nate would jump all over it, God, *Nate*. I had to get hold of copies of the photographs, first just to make absolutely sure, then to show them to Hector so he would pay attention.

I could drive to Tucson, get them from Ginny, but wouldn't Lee have copies somewhere? I wondered if Cal Thomas had ever seen them—would he have recognized Windy City? Could they all be hanging somewhere in the Thomases' house? Maybe even hanging in the hall that led to the kitchen, where I'd first talked to Sylvia and she'd shown me the Bachrach studio portrait of Lee, so young and intense, in an evening gown, and one strand of pearls.

"She left everything behind to marry the judge, she left her whole life. I don't understand why a person would do that."

I parked once again in front of the gray stone house by the bushes that no longer had roses. The rusted rake was still propped up on the wall by the door, the grackles noisy in an Arizona cypress tree. A nondescript gray car was parked just at the circle beyond the woody roses, but there was no old station wagon in sight.

I knocked on the door. I waited a long time then finally it opened. "Justin," I said in surprise. "Aren't you supposed to be in school?"

He sniffed. He looked even more peaked than usual, the skin around his eyes bluish. "I got a code," he said thickly.

"Maybe you got wet, throwing those rocks into the pool? You're all alone?"

"Sally's here. She used to be my baby-sitter. We watched *Men in Black,* but she's no fun anymore. She has to do homework. Guess what? My sister's coming tomorrow."

"Corney?"

He nodded. "She called Mom and said so."

"That's great!"

"It's okay." He looked at me hopefully. "You want to play Myst?"

"Justin?" said a voice. "Who is it?"

"It's Chloe," he said. "She's going to play Myst with me."

I stepped neatly around Justin, got into the hall, and encountered a young woman in a baggy green T-shirt and jeans. She had bobbed shiny brown hair and an ink smudge on her cheek.

"With the Victim Witness Program," I said briskly. "I was just checking in."

"Myst!" shouted Justin, desperate for attention. "Myst, Myst, Myst!"

"Justin, *hush.* I'm sorry," she said to me. "No one's here. I'm the baby-sitter. Sylvia and Mrs. Thomas took her mother to Tucson to see the doctor."

"How is she?"

"A little disoriented."

"She's not really sick!" said Justin. "She's pretending! 'Cause of Sylvia's ugly hair!"

"Oh, *Justin.*" Sally laughed. "He's got such an imagination, poor little guy."

"I'll play with him a bit," I said.

She looked relieved. "That'd be great. I've got a midterm coming up. I'll be in the kitchen if you need me."

"Myst?" said Justin excitedly when she was gone.

"Photographs," I said. "We'll play a photograph game. See how many photographs we can find in the house."

"Okay." He gave me a shove. "You sit on the couch in the living room and I'll bring them." He sniffed again and wiped his hand across his nose, leaving a snail trail of silvery mucus.

"Maybe find some Kleenex first," I said brightly.

I stared once again at Lee in pearls and evening gown.

"The powder room!" Justin triumphantly entered the room again. "These are from the powder room!"

He dumped two framed snapshots onto the couch, Lee on a horse, and a small child, maybe Justin, maybe Corney in a kiddie wading pool. Snapshots and photographs soon surrounded me. I could have reconstructed an entire history of the Thomas family in photographs and snapshots, a carefully edited history, set in a land where everyone said "cheese" and had fun.

Corney's photographs wouldn't fit with these; Corney's photographs filled in the blanks. The edited out spaces that everyone carefully pretended were not there.

"Justin," I said, half rising. "Aren't there any of *Corney's* photographs, somewhere?"

"Yes! Stay there!" Justin's eyes glittered maniacally. "You said I could bring them to you. You promised!"

"Okay, okay," I said.

He snatched a Kleenex off the end table and wiped his nose. "My room next!"

"Who's going to put all these away?" I shouted after him.

Sally poked her head around the living room door, blithely ignoring the chaos on the couch. "Well, he sounds like he's having a good time," she said. "I'm so glad you're here." She vanished, back to her midterms.

Nervously I wondered when Lee, Gladys, and Sylvia were due back.

Justin reappeared with an armload. "Here! These are my dad,

every one of them. I took all the pictures of my dad, and I put them in my room."

So that was why the judge's photograph had vanished from the living room. Justin put the pile on the couch, and pulled one out. "This is the one where he looks so dorky."

I looked down at a studio portrait; the judge, wearing his robes, smiling judiciously, looking ready for the Supreme Court. Justin took it away, thrust another one at me. "This one's my favorite."

Justin and his father stood side by side holding tennis rackets. The judge's arm was draped carelessly over Justin's shoulder. With one finger, Justin traced his father's outline. Justin's cheeks were an unnatural pink, the skin around his nose chapped and peeling. I forced myself to stop, take notice.

"I can see why it's your favorite," I said. "It's really nice. Would you like to tell me about some of these?"

Justin's face closed up. "Naw," he said. He shoved the pile away from me. "No way, Jose. Who cares?"

"You're sure?"

He leaped up, giggling. "I'm sure."

If Lee didn't rouse herself enough to take him to see someone soon, I was going to take him myself, march up to the house, drag him off personally. But for now I gave up, not only on Justin but on my search. If Corney's photographs were here they weren't in plain sight where anyone could see them but hidden away, like a family secret, where Justin wouldn't be able to find them.

"Are we about done?" I said tiredly. "You got all the rooms?"

"There's more," he said, his face smug. He was gone for a moment and then I heard him returning, laughing wildly, as he staggered into the room, hidden behind a tower of snapshot albums.

There was no more room on the couch so he dumped them on the floor by my feet and collapsed beside them. "Here's a million," he said. "A million trillion! And you have to look at every single one of them!"

"Look," I said. "I can't."

"You promised!"

I had no idea when Lee was due back, but I certainly didn't want her finding me here, thumbing through the private details of her family's life. "I can't. I have to go soon." I paused. "Tell you what— show me the newest one. Okay?"

"That one," he said in disgust. "It sucks, I'm warning you."

He pulled out one covered with blue marbled paper, only about half full. I flipped through. Corney in a prom dress, looking uncomfortable; Justin in a baseball jersey, maybe a couple of years ago; an unflattering one of Lee, sitting by the pool with Gladys. Then the history stopped, with a clutch of snapshots, shoved in loosely, willy-hilly, as if whoever put these albums together no longer wanted to bother.

I thumbed through the loose snapshots and paused at one of Corney and Lee; Corney all in black wearing dark glasses with Lee beside her in a print dress. They stood in a space that was all white except for blurred matted framed photographs hanging on the wall behind them.

"What's this?" I asked Justin.

"Corney's opening in Tucson," he said. "Mom went there for it a couple of years ago."

"Oh," I said. "Oh really?"

I thumbed through more of these, people milling, blurred photographs on the walls. "Justin, does your mom have any of the pictures from this show? The ones on the wall?"

"Naw." He made a face. "She hated them I think."

A couple of years ago, around the time Corney made her breakthrough according to Ginny. So these were the photographs I wanted; but tantalizing as they were, the snapshots were useless, the photographer more interested in the people than the art on the walls. But Lee—if no one else had seen the breakthrough photographs at least Lee had. What did that tell me?

Did I want to know? Know what? That Lee was involved some way in her husband's murder? That Lee was lost for good, the price of her freedom too high?

"But they were in the newspaper," said Justin suddenly.

"Corney's photographs? In the Tucson paper, you mean?"

"Our paper. Here. Mom's got it someplace. I can look."

There were maybe ten snapshots of Corney's opening. Waiting for Justin to come back, I lined them up on the blank pages of the album and looked at them more carefully.

Lee in the flowery print dress, standing among cool black-clad art students and their not so cool relatives; Lee, drowning in real life, but putting on a good show here, smiling at everyone. People smiled back at Lee, the still pretty mother of the promising art student. Tucson people, new friends of Corney's, replacements for the worn-out life she'd shed: among them I recognized Ginny who'd first shown me the photographs, guileless even in de rigeur black. Recognized someone else too. Standing a few feet away from guileless Ginny.

"Oh shit," I said involuntarily.

"I heard you!" said Justin, coming in the door with a newspaper. "You swore." He opened the paper. "See."

The style section of the *Sierra Vista Dispatch*. There under the headline JUDGE'S DAUGHTER RECORDS COCHISE COUNTY MEMORIES was a spread of pretty good reproductions of the three photographs. Windy City, the house where Nate's car had been parked, the small adobe. No mention though of any silent screams. Not the stuff of a family newspaper. All of Cochise County had seen the photographs, but I didn't care anyway.

I had other things to think about. Because there in the snapshots from Corney's opening, red-eyed from the flash, in baggy jacket and retro print tie, holding a glass of champagne, was Nate. Nate, at Corney's opening.

So Nate knew the judge's family—that had to be what his investigation was all about. He knew Corney. Corney seemed to me to be the most straightforward person connected to the judge. And yet she had *lied* to me. Gladys sitting right here on the couch where I sat now, came up in my mind: the pure rage in her old eyes. *"Corney,"* Gladys had said once. *"She's just like me."*

"What's wrong with you?" said Justin.

"Nothing," I said sadly.

chapter thirty-four

JACK TOWNSEND WAVED A PIECE OF PAPER
in my face. "I bought your house," he said. "We're tearing it down."
Behind me I could hear the steady *ping* of jackhammers on the roof,
ping, ping, ping, ping. "Nate!" I cried, "Nate, stop him!" I looked
around for Nate, hadn't he been here just a moment ago? I tried to
move but something lay heavy on my feet. "Nate!" I cried again. Jack
Townsend laughed. "Say hi to Craig!" he shouted, over the jackhammers.

It hit me then, a revelation—*of course*—

Faraway someone began to scream.

Of course . . . what?

I opened my eyes to the sound of rain on the tin roof, wind
gusting at my window, my phone ringing, and the revelation gone.
Big Foot lay out cold on my feet. Anxiety burned in my chest. My
phone was ringing. The room was dusky dark. What time was it?
My phone was ringing. Nola. Nola with news about Nate. I'd called
her last night, no one had answered.

"Shit," I said out loud and leaped out of bed to answer it. "Hello?"

"Oh dear. It's Flame and I woke you up. I'm so sorry."

"Flame. Hi." I sat down at the kitchen counter. "What time is it?"

"Nine o'clock."

Nine o'clock and my hands were shaking, leftover anxiety from the dream. "I'm glad you called. The rain made me oversleep. It's so dark out."

"Big storm," said Flame. "All over Cochise County. Listen, Chloe, do you plan to visit Craig again on Sunday?"

My chest burned even more. Sunday, coming up fast. "Um . . . I think so," I said.

"You don't sound too good," said Flame with concern. "Like you're coming down with something."

"It's nothing. Probably just sinuses."

"Well, I've got a nice little pot for him. They don't let them have much, but I think pottery's all right. If you would be willing to pick it up sometime . . . I'm always home."

"Fine," I said. "That'd be great. See you sometime then."

I hung up, showered, got dressed. The anxiety wouldn't go away, it pressed on my chest. I called Nola.

"They did a thorough search of the desert around the house and they didn't find *anything*. But Hector"—she gulped audibly—"Hector says there's mine shafts around there. That if he fell or . . . someone threw him down one he could probably never ever be found. He wanted to know if I had Nate's mom's address. He said they might need to be contacting her. I called the newspaper, I thought it might be on his job application. But it's not. I've been thinking, maybe someone stole his car! Maybe he went back to Ohio!" Her voice rose. "Maybe he's there now. Safe."

"Maybe," I said. "I'd like to think that. I wish I could," I added fervently.

"Don't you have *any* ideas?"

"None."

I hung up. I didn't know what to do. I had the newspaper section I'd "borrowed," should I show it to Hector? Find Corney again, confront her? Nate's car parked in front of that house meant something, but I didn't know what. No more postcards from Danny either. What was the use of anything?

I picked up the phone, dialled the number for the Buddhist colony in Vermont and even though I knew she was supposed to be on retreat, I asked for Danny's wife, Michelle.

"Chloe?"

"Michelle?"

"Yes. Oh shoot. I'd love to talk to you but I have to drive to Burlington. Danny's coming in in a couple of hours. He was out west but he totaled, *totaled* his car, he's fine but he had to fly back."

"Totalled his car?"

"It's okay. He's got good insurance. I've got to run. Call again later, okay? Bye."

Danny was okay. Danny was coming home, totalled his car and he was fine. But Nate clearly wasn't fine. The rain *ping-ping*ed on my roof. I breathed deep from my diaphragm the way you were supposed to but it didn't help. I would spend my life worrying about reckless people I could do nothing for. And it was raining.

I didn't want to spend my day doing nothing. There was something I wanted to ask Flame, and to ask her in person. The pot would be a good excuse. Was it really raining? I went out to the porch and peered up at the sky. Yes, it was. But so what? I'd driven in monsoons plenty of times.

The mountains were obscured in a mist of rain, rain leaked through a gap in the car window. I drove slowly through a wash and water spewed out from my tires. Despite my windshield wipers being on high, I could hardly see.

It seemed to me I knew all I needed to, I just hadn't put it together. Maybe I didn't want to, maybe I didn't want to know. The wipers flopped rhythmically back and forth, not quite in time to my heart. It seemed to me my heart was beating just a little off.

I pulled into Flame and Roy's and parked as close as I could get to the house. Roy, in a shiny yellow rain slicker, was just going into Flame's studio, carrying a big mop. He waved at me, grinned his dopey grin. I waved back as I opened the car door. I made a run for the house. Water dripped from the eaves of the porch, the wind chimes tinkled madly as I knocked on the door. Flame opened it almost immediately.

It was warm inside the kitchen, the windows all steamed up. "You're wet," she said. "I've got an extra umbrella. Take it when you leave. The wind blew the door to my studio open. Roy's cleaning up. He loves to clean up."

The pot sat on the kitchen table, small, decorative, a riot of sunflowers. "I hope it's not too Van Gogh," said Flame.

"I love it," I said. "So will Craig."

"I did it a few months ago and thought, oh no, Van Gogh, then the other day I looked at it and thought *Craig*. So, here it is."

I picked it up, touched the cool glaze with my fingertips. And suddenly the revelation from my dream returned, full force. How bright Flame's kitchen was, almost glaring. I took a deep breath. "Flame? Where did Melissa live?"

She smiled at me sadly. "Can't let it go?"

"No."

For a moment she hesitated, then shrugged. "In the desert. Just outside of Palominas on the road to Sierra Vista."

"Where exactly?"

"There's a little road at milepost twenty-eight, on the left. The only house, it's just off the highway." She sighed. "Melissa was a California girl. She'd only been here a few months when she met Craig. The house was never much, but she fixed it up. After she died, they never could get another renter. It sort of fell apart. Everyone knew what had happened there, after all. Craig planted some things when they first met, a desert willow. I wonder if it's still there." She looked at me. "Maybe you'll tell me."

Raindrops made small explosions in the puddles forming in the red dirt yard of Melissa's house, small, adobe, and clearly abandoned. Where windows must have been were two vacant holes. The door was nearly off the last hinge—the door where years ago Elton Harvey had knocked and she'd thought it was Craig, and she'd opened the door.

The desert willow Craig had planted was still there, just as it was in the wilting newspaper photo I had on the car seat beside me. Once again the only thing missing was the rubber baby doll. There it was, the third Silent Scream. Surprise, surprise.

Symbols. *"To Melissa,"* Craig had written. *"You were the dark rose that fades in the sun."* The photographs were little visual poems. I was so filled with weariness. I wanted to go home, go to bed. Pull the covers over my head and sleep for a thousand years. That's what all the silent screams were about. Rape sites. A rape, maybe unreported but known locally, must have happened at that second house.

Did Nate know when he drove his car to that second house that it must have been a rape site? *"Corney never explains,"* Ginny had said, *"and she hates interpretations."* In any case he must have known he was on to something.

I saw Nate, sombreros and postcards receding. Saw him turn, heard him call out to me,

"Say hi to Craig."

chapter thirty-five

MEANWHILE CORNEY KNEW NATE. IN SPITE
of what she'd said. And Justin had told me yesterday that Corney
was coming today. I wanted to know why she kept lying to me.

The road to the Thomas house was full of little puddles, rain
*ping*ed off more puddles in the driveway. Corney's van wasn't there
but Lee's station wagon was. Someone was sitting inside, in the passenger seat.

"Hello?" I called, getting out and wrestling open the umbrella
Flame had lent me, pink patterned with big cabbage roses. I walked
over to the station wagon. "Hello?"

I peered inside through the water-smeared window, rain tattooed
off the nylon umbrella. Justin was inside. He raised one hand in greet-
ing, let it fall. I made circular motions at him, and he rolled down the
window.

"Hi, Chloe," he said when he got it halfway open.

"What are you doing in there?"

"My sister came."

"Corney's here? Is she coming out, are you going somewhere? Is
that why you're in the car?"

"She's gone. She and mom went off in Corney's van. They
wouldn't let me come." His lip trembled. " 'Cause of my cold."

"Bummer."

He looked at me hopefully. "You want to play a game?"

"I'd love to, but I can't now. I need to talk to your sister," I said. "Your cold will get worse, sitting out here. Don't you want to get better so you can go places with your mother and Corney?"

Justin sniffed. "I don't care."

Of course not. He planned to sit out in the car, in the rain until his cold got really bad, turned to pneumonia, and he died. Then they'd be sorry.

"Justin!" someone called from the house. It had to be Sylvia.

He didn't even turn his head.

I thought of the hours, days and weeks and even years of close attention Justin probably needed to feel better and I felt utterly exhausted. "Where did they go?" I asked him, through my fatigue. "Your mother and Corney."

"To the Crossroads." He sniffed again. "It's a restaurant," he added.

"Sure. I've been there, it's near the Mesquite Tree."

He nodded. "They have really good milkshakes. Mom takes me there sometimes. Corney said they always went there when she was my age. When Corney was my age they had fun all the time."

"Justin!" cried Sylvia again.

"Well," I said, backing off. "I'll see you. Hang in there. Okay?"

"Here she comes," said Jason gloomily.

Wearing a bright yellow slicker, but without an umbrella, Sylvia walked toward the station wagon through the rain. Headed for Justin, she barely acknowledged my presence. Her dark cropped hair was already matted with wet, her mouth was set as if to say, "See what I have to put up with?" The raindrops streamed down her face like tears.

I hit Highway 92 and waited as an endless stream of cars went by, headlights on, going thirty miles an hour. I turned on the heater. It wasn't that cold but my clothes and hair were still damp from my run to Flame's and my shoes, socks, and the hems of my black drawstring pants were soaked from standing out in the rain talking to Justin. I finally got a break in the traffic and headed back toward Sierra Vista.

A mile or so before the Mesquite Tree, the Crossroads Restaurant was a nondescript little in structure that sold fat burgers, chili dogs, and real milkshakes. A relic of the old days before Sierra Vista bloomed into the near metropolis it was today, it had survived fast foods, Denny's, the Village Inn. It was lunch time and the parking lot was full of old pickups and old cars. Maybe it would even survive the food court at the brand new mall.

Corney's van was parked by the door. I found an empty space farther down and pulled in. Then I turned off the ignition. The rain was still falling, and cars drove by on the highway, their tires sticky sounding on the asphalt, but it seemed unnaturally quiet, without the noise of the engine and the heater blowing.

Fluorescent light streamed through the Crossroads' big plate glass window, hung with plastic ferns. I sat there in the quiet, looking in at the diners through the rain. Two men in cowboy hats gesturing at each other were directly in front of me, two moms with rowdy kids to the left. On the right two women, one laughing. They were all in twos, in that steamy oasis of warmth, which must be full of the sound of voices, cutlery clanking. No one was alone—just me sitting out in my car, a voyeur.

What was I going to say when I barged in on them?

The woman stopped laughing. I watched her pick up a hamburger and realized it was Lee. I hadn't recognized her—Lee Thomas laughing. Even now she was smiling at the other, younger woman. A woman in a cowboy hat. Corney. They sat together in their bubble of light and warmth. It didn't matter that I couldn't hear their words; their faces, their echoing gestures suggested companionship, intimacy. At least for now Lee and her daughter were just fine.

I couldn't do it—interrupt, break the spell—it might never come again.

For a moment I didn't know where I was, what I was doing except that I was far away from things that mattered. I felt like someone who wakes up out of an intricate dream, to nothing but whiffs of suspicion, shreds of beliefs. I was someone chasing after ghosts. Then the feeling passed.

I could come back later to talk to Corney. Corney wasn't the only person who knew Nate. There was still Poppy of the St. David's phone number; Poppy house-sitting the straw bale house and worried about Nate too. Under her brusqueness she'd struck me as a kind person and I'd promised to tell her what was going on. Maybe she knew how to reach Nate's mother. Maybe she knew more than she realized, and I knew more now than when I'd first seen her. We could put our heads together. I turned the engine back on, the heater started blowing. I backed out, turned toward the highway, made a right in the direction of St. David.

chapter thirty-six

AS I DROVE INTO ST. DAVID, THERE WAS A
lull in the storm. The town lay sodden under the gray sky; wet, once
bright, leaves collected in drifts along the roadway. On a telephone
pole was one of Nola's posters—HAVE YOU SEEN THIS MAN?—disinte-
grating in the rain. Amazing—Nola was really getting around. I wondered if Poppy had seen it.

On Sunrise Drive I went through a series of brand new mini-
washes, passed the cinder block houses, the trailers. The straw bale
house was a placid lump in the dark red desert dirt, matted rabbit
brush fluff lining its edges, the FOR SALE sign hanging askew.

Poppy's green Toyota wasn't there. Damn. A couple of shiny black
plastic garbage bags were piled beside the driveway, next to a gray
plastic garbage can, full, rolled up pieces of canvas sticking out of
the top. The garbage can lid lay in the street.

I parked, got out, retrieved the lid and balanced it precariously
on the canvases. I took a deep breath of the chilly air smelling fe-
cundly of damp earth. But my mouth was dry, anxiety had sucked
out all the moisture. Poppy couldn't be far, and I was prepared to
wait for as long as it took till she came home.

Just in case, I went to the front door and knocked. The curtains
were drawn closed at the windows. "Poppy?" I called. "Poppy!"

No one answered me, came to the door. Restless I walked around
to the back, through the gate to a fenced-in backyard. Caked coals,

nearly ashes were dumped into the dirt, like Poppy had had a bar-becue though I didn't see a grill anywhere. A pile of fencing, dark from the rain, and a hammer lay by the fence.

I paced the yard, listening for the sound of Poppy's car coming down the road. I walked over and picked up the hammer, wiped it off so it wouldn't get rusty. I was incredibly thirsty. Moisture filled the air but what good did it do me? I could drive to Grandma Good-man's, buy some orange juice. Or I could try the door. Poppy wouldn't care if I drank her water.

I knocked on the frame of the back door, tried it. It opened easily, as if someone had closed it and it hadn't quite caught. "Hello?" I called.

Poppy wouldn't care if I drank her water but still I didn't go in right away, instead I walked back through the gate, looked down the road. There was no sign of a car. Far away somewhere out on the main road I could hear what sounded like a truck rumbling by. Then silence, a silence that had depth and width, oppressive.

I went back to the door, pushed it open, walked into the kitchen, set the hammer down on the slate counter by the sink. The air inside smelled stale, musty. Against the kitchen window, a fly buzzed angrily. Dishes were stacked in the drainer, a kitchen towel lay on the rim of the sink. The refrigerator door was wide open. Empty, unplugged, no light on inside.

My heart beat with an extra little thump.

I took a glass from the drainer, filled it, drank it down, filled it and drank it down again.

Then I walked through to the living room with its wooden floors, its futon. The futon, all the furniture was still there, the easel too, folded and lying on its side, but objects, things that had softened, humanized the room, things I'd only noticed subliminally, were gone.

I went down a hall, opened doors; a bathroom with a toothpaste-spotted mirror, the medicine cabinet empty except for some rubbing alcohol; two bedrooms, beds stripped, curtains drawn, closets with just a wire hanger or two, chests of drawers all empty.

"Listen, you call me, when he shows up and tell him to get

in touch. I need to know that he's okay. And call me if he's not okay too. I can take it, I just need to know. You promise?"

Call her where? I found the phone, no answering machine, but, of course, the caller I.D. I pushed the review button, but not a single call was listed. I pushed star sixty-nine.

An operator said severely, "The last number to call your line was 555-2344. To call this number press one."

I did.

"Myrna Blodgett Realty speaking!" said a chipper voice.

I hung up on Myrna and went back through the kitchen, closed the back door so it caught and went out by the front.

Outside I kicked at the garbage bags, opened one and peered inside at a mess of damp goo; coffee grounds, stale bread crusts, half empty jars of mayonnaise and mustard and a broken bottle of ketchup. The other bag held newspapers, squeezed out tubes of paints, stiff brushes, and what looked like the contents of a vacuum cleaner bag, hairballs and dust.

I pulled the canvases out of the garbage can, unrolled them, stuck a rock on the bottom and top of each one to keep them from rolling back up. The fourth was the one I'd seen in the living room on the easel. It had a big "X" painted across it. I stared down at my little improvised art gallery.

Hideous muddy canvases, but not just that, there wasn't a trace of feeling in any of them. They *all* deserved a big "X." No one could be that bad. Poppy hadn't even been trying.

Myrna Blodgett, realtor, looked at me with a bright smile over an arrangement of orange silk roses on her desk in her tidy little office on the main street of St. David. "Well, hello there! Enjoying the rain?" She was all gush and fluff with her blond hair blow-dried, big flowery dress, and blue harlequin glasses.

"I saw your sign," I said. "On the straw bale house out on Sunrise."

"Of course. That's a *lovely* house. I'd be happy to show it to you."

"Actually I was looking for Poppy. Is she still there?"

"No," said Myrna, a little less shiny. "A lovely person, but I was under the impression she'd be house-sitting for a little longer than it turned out. Is she a friend of yours?"

"Yes," I said.

"A wonderful artist, of course. I love the arts. Every single one of them," she added airily, glancing at the roses on her desk.

"I was all set to buy a painting, and she's gone. I'm just *devastated*. I was hoping she left a forwarding address with you."

"Oh my no, she didn't. She's going to mail it to me. She wasn't sure of the street number. But you might be able to catch her. She seemed so anxious to go, I mean I understand her having to leave, she wasn't *nourished* by being here, we're not a very *open* community and the place she had lined up wasn't quite ready. I got her a little house-sitting job just for a week over in Patagonia, the little artist town."

"Where's that?"

"Santa Cruz County. It's about an hour away. How about if I give you the phone number there?"

"The address too," I said.

chapter thirty-seven

I COULD HAVE CALLED, BUT SOMETHING told me not to. I drove out of Cochise into Santa Cruz County and out of the storm. Though there was still cloud cover it didn't look like it had rained here; the road was bone dry.

It was dusk when I reached Patagonia. The street lights had gone on and the town, laid out on flat land with big trees everywhere had a tranquil feeling. But I still felt uneasy.

In the center of town was a square, with grass. I had no map, just an address, 101 Suahauro. I stopped at a little grocery store on a corner across from the square and got directions from a friendly middle-aged woman in a denim dress embroidered with road runners.

Suahauro was two blocks down from the square, a mixture of trailers, well-restored adobes and darling little frame houses. Halfway to 101 a big U-Haul van was parked, blocking the road, a couple of teenagers coming out from a lit-up trailer carrying a big couch. When they saw me, one of them dropped his end.

"Fifteen, twenty minutes," he mouthed. "Sorry."

I didn't want to wait that long so I parked across the street, got out, and walked. The evening was warmer than it might have been this time of year, the heat kept in by the cloud cover during the day.

Up the road a dog barked, another answered, then a chorus of dogs as I passed several houses. Then the dogs stopped. A quarter mile up the road I saw Poppy's sea-foam green Honda, bits of rabbit brush fluff still stuck on the front windshield, parked in the driveway of a little adobe with a tin roof.

It was nearly dark. All the lights in the house were off except in what was probably the living room. Clay pots full of dead marigolds lined a stone walkway to the entrance. I walked to the red front door and knocked. Waited. No one came. I knocked again. Waited some more.

I should have called ahead after all. But then I would have had to tell her about finding Nate's car on the phone. Where could she be, without her car? She'd just come here, I doubted she was cozy with the neighbors. Maybe she took a walk. Or she was there but didn't want to answer the door. The curtains were half open in the room that was lit.

I went over to the window and peered in. Electric light softened the white walls, turning them pale yellow. There was a beehive fireplace, two lumpy couches covered with bright Mexican blankets. The room was empty, tranquil and at peace. Anxiety tightened my chest. Why *had* Poppy taken off so quickly? Had she been running from someone?

"Poppy?" I called.

No one answered. Where *was* she? I walked round the other side of the house, but the windows were dark there too. Could she be in bed asleep at seven o'clock in the evening? Then I smelled burning. I sniffed, smelled it again and something else too, something familiar, homey even.

I stood stock still, listening, and heard a voice, not from inside the house, but somewhere behind. Then a muffled shout and the voice again. I backed away from the house and saw what might be a light, smoke, coming from behind a hedge of old-fashioned privet. A barbecue, that was the smell. Poppy was out back with someone, having a barbecue.

I walked round that side of the house and saw a space in the privet, where the stone walkway continued. I went through.

"Hello?" I called, turned a corner. "Hello?" I said again.

The first thing I saw was the barbecue, illuminated by a wrought-iron outdoor light. It wasn't going well, puffs of smoke obscuring everything and not much in the way of embers.

"Who's that?" said a woman's voice.

"Poppy?" I said.

The smoke cleared away suddenly and I saw, all at once, two aluminum webbed chairs, a plate of hamburgers, condiments, and Poppy in jeans and gray sweatshirt, her hair tucked up into a baseball cap and a look on her face that I could only describe as terror.

"Poppy? It's just me. Chloe."

"Chloe?" she said loudly, almost yelling.

"Chloe Newcombe. What's wrong?" I asked. The smoke prickled at my eyelids.

"Nothing, Chloe!" Poppy almost shouted again, as if I were far away. "How did you know where I was?"

"Myrna," I said. "The realtor from hell." But she didn't smile. "Why did you leave St. David so fast?"

Poppy wrapped her arms around her body. "Scared," she said.

"Of what?"

"It doesn't matter. Everything's fine now. I'm just sitting out here with this old grill." She batted at the air. "Too much smoke."

"I heard voices," I said.

"Voices?" Poppy laughed. "There's just me out here, all alone." She looked embarrassed. "I talk to myself a lot. I'm making a batch of burgers on the grill, then I'll freeze most of them. I swear, Chloe, sometimes I think I'm probably going crazy, living alone all the time."

She stood up, rubbing her back. "Ouch," she said, beginning to walk stiffly around the backyard. "See?" She gestured at a line of rose bushes near the back, at flower beds, full of dead flowers. "It's nicer here than St. David." Her intended tone was clearly meant to be conversational but her voice seemed shrill and oddly loud. Maybe she was going deaf.

She walked across the yard to the roses. "Peace roses, my favorite. There was one blooming the day I got here." She spoke too quickly in her loud voice, words running together. "Don't you just love peace roses, Chloe?"

"Yes," I said in a calming tone of voice. "Yes, I do."

She kicked at one of the bushes with her white running shoe. I didn't remember her being quite so strange. Jesus. But I'd promised to give her any news about Nate. Did she expect bad news? Was that why she looked so scared?

"Poppy, listen," I said. "Listen to me, okay? I came to see you to tell you they found Nate's car." She looked so uncomprehending, I raised my voice. "They found Nate's car out in the desert."

"They found Nate's car out in the desert," she repeated, like an automaton. She took off her baseball cap, put it on again. "Who did?"

"Some kids. They called the police. It had been there for a while."

She turned her back on me, and said in a wail, "They found Nate's car!"

She was so weird. I shouldn't have come alone, I should have brought someone. Nola, at least. Suddenly I missed Nola. Compared to Poppy, Nola was *fun*.

"Poppy," I said. "Wouldn't you like to sit down?"

"No. I'm fine. They found his car, I guess that's a pretty bad sign."

"Yes," I said. "Listen, Poppy, someone has to talk to Nate's mother. Do you have any idea how I can reach her?"

"No idea at all. Didn't I tell you that before?" Poppy left the roses and walked toward me. "Chloe, I'd invite you to dinner but"—she gestured at the plate stacked with hamburger patties—"there's not enough."

"I thought maybe he'd mentioned what town she lived in, in Ohio?" I persisted.

Poppy looked distracted. "What?"

"The town where she lives. In Ohio, I know she lives in Ohio. By herself in a big old house. Nate never mentioned her? If I knew the town," I said, talking slowly, trying to get through, "I could call all the Pendergasts that live there. And there are other things I wanted to talk to you about. Did Nate ever mention someone called Corney?"

"Jeez, I'm sorry, but right now I can't think." Poppy clutched her head, knocking her baseball cap awry. "Chloe, listen, you have to go. I need to be alone right now, okay?"

I backed off. Everything felt so unreal, as though Poppy and I were actors who hadn't quite learned their lines, in the spotlight opening night and the cue person had vanished. It was like at the Thomas house, except there the actors had been pros.

For a second there was dead silence. The tension in the air was palpable. Then from behind the roses, I heard sounds, scuffling.

"What's that?"

"Animals," said Poppy wildly. "This house backs onto empty land. There are so many out there. Skunks, deer, rabbits. *Javelina!*" she shouted. "Anyway you better go. I have to adjust. Call me in a couple of days, okay? You have the number here?"

"Myrna gave it to me," I said.

The creep and scuttle beyond the roses got louder, not little desert animals; a horse, or maybe a cow.

"Bye!" said Poppy

"What *is* that?" I asked.

"Nothing," said Poppy very loudly. "Nothing, Chloe. Just kids, they hang out back there."

If not a horse or a cow, then kids, not creeping but plunging through the desert. Close. Just behind the thorny barrier that protected the civilized world. Behind the peace roses. Poppy gave a little moan. The tension in the air changed to panic. What looked like a bunch of sticks appeared at the opening. Burnham Wood, I thought idiotically.

Poppy took a few steps toward the fence. "Timmy!" she cried. "No! Go back!"

Timmy?

"No what?" said the person, Timmy, in exasperation. "I got mesquite." He dropped the sticks.

And I could see his face, his teddy-bear face.

For a moment I stepped into my earlier post-dream experience, but the dream was still going on, things happening with eerie nonchalance, without impact. His fifties nerd cut was growing out a bit, turning into early sixties Beatles, his ancient madras jacket covered with bits of kindling.

"Nate," I said.

chapter thirty-eight

HE LOOKED AS SURPRISED AS ME. "WOW. HI, Chloe."

"Who the hell is Timmy?" I asked.

He crunched toward us in his thrift store running shoes. "Nobody." Suddenly he grinned. Nate, wonderful, rotten, silly, horrible Nate.

"It's his new alias," said Poppy. "I have to call him that all the time, so I won't forget."

"Why?"

"Chloe, he's in terrible danger."

"But you're alive," I said. "My God, you're actually alive." I sat down abruptly on one of the chairs. "I was so *worried*." I looked at Poppy. "You weren't going to tell me? You were just going to let me leave?"

"He told me not to tell *anybody*."

"Poppy," I said aghast. "You're an *adult*. And Nate, Jesus Christ," I ranted, "I've been all over the county looking for you. You really are a jerk, do you know that? An irresponsible thoughtless jerk. And what about Nola? You might at least have thought about Nola."

Nate hung his head. "I know. I feel awful about it, I really do. But she can't know about any of this. She's too sweet and trusting. I think about Nola a lot."

"You have some explaining to do, big time. They found your car today."

"Finally," said Nate.

"Finally? Want to tell me what's going on?"

"I got in . . . over my head." He sat down on a clump of weedy grass. He looked tired. "I was going to be the Woodward and Bernstein of Cochise County, you know? Guess that's what every dumbass kid reporter wants to be." He tugged at a blade of grass. "I'd do it differently, now, play my cards with a poker face."

"And B.W. told you he saw a woman on a bicycle, right around the time the judge was killed. A woman with long dark hair. Do you think it was Yolanda?"

"Ha!" said Nate. "It was a wig, they found a strand of it—Dynel. One of the few things Hector told me. It could have been a lie of course. So I wouldn't bug Yolanda anymore. Right after I talked to you in the parking lot, remember? When I told you I'd discovered something by accident? Something pretty hot?"

"Of course I remember."

"This person I went to see, I thought they had more information, but what they really wanted to do was warn me. I'd gotten certain people pissed off, they said. Really pissed off. Dangerous people. You could be dead, they said, in twenty-four hours."

"*What?*"

"That's what they said." Nate ran his hand over the top of his head, nervously, not a smirk left in him. "They were pretty convincing."

Poppy picked up a stick and poked at the grill. "You know the fire looks okay now. I think I'll put on some burgers and the three of us can have dinner, relax." She plopped burgers onto the grill. "You heard what he just told you. His life is in danger. He wants people to think he's dead."

"I want to know why you picked that house," I said.

"Corney—the judge's daughter—"

"I know about the three photographs," I interrupted. "Nate. You know Corney, don't you? She said she didn't know you. Why did she lie?"

"Corney can be squirrelly, haven't you noticed?"

"No," I said. "Was she involved in some way?"

"Not at all. Leave her out of this, okay? I know what happened to her at Windy City. I know what the photographs meant. That day when I went to Windy City—it was amazing, I remembered them right away. And as far as I could tell no one else was making the connection. I didn't want to just run, tail between my legs so I left my car at that house, because I thought maybe, just maybe, it would flush someone out."

He sighed. "I hung around hoping—but it took too long to find the car. Every day I was in Cochise County was a risk. And Nola was hanging my picture all over the county for God's sake. I'm leaving tonight. I'm going to disappear."

"You haven't told me anything really," I said. "Just that the photographs must be somehow connected to the killer. But how? It doesn't make sense."

"But it's a step in the right direction, I'm sure of it. You can help," he said. "You can tell Ollie about the photographs. He can do a story. A chance to redeem himself and make a big contribution. What the photographs mean. What it was like to be a rape victim in Judge Thomas's courtroom. People should know that." Nate's voice rose. "They need to know that. Everything out in the open. The man was a creep, he deserved what he got."

"But surely," I said, faintly, surprised at his passion, "the punishment should fit the crime."

"That's right," said Nate. "It should."

"That fucking judge, I'm glad he's dead." Craig had said that. Did Nate know about Craig's connection with the judge?

"How's Craig?" said Nate as if he'd read my mind.

"Craig?" said Poppy.

"If you really want to know," I said wildly, "he's checked himself into rehab. He's addicted to painkillers. That's why we weren't getting along. He doesn't know about any of this. And Corney, do you think she'd like all that stuff about her personal life to be public?"

"Corney's a trooper." He frowned. "But Craig. Wow. Poor guy."

"Craig?" said Poppy again but neither of us paid any attention.

Nate stood up. "Look. I think I better go now. I'll take a couple of burgers with me."

"What if they're not done?" said Poppy. "*E. Coli.*"

Poppy and I stood by her car and watched as Nate slung on his backpack, brand new so he could leave his old one behind and freak out poor Nola even more. Poppy gave him a hug. "Stay safe," she said.

I gave him a hug too. He smelled like wood chips and the desert. "You're going to hitchhike?"

"He's got a car, further down," said Poppy.

"Go home and get a good night's sleep," Nate said. "Think about things. You're a victim advocate, there for the victims, remember?"

"It smells like rain," said Poppy nervously. "Better get going."

"One more thing," said Nate.

"What?" I asked.

"You go to visit Craig, don't you? You're not just going to give up on him in his time of *need.*"

"It's not that simple. Jeez. Look, Nate, is there something important you're not telling me?"

"It's a long story. But you're going to see Craig soon?"

"Sunday," I said.

"I think you two should have a long talk."

"Why?"

"Bye now." He started off down the road.

"Why should Craig and I have a long talk?" I yelled after him. "Why?"

But he just kept going and soon he was lost in the darkness.

chapter thirty-nine

FROM THE WINDOW OF THE DINING ROOM in the Mountain View Rehab Center, the haiku clouds moved across the mountains with a kind of stately grace. They looked exactly the same as before, as if there were some giant video in the sky, always running for the benefit of the patients at Mountain View Rehab.

Craig sat beside me. He was losing his tan. I reached into my purse and pulled out the little pot. "Present for you from Flame," I said.

"Wow." Craig turned the sunflower pot over and over in his hands. His face shone. I had a friend once, a perfectly regular person, who got involved with Maharishi Mahesh Yogi. He began to meditate all the time. After a few months his face looked just like Craig's. "Mexican sunflowers," he said.

Mexican sunflowers. Just like the ones he'd planted by my driveway, so many months ago, not long after we met. We'd gone out to dinner, had warm seafood cocktails, listened to the jazz singer doing "I Only Have Eyes For You." *"Everything does better,"* Craig had said then, *"if you pay attention to it."* But I hadn't even made the connection. And I'd brought him nothing but myself. The bitchy skeptical girlfriend. Flame was the one who truly cared for him.

"I'm glad you're here," said Craig. "You know something? All along I keep thinking you're going to back out."

"Why do you think that?" I sipped my iced tea sweetened with fructose.

He shrugged. "You seem ambivalent."

"I guess I am. But I'm here."

"I know. Thanks."

There was an awkward silence. He hadn't been gone that long, but it seemed as though we were going to have to learn how to talk to each other all over again.

Craig cleared his throat. "Look," he said. "I know I'm harping on this but I keep feeling you've been blocking me. If there's anything you want to say you should say it."

For a moment, my throat closed up. Then I said, "Nothing really." I looked at him. "What about you? Do you have something to tell me?"

"What I have is what I just said. You. Blocking me. Holding things back. Jesus Christ, Chloe, I'm here to deal with my whole fucking life. This is the best time for total honesty."

There was another silence.

"Okay," I said, finally. I took a deep breath. Nothing could be more calming than the clouds on the mountains, but my breathing felt shallow.

"What?"

"Tell me about Melissa."

Craig's face blanked out. "Whew." He stood up. "Let's take a walk."

"Okay. In the beginning, what I liked most about her, was she was so lighthearted. Always playing music, singing around the house. I never felt like she *needed* me, more like I was a choice."

"Um," I said.

The path curved around desert willow, little stone benches. We came across a lizard on a bench, warming in the sun. "Hey there, Miss Lizzie," said Craig, as it scuttled away. He looked at me. "How much . . ."

"I read the file, the police reports and all that."

He sat down on the bench.

I sat beside him.

"The night it happened," he said, "I was supposed to come over around seven-thirty, but I got involved with planting tomatoes in the greenhouse. I remember looking at my watch and it was almost eight-thirty and I thought I'd better call but then I decided to take a shower first." He paused. "The lights went out at her place, all the clocks were stopped. At eight-thirty-five. If I'd called . . ."

There was a silence.

"Never mind," I said.

"Later she told me she thought she'd blown a fuse. When she heard someone outside, she didn't even look out the window first because she was sure it was me. She didn't tell me this, but I've imagined it over and over, her opening the door, with that look on her face I used to call her I-need-home-repair look. I guess it was manipulative but it was so cute." Craig clenched his fists. "Shit."

The pink haiku clouds drifted effortlessly over the mountains. Across from us, a bank of red marigolds blazed in the sun.

"When I got out of the shower, I called her but no one answered. I didn't want to drive over there if no one was home. When the cops called from the hospital and told me, I drove there like a maniac, then sat in the waiting room and waited. They were doing that rape kit stuff, but nobody would tell me anything. I sat there and stewed, getting angrier and angrier. Then they took her over to the sheriff's substation in a police car and I had to follow, they wouldn't let me talk to her. They had to make sure I wasn't . . . a *suspect.*"

"That's awful," I said.

"She told me later. I drove her home when they finally got done questioning her. I was so angry she was afraid of me. She wouldn't let me near her. I spent the night on her couch." Craig kicked at a rock by the bench.

"I guess I wasn't much help and then later when I tried to be, I always felt sick with guilt. I knew better intellectually, but I kept thinking of her opening the door because she thought it was me."

I didn't say anything.

"Then things got a little better between us until the trial and I had to see that guy day after day, and that set me off again, I was so mad I could hardly speak to Melissa. Then the guy *got off*, because the judge denied some motion, that same goddamn judge . . ."

"I know," I said. "Craig, a detective came to see me, Mark Flannery. He wanted to know where you were, the night the judge was killed."

"Like after five years I'm suddenly going to kill the guy?" said Craig reasonably. Oh, so reasonably. "I didn't like that judge but what was done to Melissa was already done. The guy who did it is dead."

He shrugged. "Looking back I can see I blew it from the beginning, it was me, me, me—that's all I really thought about. I guess I didn't love her anymore, I mean not in any good way. But I kept trying to fix it, I was even going to ask her to marry me, then she . . . she OD'd."

I put my hand on his arm. "It wasn't your fault. You know it wasn't your fault, Craig."

"Sure. I know."

The sun was suddenly so hot, I was weary to my bones. Why had Nate wanted me to talk to Craig? Did he think Craig had done it, that he'd confess to me? It seemed like he hadn't finished.

"What else?" I asked.

"The funeral. It was in California. She was from L.A., out in the Valley. I flew there, met her family. Her father was dead, so it was just her mother—she died a couple of years ago, Melissa's sister and Melissa's son. She was married once, like all of us. Her boy was grown up, going to UCLA, I'd never met any of them before. By then I was so depressed, I was a zombie. Not that anyone noticed, they were all zombies too. Her mother was zonked out on some kind of tranquilizer and Timmy and Poppy—"

The pink haiku clouds should have exploded right in front of us, but they kept on mindlessly floating *"Who?"*

"Timmy and Poppy. I told you. Her son and her sister."

Poppy. So Poppy was Melissa's sister. Damn pink clouds. Poppy had called Nate Timmy—an alias–she'd said, but it wasn't. It was his real name. He was Melissa's son. That was why he hadn't wanted to come to dinner, when I'd invited him that day at the cafe, to meet Craig. He'd already met him. Why hadn't he told me that? Because he was pretending to be someone else. I closed my eyes.

"We went out to dinner before I left, just the three of us," Craig went on. "Some Japanese place."

"You can tell Ollie about the photographs," Nate had said. *"He can do a big story."*

I folded my arms on my stomach and bent over on the stone bench. *"No."*

"Well, I *like* Japanese," said Craig, "usually. But we ordered all these strange fishy seaweed dishes no one ate. Timmy and Poppy kind of cornered me—something I said—and it turned out Melissa had never told any of them about being raped. Not one word. They made me tell them everything about it, all the details."

But I kept hearing Nate's voice, passionate. *"What it was like to be a rape victim in Judge Thomas's courtroom. People should know that. The man was a creep, he deserved what he got."*

"Oh, Craig," I said in anguish. Because I saw it all so clearly now—Nate had come to Cochise County to kill the judge.

Nate had killed him where Corney, Cal Thomas's daughter, had been raped. Nate had been hoping for a big story, JUDGE KILLED AT SCENE FROM DAUGHTER'S ART PHOTOGRAPH, something like that. And when no one made the connection, he left his car in front of a rape scene from another of Corney's photographs. Because sooner or later, someone would notice, and it would all come out. What the judge had done to Melissa.

Someone had noticed. Me. Now I was supposed to go tell Ollie, the reporter.

What would happen to them, Poppy and Timmy-Nate?

"Oh, Craig, oh, Craig," I said.

"Yeah, it was pretty bad. But you know, I'm glad I told you all this, every time I tell the story it gets easier." He looked at me then. "My God, Chloe, you look terrible. What's wrong?"

"I'm sad," I said. "I'm very sad."

"Don't be sad!" said Craig. "This is all temporary, things will be the way they were. We'll have more film festivals. Soon it will be winter. We've never spent a winter together. It's a good time to plant. A lilac bush! How'd you like a lilac bush next to your sunflowers?"

He sounded like the old Craig again. But I was too sad. It overwhelmed me, filled me up and there was no room for anything else. No wonder Corney had denied knowing Nate. She knew him as Timmy, not Nate. Corney must have told Nate her rape experience and inflamed him further. And Nate-Timmy had sought me out, Craig's girlfriend, from the beginning. He had sought me out and set me up for just this scene.

Then suddenly in the midst of it, sitting there on the bench, in front of the red marigolds, backed by the haiku clouds I had a little satori. I'd been running around, chasing after other people's secrets yet the themes of their lives had echoed the themes in mine, displacements for what I didn't want to face.

Pay attention, said the satori, *this is* your *life*.

"You have to do one thing, just one," said Craig, "to have all this. You have to come to Family Week."

"I will," I said. "I will. I promise."